Bra over Jumper

My Mum has Alzheimer's

Marion Birkenbeil

IngramSpark

Published by agreement with IngramSpark

English translation copyright © Marion Birkenbeil 2023
First published with the title BH über dem Pulli in Germany 2023

This is a work of fiction. The story is set in 2017 and includes actual names of places such as Brisbane, Coolum Beach, Marcoola, Noosa and Pacific Paradise. However, the entire plot, all characters, dogs and nursing homes are fictional. Some organisations mentioned in the novel, while real, are used fictitiously without any intent to describe actual conduct.

Book Layout © 2023 BookDesignTemplates.com
Cover Design and Cover Image by Marion Birkenbeil

Bra over Jumper/ Marion Birkenbeil -- 1st edition
ISBN 978-0-6459818-0-3 (Paperback)
Also available as E-Book: ISBN 978-0-6459818-1-0 (EPUB)
A catalogue record for this book is available from the National Library of Australia

Prologue

Michael, 47 years of age, is living on the Sunshine Coast in Queensland, in a beautiful part of Australia. However, his life is not always cheerful. After fifteen years of marriage, his wife Tina wants to split up and stay in their house. Fortunately, he finds a small rental property and keeps the company of his beloved dog. But he becomes increasingly worried about his mother in Brisbane, since she suffers from Alzheimer's disease. One day she almost starts a kitchen fire by accident. What should he do? He and his brother have to find a solution, and fast!

Just when Michael thinks he has everything under control, a mysterious murder happens nearby. Someone finds a half-naked, lifeless woman in a park in Coolum Beach. Who killed her, and why? Michael is horrified, as Tina is living in this normally peaceful seaside town. It turns out that the murdered woman was a nurse named Maureen. But many months pass by without any hints about the culprit and his motive. Maureen's sister and her parents are inconsolable.

Michael and Tina can't forget the gruesome deed either, and Tina is more anxious than ever before. And then an acquaintance of them disappears without a trace.

Meanwhile, Michael's mother no longer recognises her own sons ...

Bra over Jumper

has been translated into English from Marion's original German version called BH über dem Pulli, published by Books on Demand in Germany, August 2023. Marion Birkenbeil translated this book by herself, assuming full responsibility for any errors which may have inadvertently occurred. Apologies for all mistakes and any phrases that may sound odd to a native English speaker!

BH über dem Pulli

By

Marion Birkenbeil

ISBN-13: 9783753402956   Paperback, 288 Pages

ISBN-13: 9783757851057   E-Book (EPUB)

Books on Demand.   Language: German

An Australian crime novel from the Sunshine Coast

1

The sky was grey and no breeze moved the blades of grass in front of Nellie's nose. She dozed off and woke up with a start when a fly buzzed around her. Nellie snapped at the pesky fly but missed it by a hair's breadth. The 11-year-old border collie sighed and nodded off again.

"My dear Nellie, I love you so much!" I whispered, looking at her pretty face with its white muzzle and already slightly greying eyebrows. Her brown and white long coat urgently needed brushing. Once again it was covered in seeds after our last walk, and a twig was stuck firmly in her bushy tail. Quietly, so as not to wake Nellie, I folded up the newspaper, stood up from my comfortable garden chair and went into the house for a drink. The sultry weather in Australia was still getting to me, even though I had emigrated from Ireland forty years ago, together with my parents and my brother Patrick. My hair was reddish-brown and resembled Nellie's hair colour, but was cut short and easier to tame. However, it often looked like a mess too, because I kept running my fingers through my hair whenever I was overcome by despair. Last night, I hardly slept a wink. In addition to many other sorrows, I was deeply concerned about my 82-year-old mother. How would she cope without her husband? Eddie, my dad, had passed away the year before, finally released from an incurable disease that had confined him to bed for months. Marie, my mum, had looked after him lovingly, although she was not exactly the most patient person and preferred to dig around in the garden. Every now and then, a carer had come to assist her, and Patrick and I were very grateful that our father didn't have to move into a nursing home. In the end he died peacefully at home, with Mum by his side. But we all missed my dad sorely.

While I was drinking an orange juice in the tiny wooden house that I had been renting for a few months, my thoughts drifted into the past ...

Right after Dad's funeral on a large cemetery in Brisbane, my mother turned around searchingly, asking no one in particular: "Where's Eddie?"

An elderly mourner gasped audibly, and my brother Patrick and I looked at our mum in dismay. Her eyes were teary, but seemed strangely empty. Before we could reply, her expression changed. She frowned and said ashamedly:

"Oh, I guess I'll have to get used to Eddie not being with me anymore."

Patrick hugged our mother while I sobbed away again, desperate for a fresh tissue. How could a mature man cry so much? But my brother, who was two years older than me, had also sobbed like a little child during the sermon ...

Not for the first time, I asked myself whether that day had already been the beginning of my mother's dementia. Can shock and grief trigger Alzheimer's?

In spite of her age, my mother had been amazingly active. She regularly attended exercise classes for elderly women, went swimming with a few other seniors once a week, worked tirelessly in the garden and met up frequently with various friends. Therefore, Patrick and I had always assumed she would manage fairly well without her husband. But her health went downhill after our father's death. She became more and more forgetful and often seemed depressed and introverted. She hated the emptiness and stillness when she was alone in her flat. And every time she returned home, she half expected to see her husband on the couch in the living room as she'd been used to. But no one was there – silence reigned ...

A shrill bark snapped me out of my musings and I spilled some of my freshly squeezed orange juice all over my freshly washed white T-shirt. Crap!

"Nellie, stop!" I shouted. "What's wrong, girl?"

Her barking increased to a joyful howl, and shortly afterwards I heard a familiar-sounding voice. It was Tina, my ex-wife. Actually, we were still married, but we separated about five months ago – after fifteen years of marriage and too many frustrating arguments. She stayed in our house by the sea, I moved into a tiny house in the hinterland of the Sunshine Coast, not far away from Coolum Beach. The rent for my new home was unbelievably high, just usurious! But I got to keep my beloved dog, and at least I had my peace now. Fortunately,

Nellie only barked when someone came to visit, and usually she stopped again quickly. As always, she was thrilled to see Tina this afternoon, while I was feeling uncomfortable, partly because I was only wearing undies in this heat. After all, I hadn't expected a guest.

"Hi, Tina!" I croaked. "What a surprise! Wait a sec, I'll quickly put on some pants!"

"Don't bother, I'd seen you naked before!"

Tina smirked. She gave me a fleeting kiss on the cheek, and a scent of shampoo wafted around me for a moment. Nellie pressed her whole body against her legs in delight, and Tina stroked her tenderly. I hurried into the bedroom to change my T-shirt and to slip into my favourite comfortable shorts, which I had carelessly thrown on the floor the night before. My untidiness had been one of the many reasons for our arguments. What I considered as cosy often meant an unacceptable mess for Tina.

"What's new?" I asked. "Would you like a coffee?".

"Yes, gladly!" Tina straightened up from her bent position and brushed her wispy black curls out of her face.

Nellie laid down on her back, rolled from side to side and kicked her legs, making funny sounds.

"Nellie seems to be very happy!" Tina smiled briefly, but then she said in a strict voice: "Michael, you have to look after your mother! It can't go on like this!"

"Why? What happened?"

"Your mum slipped and fell down in the bathroom yesterday. Her neighbour called me this morning. She was terribly upset and said Marie had a black eye."

"Oh no!" I exclaimed. "I hope she hasn't broken anything! But why didn't Linda notify me as well?"

My mother had lived in Brisbane for many years, renting a unit on the top floor of a two-storey house. On the ground floor, Linda and Ken lived with their two daughters. Linda was very nice, but I regarded Ken as a macho whom I didn't like very much. My parents, however, had got along fine with the couple. Ken had often hosted a barbecue on a large terrace, where they all drank and sang to their hearts' content. My father had been endowed with a velvety, wonderful-sounding voice. And the others? Well, they had sung along and had fun, even if they had warbled rather loudly than beautifully.

"Well, you must have forgotten to switch on your mobile phone again," Tina now said a little snappishly. "But Linda has informed Patrick, and he's already on his way to your mum's."

Where was my darned smartphone? I ran into the bedroom, then back to the living room, rummaging among unread newspapers and books on the table, then in the crevices of my old armchair without finding it. Once again, I ran my fingers through my hair. While Nellie watched me intently during my frantic search, Tina looked at me with that slightly contemptuous facial expression that I absolutely hated. Eventually I found the phone in the bathroom – without power, of course. As soon as I turned it on and charged it, it rang.

"It's Patrick!" I told Tina, who was busy making coffee for us.

My brother started babbling: "Hi, Michael! I'm at Mum's. She fell down yesterday and she looks terrible! Her face is shimmering in thousands of colours and she's got a nasty scrape."

Then he continued in a whisper:

"I don't think we can leave her alone much longer! Do you know what she just did? She intended to boil water for her instant coffee. But she tried to heat the electric kettle on the gas flame of her stove, imagine that! It smelled awful when I arrived, like burnt rubber. And in general, she's looking miserable! She must have drunk far too little water in the last few days, and we had such a tremendous heat."

"Poor Mum!" I said despondently.

What should we do? Our mother hardly ever drank water, but just coffee and now and then a little liqueur or a glass of wine with the neighbours or friends. When we tried to encourage her to drink, she always replied:

"Water is for washing!"

And now she almost set the place on fire! What would happen next? Like many times before, I felt a strange, unpleasant fluttering in my stomach. At least Mum wasn't all alone; she had the neighbours in the house, and Patrick and I took turns visiting her at the weekend. Unfortunately, Patrick and his girlfriend Sarah didn't live nearby either, but on the Gold Coast. Tina called my mother occasionally, and she'd also visited her a few times after our separation. However, the two of them didn't exactly have the best relationship. My mother got along much better with Sarah, who was gentler and calmer than Tina and didn't contradict her as often.

Tina now kindly handed me a huge cup of latte.

My brother was still chatting away. "The other day Linda had to call the police because of Mum!"

"What?" In shock, I almost spilled the coffee too.

"Yes, Mum came back from shopping and couldn't find the key to her flat. Helplessly, she stood in front of her door, slowly getting into a panic, and in the end, she was shouting and arguing loudly with another neighbour. Linda didn't know what to do and in desperation called the police. When they arrived, it turned out that Mum had the key hanging from a shoelace around her neck – under her blouse!" Patrick chuckled briefly. "But now I'd better look after Mum and see what she is up to! I'll tell you more another time, okay? Bye!"

I felt terribly helpless, drained and tired, but suddenly I was grateful for Tina's presence. With Nellie at our feet, we drank our coffee in the garden and discussed how we could help my mother.

2

The old man was tanned, lean and spry. He had thrown a towel over his shoulder and walked briskly. Like every morning, he wanted to go for a swim, even though threatening clouds were gathering in the sky and a thunderstorm was forecast. He was 85 years old and had long ago made it his goal to keep his body and mind in a good state and to maintain a healthy lifestyle. It was not always easy and required hard discipline. At his pace, it usually took him about half an hour to walk from his house to the beach. On the way, he ate a banana and hoped he wouldn't meet the disobedient huge mutt again, the one that had already jumped up on him twice, trying to snatch a piece of banana. Both times its owner, a scrawny young man, had managed to pull it away only at the last moment. That dog was such a big monster with its wet, long tongue!

His wife liked poodles and schnauzers best and was generally quite fond of animals. She had always been a kind and cheerful woman, but recently she was cranky at times, getting easily upset over little things. She was very forgetful and often asked him the same questions over and over again. Besides, she had become hard of hearing and couldn't understand his answers anyway. He should really take her to an ear specialist soon. Maybe a hearing aid would help? He sighed and kicked a crushed Coke can off the pavement into the gutter.

As soon as Tina had gone home after her surprise visit on Saturday, I felt lonely and lost, and Nellie ran restlessly around the garden. She was visibly suffering from our separation and hardly understood why her mistress and master had fallen out. Did I understand it? In a way, I still loved Tina. She was smart and amusing, had quite a good figure, naturally wavy long hair, pretty boobs and beautiful brown eyes that shimmered warmly when she was in a good mood or animated. And she was fond of animals, which was especially important to me.

I think I inherited my love of nature from my mother. She was a dominant and strict person who had also liked to boss Dad around, but had a soft heart for animals. I wondered if I should give her a little dog for company. Oh no, better not, she was already too old and confused. She would probably feed it at least five times a day and forget to provide fresh water. Or she would give it unhealthy stuff to eat. She could hardly take care of herself anymore! I had recently caught her eating vanilla pudding with a somewhat yellowish, unsightly cream for breakfast, and I had the impression that she hardly cooked herself anything proper for lunch.

What will happen next?

My job at the library made it impossible for me to care for her full-time, and my current rental property was far too tiny for a second person. Tina would have enough space in her big house, but was certainly not willing to accommodate her mother-in-law. Besides, she too had a job she didn't want to give up. Patrick and Sarah were also both employed. Furthermore, they had three children aged 15 to 21 still living with them. Should we look for a professional carer for our mother? But Mum's unit had only one bedroom and was overall hardly suitable for old or disabled people. For example, she had to climb laboriously into a bathtub to take a shower. And we would have to employ not just one but several people for a round-the-clock care.

What should we do?

Over and over again, I felt like treading water and tearing my hair out. This brooding was really maddening. We should probably take Mum into a nursing home soon – as hard as that was for Patrick and me. Just thinking about it made me feel sick. But other relatives, friends and also Linda and Ken had been urging us to do so for a long time. And what else could we do? I decided to look for a decent aged care home that she would like. I also planned to use my upcoming vacation to move into Mum's unit in Brisbane.

Patrick was pleased with my ideas. He told me that he had given Linda a spare key so that she and Ken could look after our mother in case of an emergency. Although I found Ken a bit arrogant, I had to admit that he and his wife were trustworthy and helpful people. In the past, they had often assisted my parents with the shopping after we had sold Dad's old rusty car. Mum had never had a driver's licence. She'd used to cycle around, ignoring all traffic rules, and it was amazing that she had never had an accident. But in the meantime, she had given up cycling because her knees hurt too much and her sense of direction was deteriorating badly. She also found it increasingly difficult to climb stairs.

I sighed and let my dog back into the house. At 11 years old, she was no spring chicken either, and sometimes quite stiff when she got up after a nap. She had even limped a bit recently, but luckily recovered well. Now Nellie brought me a tiny twig from the garden, looking at me expectantly. Despite her old age, she was keen to retrieve balls or sticks of all sizes. I always had to be careful that she wouldn't overdo it, otherwise she would whizz around to the point of total exhaustion.

3

In the following weeks I spent many hours researching aged care facilities in Mum's area. Patrick and I discussed several possibilities at length, without coming to a decision. And then suddenly I had an inspiration. It would be much better if my mother were near me! She had lived in Brisbane for a long time, but it was getting harder and harder for her to recognise people. Some friends had already distanced themselves from her. They probably found it too much of a hassle to communicate with her, because, due to her dementia, she was often at a loss for words. Moreover, my mother almost didn't make it home one day because she was hopelessly lost. At some point she would not be able to find her way around at all. So why should she stay in Brisbane?

An examination by a neurologist and various medical tests by specialists had meanwhile confirmed that she had Alzheimer's disease. Many brain cells had already died – it didn't look good. Unfortunately, there is no cure for this wretched disease yet. However, my mother was prescribed a medicine to alleviate the symptoms. And she was told to drink more water. Well, that would have to be instilled in her with the patience of an angel! Even when I mixed fruit juice into her drinking water, she would just scream, "Yuck!" and sip the liquid like a little bird. She didn't like tea either.

My holiday started today, and I had already packed everything for my trip to Brisbane. Thoughtfully, I looked out of the window, which was in desperate need of cleaning. My house was tiny and had only one bedroom (with access to a shower and toilet) and a rather primitive kitchenette in the living room, but I loved the garden. It was a bit overgrown and had lots of dense shrubs and a few old fruit trees. There was a small pond in which Nellie sometimes cooled off and where the frogs croaked loudly in rainy weather. Birds of all kinds often frolicked in a bottle-brush tree. Some nibbled at the red blossoms, others intoned a deafening song. Originally, this house had been supposed to be a holiday cottage only. The owners, an elderly couple, lived right next door in an old Queenslander, a large, white-painted wooden house with a verandah on three sides. They were lovely people, and I had been lucky to find anything to rent at all, as flats were in high demand on the Sunshine Coast and in the surrounding area. And my beloved dog was allowed to move in with me!

I finished my tea and decided that the window cleaning would have to wait. It was still very early in the morning, and just now the first rays of sunshine were breaking through the clouds. Nellie nudged me impatiently with her head to remind me of our walk. I had promised her to take a detour to the seaside prior to our journey to Brisbane. So, we took a long walk on the beach in Coolum Beach and then drove off in my old Toyota. The traffic was quite busy and got worse as we got closer to the city of millions. Bumper to bumper – stopping, starting, stopping – just annoying! How many inhabitants did Brisbane have by now? 2.3 million or even more? In any case, the city where I had spent my youth and which I had loved seemed like a busy nest of ants now.

Finally, we arrived at our destination. Patrick and I both had a key to Mum's flat. Nevertheless, I rang the doorbell twice in quick succession before climbing up the stairs with all my luggage and a shopping bag full of groceries. Mum opened her front door and Nellie greeted her warmly, wagging her tail wildly and emitting droll, excited sounds. I, however, stared at Mum in dismay, and the sight of her outfit left me speechless. She was wearing a wine-red, home-knitted jumper, and a beige-toned bra over it!

She stroked Nellie, looked at me critically and said quite reservedly and politely: "Good morning!" and I realised that she didn't recognise me at all. I gulped in trepidation, wondering whether to hug her or not. After all, I didn't want to frighten her.

"Hello, Mum!" I said softly.

Her grey-green eyes seemed strangely empty and sad, far away, like at Dad's funeral, but then they returned to the present. She smiled delightedly, took me in her arms and said lovingly: "Hello, little one!"

Funny, as she barely reached my chest.

"Have you had breakfast yet?" I asked her. "I brought fresh bread and your favourite jam."

How thin she had become! She kept pulling up her shorts, which were too loose. I grinned a little sheepishly.

"Mum, you've put your bra on the wrong way, it's supposed to go under your jumper! And anyway, isn't that much too warm? Why don't you put on a T-shirt?"

Without waiting for an answer, I went into her bedroom. Phew, it stank horribly! I tore open the window and took a light, airy T-shirt from her wardrobe.

"How about this one?"

My eyes fell on her shoes standing beside the unmade bed. I discovered something white in one of them, and now Nellie sniffed at it with interest.

"Bah!"

I admonished her, pulling a pair of dirty undies out of the shoe that my mother had apparently stuffed in there.

No wonder the room smelled so terribly of faeces! I helped Mum change, not being very adept at it and awkwardly fiddling with the bra. We both had to cackle. Then we sat down in her cosy kitchen. I made us something to eat and later baked a cake, while she rummaged around in her wardrobe and dusted her furniture in the living room. Unlike other old people, she never took a nap and was still as eager to work as ever.

In the afternoon, we went to her garden where she proudly showed me her flowers, herbs and vegetable plants. The thought of tearing her away from her beloved home and garden, where she'd lived for so many years, almost broke my heart. And yet she could not stay here much longer! For a while we weeded in peaceful unison while Nellie slumbered underneath a tree. Linda, the neighbour, came over for a short chat before we returned to Mum's flat.

"And now we've earned a piece of cake as reward for our work!" I said to my mother and started to cut my homemade apple cake.

But she looked at me in horror and shouted:

"No, we can't eat that! We have to get the permission of that man first."

Only after some confusion on both sides and further protests from my mother did I realise that there were two different persons in her mind. Right now, she regarded me as her son but the baker from the morning (who was me) as a stranger. Finally, I convinced her to have some cake and was pleased with her obvious enjoyment. She had always loved sweets and used to bake vast quantities of delicious cakes. Afterwards, we played two rounds of Ludo, which she won, as happy as Larry. In the evening we watched a quiz and then a romantic film. I noticed that she could no longer manage to turn on the TV, let alone choose a particular program. Several times I patiently tried to explain the remote control to her, but it was useless. Darn dementia!

4

I woke up the next morning feeling very tired. My mother was standing right next to the sofa where I had spent the night, gazing at me intently – almost as if she wanted to find out who was sleeping on her couch. A glance at the big clock on the wall told me it was only 6 am. Even Nellie was still blissfully asleep – curled up into a cute bundle of fur on the carpet under the living room table.

"Good morning, Mum, you're up early!"

I yawned, and my head ached. I hadn't slept very well and had been brooding far too much again.

"Good morning!" she grinned at me mischievously.

She was still in her nightgown and her grey curls were disheveled. I got up quickly and stretched.

"I'll make us breakfast, okay? And afterwards we'll take Nellie for a walk."

Nellie woke up and pricked up her ears, and my mother stroked her tenderly. She seemed content, but when I came out of the bathroom, I found her crying in the bedroom.

"What's wrong?" I asked anxiously.

"I want to go home!"

"But you are at home! You've been living here for many, many years! Since you and Dad emigrated from Ireland back then."

Looking nervous, she opened her wardrobe, from which she randomly pulled out various trousers, blouses and T-shirts and laid them on her bed.

"It's strange that my clothes are in the wardrobe, although I don't even live here!" she said in a shaky voice.

The next moment, she announced resolutely:

"And now I'm going home to Mummy and Daddy!"

Only now did I realise that she wanted to go to Glenbeigh in Ireland, her old home, where Patrick and I were born. Should I explain to her that she had been living in Australia for about forty years and that her parents were no longer alive?

As she reached for her shoes, I quickly suggested:

"Let's have a coffee first!"

Fortunately, she allowed herself to be led into the kitchen, but refused to take more than three sips of water. She drank a cup of coffee with a tiny bit of milk, so at least she had some liquid! After breakfast, I put her clothes back into the wardrobe and made her bed. In the process, I discovered a dirty, crumpled-up pair of knickers at the foot-end of the bed.

Before we left the flat, Mum combed her hair carefully. We went for a nice walk. My mother admired many flowering plants and Nellie sniffed at countless shrubs at length. I liked this part of town that still had its original character. Many old canopy trees provided pleasant shade. It was already quite warm, but a bit windy. Now and then wonderful scents of the blossoms of the Ivory curl trees and Frangipanis wafted around us. Mum walked at a brisk pace, often waving her cane wildly to draw my attention to something, such as a special flower, a rusty tin roof, a colourful window pane with leaded glass, a shabby house in desperate need of a coat of paint, or a pretty ornate balcony railing. She had always had a special eye for little things that she could enjoy. The heat didn't bother her.

On the way, an elderly lady called out kindly, "Hello, Marie!", but my mother had no idea who she was. When we returned, I prepared lunch and Mum took a small watering can to look after her houseplants. Unfortunately, she seemed to do this too often, because some coasters were already close to overflowing, and even a pot of artificial flowers was eagerly watered.

In the afternoon, we were sitting in the living room having coffee and cake when she asked me out of the blue:

"Are your parents still alive? And where do you actually live?"

For a moment I was speechless, and I gulped in trepidation. So now she really didn't know who I was!

"Mum! I'm Michael, your son!"

"What? That can't be!" Mum looked at me, stunned.

"Yes, look here!"

I stood up and showed her the framed family photos on the wall, which included Patrick and me. She inspected the photos and me in turn, still in disbelief. Her narrow face looked helpless and frightened, and I struggled to keep my composure. I almost wanted to cry like a little child.

But suddenly she embraced me and called out:

"Oh, my child!"

Then she smiled at me lovingly, though still with a slightly doubtful expression, and asked:

"You are my child? How old are you?"

5

Today the old man was on the road much later than usual, as there had been a crazy downpour in the early morning. Only after the rain had completely stopped did he set off for the sea. On the way, he ate his daily banana and was pleased not to meet any dogs longing for a piece of it. A bright flash of lightning rushed across the sky. At the same moment, it began to rain cats and dogs again. Oh no! He hurried to find shelter under a roof of the shops nearby and carelessly threw away the banana peel. He decided to postpone his hike to the beach and treat himself to a cappuccino in a street café. The rain slapped heavily on the canopy as he looked for a seat. Finally, he found a vacant chair. It was a little damp from a gust of rain, but he simply sat down on his towel. The café was well attended. Next to him, four middle-aged people were talking animatedly, dressed like businessmen.

A young couple at the next table were busy with their smartphones, wolfing down their breakfast at the same time. The air smelled of coffee, toast, eggs and bacon. A pretty blonde-haired woman kept looking at her watch, as if she were expecting someone, and seemed a little nervous. The waitress now brought her a cup of tea and had to step over a fat dog that was comfortably dozing off. Its owner, who was also quite chubby, apologized and pulled his drowsy dog closer to him so that it would no longer be a potential trip hazard. He smiled kindly at the old man, but he quickly looked away. The old man had a queasy feeling that he could not explain.

In the opposite corner of the street café, half hidden behind a large flower pot with an evergreen dense bush, sat a young woman with long hair and a floppy hat. She began to play the guitar and automatically the old man tapped his feet to the rhythm. Gradually a smile spread across his sullen, gaunt face. For the first time in a long while he thought of his friend Eddie, fondly remembering how often they had sung together when he and his wife had lived in Brisbane. After finishing his cappuccino, he walked to the sea. His heart was strangely lighter, and the rain had subsided and didn't bother him at all. He whistled happily to himself, barefoot, with his slippers in his hand and his towel around his shoulders.

* * *

Tina had arranged to meet her friend Katja on Sunday morning. Unfortunately, she overslept, and now she had to hurry to get to the café in time. After a cat wash, she quickly got dressed and jogged off. She had slept badly and had a strange dream in which she was trying to protect Michael from an aggressive, drunken man with a huge beer belly. Afterwards, she had tossed and turned restlessly in bed for ages before she could fall asleep again. Although she had initiated the separation from her husband, she kept noticing that she still had special feelings for him. During her last visit, when he had spoken of his mother with grief, she would have liked to hold him close and comfort him. He had looked so helpless and vulnerable, with his downy reddish hair and striking cornflower-blue eyes that made him seem younger than his 47 years. And although she didn't like his mother very much and had often quarreled with her, she was still worried about her.

Oh, darn, now it was starting to rain and she had no umbrella with her! She ran even faster, crossed a road, and then slipped on a banana peel and fell down. Struggling to get up, she cursed. What idiot had thrown a banana peel on the pavement? Stupid slippery thing! Her knees were bloody and her right wrist hurt.

"Did you hurt yourself?" a concerned voice asked, and a man gently grabbed her elbow.

"Um, no, it's just a scrape!" said Tina.

Embarrassed, she gazed at the man who was eyeing her critically. He had expressive brown eyes that involuntarily fascinated her. His warm hand on her arm gave her whole body a pleasant tingling sensation. She felt her heart racing and her cheeks flushing and knew for a fact that it was not from jogging. She had a crazy need to snuggle up to this stranger. How dumb was that? After all, she had only recently broken up with Michael and didn't really want to get involved with another man in the near future.

The helpful guy continued to hold her until she was safely back on her feet. Then he bent down to pick up the banana peel.

"Aha, there we have the culprit!"

He grinned, his teeth flashing white in his beautifully shaped, deeply tanned face. With his other hand he held a huge umbrella over them both.

"Would you rather I accompany you?" he asked, laughing a little mockingly. "Though you're already soaking wet anyway. Where are you off to?"

"Oh, umm, well ..." Tina stammered and tried to regain her composure. She wasn't usually so shy after all! "Thanks, that's really nice of you! But nah, I want to meet a friend and I'm way too late anyway, so I'd better dash off quickly. Bye!"

And she scurried off. She felt like a chicken on the run and hoped she wasn't looking too nonathletic. The nice, handsome man appeared so fit and well-toned!

Katja was still waiting in the café and was beginning to get impatient. She kept glancing at her watch and had already finished her tea when Tina finally arrived – quite soaked and with bloody bruised knees.

"What have you done?" Katja asked, aghast.

"I actually slipped on a banana peel, how silly!"

Tina used a tissue to wipe blood off her knee, grimacing as a sharp pain went through her wrist. And then she saw the man with the umbrella approaching, tossing that evil banana peel into a dumpster with momentum. Again, she blushed. What was the matter with her? She was no longer a teenager, but already 44 years old!

Katja followed her gaze and called out: "Hello, Philip!"

She waved wildly, almost knocking a tray out of the waitress's hand. Hot coffee spilled out of a cup and splashed onto Katja's arm. At the same time, they both uttered a cry of terror and the young waitress suppressed a curse.

"Excuse me!" said Katja, gratefully accepting a few napkins from the waitress, who was now putting on a friendly face again.

The man paused for a moment, folded his umbrella and went to them. "Hi, Katja!" Then he turned to Tina and grinned. "Hi! Well, I could have escorted you under my umbrella!"

Katja frowned uncomprehendingly. "Tina, this is Philip, my new colleague."

"Yes, we have just met," Philip replied.

"He was my savior when I slipped," Tina explained to her friend. And without thinking, she suggested: "Why don't you sit down, Philip, and I'll shout you a coffee!"

Oh dear, I wonder if that's okay with Katja, she thought the next moment.

But her friend seemed pleased, and when Philip agreed and looked around for a vacant chair, Katja whispered: "He seems to be a very nice man!"

She winked at her conspiratorially and Tina felt like a silly young girl for the second time that morning. Philip could only get hold of a wet chair that he carried to their table.

He cheekily grinned at Tina. "Actually, you should sit on it, because you're already wet anyway."

"Here!" Katja handed him a napkin so that he could dry the chair.

Tina found his smile and laugh lines incredibly attractive, and also his twinkling eyes and thick brown hair, which was greying ever so slightly at the temples. How old could he be? Maybe in his mid or late forties?

Katja leaned back and brushed her light blonde, silky hair behind her ears. She was a pretty, petite woman next to whom Tina sometimes felt clumsy and awkward. And right now, Tina felt pretty ugly with her soaking wet hair and the T-shirt sticking to her body. But Katja chattered blithely away, and soon all three were engrossed in conversation.

The young woman with the floppy hat continued to play the guitar for a while. She was wearing an airy summer dress and sandals. Her songs were soft and melodic, and her pleasant background music didn't interfere with the conversation of the other guests. At one point she faltered briefly when she felt the gaze of an old man who was watching her curiously but quite seriously. A little later she noticed that he was looking at her again (or still?), but this time with a slight smile on his gaunt face. She left the café as soon as the rain stopped. The big man and the fat dog also got up and walked away.

* * *

Every now and then, the old man longed for his home in Ireland, the green hills and the pretty stone houses, the mossy, enchanted-looking forests and the intense, dramatic display of colours, modified by clouds, sun and shade. And he missed the pubs where young and old people met and sometimes spontaneously played music together. It was on one of these happy evenings that he had met Julie, the funny, spirited tourist from Australia with whom he had fallen head over heels in love and whom he had later married. It was because of her that he had emigrated from Ireland many years ago, when he was still a young lad.

The girl with the floppy hat in the café reminded him a little of those times and of the young Julie, who could also play the guitar well back then. Now, as he was walking past the new apartment complex that had recently been built in the centre of town, he was singing a song he had often sung with Julie and Eddie, his Irish friend in Brisbane. Shortly after, he reached a park and then the beach at Coolum Beach. The sea was grey and calm today, almost like a huge lake, and due to the rainy weather, there were no people in the water. By now it was just drizzling. There was lightning in the distance and he heard a low rumble of thunder, but the storm was further away.

The old man loved the Sunshine Coast in Queensland, no matter what the weather was like or how high the waves were. There were beautiful, long sandy beaches, and the relatively warm seawater was inviting for a swim even in winter – if you weren't too sensitive. Now he enjoyed the feeling of freedom and adventure as he walked through the gentle waves, felt the sand under his feet and then let himself slide into the water. It had a pleasant temperature on this summer day. He dived under the next wave and swam briskly. Later he swam on his back and the rain mixed with the salty spray on his smiling face.

Two lifeguards on the beach were watching him, glad that the old man was swimming in the section between the flags as he should. Only a few days ago they had had to rescue a careless, quite tipsy German tourist. Instead of obeying the beach rules, he had jumped into the water at the wrong spot, promptly getting caught in a dangerous current that had quickly pulled him offshore. Fortunately, they had seen him in time and had immediately raced to his aid in a motorboat. However, this arrogant guy hadn't even thanked them for their rescue operation but had even become rebellious!

6

When I woke up on my second morning in Brisbane, my mother was standing next to me again, watching me. It was almost scary! My back was hurting, probably from the sleep on the soft couch. Outside, a bird warbled merrily and the curtain at the open window billowed in a light breeze. It was 6 o'clock.

Mum asked: "Where's the little one?"

"Who? Do you mean my dog?" I was perplexed.

Nellie was lying next to me on her side, her legs propped up against the couch. Because of her white paws it looked like she was wearing socks.

"No, the little one! We were playing Ludo yesterday. Where is he?"

I detected a hint of desperation in Mum's voice and replied: "But I'm here! I'm Michael, your youngest son!"

Incredulous and confused, she stared at me; incredulous, confused and still rather sleepy, I stared back. Who did she think I was, a stranger? Who had cheekily slumbered on her sofa in the living room?

I had to grin.

"Yes, you won the game last night! And this afternoon we'll play another round, okay?"

"Yes, we will!" she was beaming now.

We had breakfast, went for a walk with Nellie and shared the daily newspaper. Mum read many articles repeatedly, forgetting the contents straight away each time. She seemed in good spirits, and it was a cosy morning until my mother became sad and restless again, desperately wishing to wander home to Mummy and Daddy – on foot to Ireland!?

By now I had learned that there was no point in just distracting her and bringing up another subject. It was a better solution to calmly explain where she was and what had happened in the past – though I mainly talked about cheerful and positive events. Once again, we looked at the pictures on the living room wall, and then we flipped through several photo albums. There were plenty of photos of herself and her family in Ireland. We saw other relatives and friends, her first dog called Bobby, my dad and his family, and of course Patrick and me at different ages and sizes. What a chubby baby my brother had been! But cute with his sky-blue eyes and the black curls which he must have inherited from our mother. I resembled my father, who also had reddish-brown hair and a rather slim figure. Mum had been stocky for a while, but had lost many kilos in the meantime.

Although, like my parents, I was quite thrifty, I wanted to take my mother to a restaurant today. Before we left, I quickly went to the bathroom. When I returned to the hallway, she was standing there, neatly combed, and smiled at me. "I'm ready!"

"Oh!" Once again, I was flabbergasted.

Mum had already put on her sturdy shoes, but was only wearing socks, a fancy blouse (over her bra) and knickers!

"I don't think they'll let you enter a restaurant like that. You need a skirt or some pants," I explained, not quite sure whether to laugh or to cry.

Unfortunately, Nellie had to stay home, as Mum and I intended to visit the beautiful botanical gardens at Mount Coot-tha after lunch, where dogs were not allowed. After a short deliberation, I asked Linda, Mum's nice neighbour who only worked part-time, to look after Nellie in the early afternoon. During our chat, I learned from Linda that she and her family would soon be going on a holiday for a fortnight. Immediately I felt queasy. What should we do? There was no way I was going to leave my mother all alone in the house. She could accidentally burn it down! Or she could fall down again, hurt herself and stay there helplessly for who knows how long – or she could even break her neck from a fall on the stairs – the wildest fears ran through my head.

I soon realised that Mum had got used to having me around as a flatmate, no matter if she regarded me as her son or as a friendly, helpful stranger. One rainy afternoon, I did some grocery shopping and found her in sheer despair upon my return. She had thought I had been gone for ages, and it took a while to calm her down. Luckily, Nellie made her giggle when she expectantly placed a ball of wool at her feet to play with. Mum used to knit jumpers and stockings in the past and still had a big basket full of socks and colourful wool scraps.

Mum loved Nellie and Nellie loved her. The two of them could cuddle together for hours. Every now and then, my dog would sit on her lap with a rapt expression, although at 19 kilos she was actually a bit too big and heavy for a lap dog. Nellie had never been allowed to jump onto an armchair or a couch before, but for Mum's sake I turned a blind eye. However, I woke up the next night because Nellie was snuggling up to me on the couch. Tina would have freaked out if a dog had shared the bed with us!

Overall, the days with my mother were emotional, but actually very harmonious as well. Although her flat was small, we didn't get into each other's hair. When I was busy cooking, vacuuming, cleaning or doing laundry, she rummaged around in her cupboards, wiped the dust off her many knick-knacks in the living room or watered her houseplants, and we also worked well together in the garden. Communication wasn't always easy, though, as sometimes Mum used wrong words or could barely utter a complete sentence.

But she also had amazingly lucid moments. She seemed much gentler and more soft-hearted than before and was easily touched. In my childhood, she had always seemed strong as an ox, stubborn as a donkey and incredibly brave, and I had hardly ever seen her cry. Now tears came to her eyes quickly when sad or tragic stories were shown on television. During one particularly heart-wrenching film, both of us sobbed. And many a night I cried softly, still dreading the thought of shipping her off to a nursing home.

Had I changed as well? I had never considered me as maudlin. Even during the many ugly arguments with my wife, only Tina had often cried loudly or screamed hysterically, while I had mostly remained silent and petrified. Strange, Tina hadn't contacted me for a long time, I mused. How was she doing?

At that moment my mobile rang. Was it Tina? Nope, it was someone from an aged care home on the Sunshine Coast, my first choice of the various homes I had made enquiries about. Funnily enough, it was called 'Puzzle House', and it was only a few years old. I liked its location in a large park that also allowed visitors with dogs. Best of all, it was in the immediate vicinity of my former home (now Tina's) and nearby from my current accommodation, just fifteen minutes drive away. I rejoiced inwardly to hear that a place had become available there! At the same time, my knees felt wobbly, and I was anxious that my mother could overhear my chat to the friendly sounding man on the phone. I had just finished the call when she approached me, asking curiously: "Who was that?"

Oh boy, what should I say? I swallowed nervously and my ears seemed to glow. Should I lie to her? When Dad had still been alive, she had said she would quite happily move into a residential aged care facility later on. But in the last few months, whenever relatives or friends had tried to persuade her to actually do it, she had vehemently rejected all suggestions with a grim face.

Quite spontaneously, I now replied:

"I have booked a holiday resort for you – close to my house and very close to the sea. Since Linda and Ken are planning to go on vacation and I'll have to go back to work soon, you would otherwise be alone here in the house for a fortnight."

I felt lousy and mendacious, and a bout of nausea overcame me, but I was still grateful for this excuse.

7

Unfortunately, I couldn't think of an excuse when Linda and Ken invited Mum, Nellie and me for dinner on Friday. As I'd said before, I didn't like Ken very much. He used to flirt shamelessly with Tina whenever we met him in the house or in the garden. Well, maybe he wasn't a macho at all, but I was too jealous? Ken was quite good-looking and a strong, skilful man – and about ten years younger than me. When I was at school in Brisbane, other kids had often teased me about my reddish hair, and I had been quite skinny. Because of their taunts – and perhaps also as a result from being under the wings of my strict mother – my self-confidence had suffered immensely. Sometimes I wondered why the pretty, dynamic Tina had chosen me of all people as her husband, and I had never liked it when she looked too deeply into another guy's eyes. At a birthday party many years ago, Tina had danced exuberantly with a handsome man whom I would have liked to smack during their third dance together. Was I myself a typical macho, possessive and nasty? Ken couldn't be that bad, since he was always extremely friendly and helpful. Anyway, I tried to look on the bright side.

And indeed, my mother and I now spent an amazingly cheerful evening with the neighbours and their two daughters, who were a bit naughty but very cute. One was 9, the other 12 years old. Linda dished up plenty of delicious food and Ken gave us too much wine to drink, so that by the end Mum and

I were quite tipsy. At an appropriate moment (when Mum was on the loo and the children had gone to their rooms) I informed Linda and Ken about my new plans regarding my mother. They were sad and relieved at the same time. In a soft voice, Linda told me that her kids regarded my mother as their third grandmother. They would all miss her!

Later in the evening, when Mum was already snoring loudly, I called my brother. We had a long conversation and were both very agitated. Our Mum would move to a nursing home – and not just for a fortnight, as I had led her to believe! That night I cried bitter tears.

On Saturday, I woke up, slightly hungover, from a paw scratching impatiently at my arm. Ouch! Nellie let me know that she had to do an urgent business. To my surprise, Mum was still fast asleep and not watching over me yet. Quietly, Nellie and I left the house for a short walk. Worried that Mum could do something stupid in my absence, like putting the kettle on the gas stove, I started to run.

"Hopefully this will file down your sharp claws!" I called to Nellie and smiled at the astonished expression on the face of a passer-by. She certainly thought I was crazy to talk to my dog – what I did all the time! I decided to buy a loaf of fresh bread in a bakery, and when I opened the door I bumped into Roger, an old school friend. Immediately my guilty conscience stirred. Although I had been in Brisbane for almost a whole week, I'd never contacted any of my friends. And why not? Only now did I realise the reason: I was embarrassed for my mother's irrational acting and her mood swings! How would my friends deal with her Alzheimer's disease? Well, I would try it out. So, on the spur of the moment, yet a little apprehensive, I asked Roger to visit me. Back at my mother's, I was glad that Mum hadn't missed me yet. She was still a bit tired, but in good spirits. Spontaneously, I also invited Glenn, another friend from my school days, to come over for a chat.

As soon as my mates arrived, I was ashamed of my previous doubts. Their behaviour towards my mother was completely natural. They waited patiently or helped her when she couldn't find the right words, and they responded in such a nice and sensitive way to my mother's new sudden bout of sadness that I was deeply touched.

When they said goodbye, Mum said in a warm and moving voice: "It was so nice to have met you!"

She regarded them as strangers. And yet, Roger and Glenn had been close friends in my school time, and they had also come to Dad's funeral. But my mother couldn't remember any of that.

She seemed to think more and more often of earlier times and of her own childhood. It was a pity that her siblings lived so far away! Her brother had immigrated to America as a young man, and her sister had stayed in Ireland. Although they were older than my Mum, both of them were still relatively fit, both mentally and physically. A couple of times I tried to contact them via Skype, but despite our best efforts, Mum was not at all interested in communicating with a screen.

* * *

It's fascinating how our brains work. And sad how they deteriorate with age – worse for some. So far, my short-term memory was still pretty good. Nevertheless, I was afraid of developing Alzheimer's at some point. There are certain medicines that might slow down the course of the disease, but unfortunately (as far as I know) they can't stop it. Is this particular form of dementia actually hereditary? Are there preventive strategies? How do you keep your mind sharp? Perhaps with crossword puzzles, learning new languages, 'Scrabble' and similar games like 'Upwords' and 'Wordfeud'? Or with sufficient exercise and a healthy diet rich in vitamins and low in fat?

After reading various articles about this topic on the internet, my head was spinning. People who kept mentally active, socialised and played a musical instrument were said to be less likely to develop Alzheimer's disease. Juggling was supposed to be an effective brain training. Some recommended the frequent consumption of berries, nuts and fish, others believed that turmeric (preferably mixed with black pepper) was very healthy and could possibly also improve the memory. But how much would you have to consume? I wondered. Too much of anything could possibly be detrimental.

Nicotine was said to be harmful to the brain. Other risk factors mentioned were old age, genetic predisposition (oh my!), diabetes, depression, high blood pressure and high cholesterol. And what about alcohol? It would kill brain cells if you drank too much too often, thus also damaging your liver.

Apart from the occasional glass of beer or wine, I didn't drink alcohol. And neither my mother nor I had ever smoked or taken drugs. Unlike Mum, I drank plenty of water and tea. So, I fervently hoped that not too many harmful protein deposits would accumulate in my brain, and that my nerve cells in the cortex and deeper brain structures wouldn't die too quickly.

Incidentally, I had long ago started sprinkling a bit of turmeric into our dinner, much to my wife's annoyance. But Tina had often complained anyway. She'd found my delicious meals too hot! She preferred everything bland, seldom using any spices besides salt and pepper. While I was a vegetarian and quite fond of exotic dishes such as Thai or Indian food, she liked to eat potatoes and steaks. Well, people will always argue about taste, and now we both cooked for ourselves and could choose whatever we wanted ...

These thoughts made me grin wryly. Although Tina and I were separated, she kept coming back to my mind. After all, we had spent a very long period of our lives together and had loved each other dearly in the beginning. I would certainly not be able to forget her so quickly. Or maybe I would, if I also got Alzheimer's. It was a frightening idea that one day I might not even recognise Tina! My wife, with whom I had been so intimate and familiar ...

Did Mum still think about her Eddie, my father, very often? She had rarely spoken of him lately. Recently, however, she had suddenly looked at me with a very clear gaze and said:

"I had a great life with Eddie. He was a wonderful husband and always so sweet and gentle!"

*   *   *

During a long telephone conversation with my brother, Patrick suggested we should invite Mum's four best friends over for Sunday afternoon. He promised to visit us with Sarah as well and offered to bring a big cake. I didn't feel like having a party, but I quickly agreed. After all, who knows when the old ladies would ever see each other again? So, I tidied up the place, packed a few things and helped Mum take a shower – which was a rather complicated procedure. It was difficult for me to get her into the bathtub, and the two of us only managed it with some embarrassment and silly giggles. My mother was not quite as prudish as my father used to be, but I had never seen her stark naked before in my life.

8

The young woman no longer had a floppy hat on her head, and she lay exposed and motionless under a stately, broad Moreton Bay fig tree in the park near the library. Her eyes were closed. Her long auburn hair surrounded her pale face like a fan. A leaf came loose from the tree, gyrated in the light breeze and fell onto her leg. Except for a pair of knickers and a bra, she was naked. The old man squatted beside her and stroked her arm. Very gently, he lifted her head and carefully slipped his folded towel underneath. She was so beautiful! In his memory he could still hear her lovely guitar melodies, and very softly he hummed a song, almost lulling, as if to soothe a baby.

He was startled when he heard some panting and snorting at his back. The next moment, a large dog sniffed at the woman's hair, but was hastily pulled back with a horrified yelp. The old man recognised the puny young man and the dog that liked to eat bananas. The dog's eyes were golden brown, gentle and sad, its owner's eyes golden brown and wide with shock. Stunned, he stared at the lifeless, half-naked woman, then at the old man, then at the woman again, and he had to retch. With more strength than the old man would have thought him capable of, he yanked his dog even closer to him and ran off at lightning speed. The skinny guy stopped after about twenty metres, watched the old man suspiciously and pulled a mobile phone out of his pocket. The dog peed on a post. Just now, the sun was rising brilliantly over the sea. It coloured the sky yellow-orange and made the waves glisten, and it was a picturesque sight. But the old man did not go swimming that early morning. He stayed with the young woman until the police arrived.

*   *   *

Tina could hardly believe that she had unexpectedly fallen in love! With Katja's colleague from the post office in Pacific Paradise! How paradisaical! And funnily enough, she had only met him because of an old banana peel! In any case, his caring behaviour during her little accident had prompted her to spontaneously invite him for coffee. Despite her initial embarrassment and her rain-soaked clothes, she had thoroughly enjoyed the time with Katja and Philip in the café on Sunday morning. She had laughed more heartily than she had in a long time, and they had happily exchanged their phone numbers. That same afternoon, Philip had called Tina to inquire about her wrist, and just the sound of his voice had excited her in a wonderful way. The very next evening, she had already met him again (this time without Katja). They had waded barefoot through the water on the beach in Mudjimba, and after a while he had taken her hand. Later he had kissed her very gently and only briefly, but nevertheless so erotically that her whole body had tingled.

And what now? Before meeting Philip, Tina had firmly resolved to refrain from dating. First, she really would have to sort out her messed-up relationship with Michael. Should she tell him about Philip? After all, Michael was still her husband! Perhaps it was bad timing, as he was worried sick about his mother. Poor Marie! Tina had never managed to address her as 'Mum'. At times, she had almost hated her mother-in-law who could be very hurtful, quarrelsome and unyielding. And yet Tina had always admired her enormous energy and drive, her cheerfulness and inquisitiveness, and had also often laughed with her. But now things were going steadily downhill. During her last visit, Marie's eyes had no longer been shining but had appeared dull and depressed. Could Michael cheer her life up a bit? He was a good-natured person and loved his mother dearly. Eddie, his father, had also been a kind-hearted, dear man; she had liked him very much. It was a pity that he had already died. One should enjoy one's life while it was possible!

Tina sighed. She and Michael would finally have to achieve a settlement concerning their joint property and finances. The thought of a final divorce, however, made Tina feel queasy, and she was downright afraid of a discussion. Michael never got loud or even violent. On the contrary, he usually got very quiet when they argued, but his stubborn silence drove her up the wall even more. Unfortunately, they had had far too many arguments in their fifteen years of marriage. It was hard to believe they hadn't separated sooner. And yet she missed him more often than she would have guessed, and she found it hard to live alone in the house. Even cooking just for herself was not much fun.

Lost in thought, she hadn't even noticed that it was already getting dark until her stomach was growling audibly. She sighed again, switched on the light and went into the kitchen to cook something for dinner. Maybe steamed vegetables and a steak? She reached for her heavy, cast-iron pan – and promptly dropped it with a yelp. The pan crashed to the tiled floor with a roar. What a bummer! She hadn't even thought about her aching wrist! Was it sprained? She should indeed go to the doctor, as Katja and Philip had already advised her. At least there hadn't been any hot oil in the pan that could have burnt her feet, but now there was a crack in a kitchen tile! Damn! Should she just smear some glue into it? Michael would freak out! He and his brother Patrick had laid the tiles in the kitchen and dining room themselves, and both had been proud as fools of their work.

Frustrated, Tina stared at the damaged tile as another problem popped up in her mind. The big one that she kept trying to push away. Ultimately, she would have to put her house up for sale in order to pay Michael his share – that would be the half of their shared possessions. Therefore, the kitchen (including the tiles) should be spotless and the whole house should look as tiptop as possible. But did they really have to sell the house? She would love to stay here!

She had lost her appetite, and only with difficulty did she suppress a sob.

9

Nellie licked up the last crumb of cake from the floor with relish. Patrick and Sarah had brought a delicious home-made cheesecake. The Sunday afternoon with Mum's friends had been nice, although all four of them had talked terribly loudly and my mother had been very confused. In general, she had been rather quiet. But she had eaten her slice of cake with appetite, and several times she had giggled happily. Nellie had loved being the centre of the old ladies' attention, obviously enjoying all the cuddles.

The next morning, Mum and I packed our bags and drove to the Sunshine Coast. Patrick and Sarah would have liked to come along to Mum's new home, but with heavy hearts they had already gone back to the Gold Coast the night before. They had to work on weekdays and couldn't take time off. However, for Mum's sake, we wanted to avoid a big fuss anyway. Nevertheless, I had the feeling that Mum knew very well that she wouldn't just be off to a two-week holiday today.

On the highway, a soft drizzle started. Mum and I were silent most of the time, indulged in our thoughts while the windscreen wipers squeaked softly. Nellie slumbered in the back seat. I felt excruciatingly queasy and could have cried, but I pulled myself together and concentrated on the traffic, which fortunately was not as heavy as the one coming from the opposite direction.

Finally, we arrived at the nursing home called 'Puzzle House' that was part of a fairly new aged care facility. I parked and took a deep breath to calm myself. The residential complex consisted of several single-storey brick buildings separated by gardens and courtyards. There were many shade trees, tall palms and exotic-looking plants, and it almost looked like a cosy holiday resort. The buildings were rendered and painted in a variety of colours like sandstone, light blue, pale yellow or ivory, and most had tiled roofs and solar panels. The whole retirement village was close to a forest, quiet and secluded, yet within walking distance of a shopping centre, complete with post office, doctors, cafés and restaurants.

Even from the car I could catch a glimpse of the beautiful gardens surrounding the main building. The rain had stopped by now and the sun was cautiously peeking through the clouds. In the distance we heard the babbling of a water feature. At the sound, Mum promptly said she had to go to the loo. As a precaution, she had put on a nappy in the morning, but I still hoped she would make it to the toilet in time. I quickly helped her get out, leaving her luggage in the boot for now. A bald man walked by and grinned at us with a toothless smile. In front of the main entrance, several seniors were sitting on benches or in wheelchairs next to some tall, nicely planted flower pots, chatting animatedly.

"Looks nice, doesn't it?" I asked my mother in a cheerful tone, but my voice was hoarse.

Mum nodded, although she was looking intimidated. At the reception we were greeted in a friendly manner and I immediately inquired, somewhat sheepishly, about a toilet for visitors. After the pee break (phew, just made it!), a short introduction and some formalities, a young nurse named Yolanda took us to Mum's new flat. It was a relatively small room with a single bed, a built-in wardrobe, a side cupboard and its own bathroom and toilet – all senior-friendly, of course, so you could just walk into the shower without having to acrobatically scramble around. A rather large television hung on the wall.

While I observed everything and Nellie sniffed at the floor, Mum went straight through the room to the garden door and exclaimed excitedly: "Oh, I have my own verandah!"

I followed her and was amazed and pleased with the sight. We saw a fenced garden with a tiny lawn and many shrubs, which Nellie explored at length. There was a paved seating area that was covered and had a small round table and two chairs. A brick wall served as the partition to one of the neighbouring gardens, and a solid perforated shelf was attached to it. It was empty besides a tiny watering can and a terracotta pot with a wilted geranium.

"Um, someone must have forgotten to clean the shelf," Yolanda said, smiling apologetically.

She looked nice with her reddish apple cheeks, friendly blue eyes and thick auburn hair (almost exactly the same colour as Nellie's and mine!) that was tied up in a thick plait. Her turquoise and blue coloured work clothes suited her well and showed off her attractive curves. To my surprise, my mother resolutely grabbed the empty watering can, filled it in the bathroom and watered the lonely, withered geranium.

I winked at Yolanda and said: "No problem, my mother loves flowers!"

I would certainly bring all the potted plants from Mum's unit in Brisbane that she hadn't drowned yet.

Yolanda explained us all sorts of things, for example, how Mum could call for help in an emergency, and then showed us the main building. It was divided into different wings and had several common rooms and dining rooms. The walls were not white and sterile, but painted in different bright colours and decorated with countless pictures and photos. The air in the corridors smelled a bit like cleaning products and disinfectant spray, but also tantalisingly of pastries and coffee. Somewhere in the distance we heard an alarm of some kind, probably a call for the nursing staff (hopefully nothing bad had happened?), somewhere else something rattled. Yolanda chatted away incessantly, talking about group activities such as painting, handicrafts, singing and 'sports on the chair', but I could tell that Mum was tired. And I couldn't stifle a yawn, either.

Yolanda was grinning at me. "It's almost time for a second breakfast. Would you like something too?"

"Yes, that would be great!" I replied.

"Today we'll have a special event at half past ten with a musical performance in the main hall. Unfortunately, your dog is not allowed in there. Maybe you could just take it to your mother's room for the time being?"

"How sweet!" screamed an overweight woman in a wheelchair when she caught sight of Nellie, rolling towards us at breakneck speed.

I was about to save my dog and myself with a side-step when she braked abruptly, very close to my toes. In sheer delight, she bent down to Nellie and stroked the diamond-shaped white spot on the back of her fluffy soft head, which I also found particularly cute.

"Marie, we'll go to the dining room, okay?" suggested Yolanda, taking Mum gently by the arm.

I had a hard time separating Nellie from the dog-loving lady, and shortly afterwards I met other seniors and a carer who too were quite enthusiastic about Nellie. When I finally looked around for my mother in the dining room – without the dog – she was already sitting at a table with four other residents. One man was dozing with his mouth wide open and one woman was staring apathetically at her empty plate, while two other women were asking Mum about her life with great interest. It would be so nice if she could find new friends here! Gradually the room filled up and then we were given small pieces of cake, some fruit and lukewarm coffee or tea. Mum crumbled the delicious cake with her fingers, munched away and seemed momentarily content. The man woke up and sipped his tea rather loudly.

My brother had advised me not to stay too long with Mum so that she'd more quickly get used to the nursing home, her new flatmates and carers, but I found it extremely difficult to leave her alone. How would she cope? Who would comfort and reassure her when she became sad and anxious again? I gulped down my last drop of coffee (thin instant coffee, yuck!), but couldn't get rid of the thick lump in my throat.

I hugged my mother goodbye. "I'll come and see you tomorrow afternoon, okay?"

"Okay!" my mother mumbled, and her eyes filled with tears.

Before I would start bawling in front of everyone, I took to my heels and went to Mum's place to pick up Nellie, who was supposed to be waiting dutifully on the patio. But when I got there, there was no dog in sight. Where was Nellie? Had a staff member opened Mum's door, allowing her to escape in a flash? Was she now running through the nursing home looking for me? Or was she just blissfully sleeping under a bush somewhere? At her age, she sometimes had an amazingly deep sleep.

"Nellie!" I called and explored the garden. Only now did I discover that it also served three other senior citizens in this wing of the building. It wasn't quite the private oasis for Mum as I had assumed. But it was pretty here, and fortunately the garden was fenced off from the street, so that my mother couldn't just run away if she suddenly decided to march off to Ireland or somewhere else. And because of the high pool fence, Nellie couldn't be too far away.

As I followed the curved path and turned off to the next patio, I heard a soft voice. Apparently, somebody was still in his flat and not in the dining hall. Could Nellie be here? Timidly, I knocked on the open door and looked into the room. A scrawny, ancient looking woman in a nightgown was hanging out of her bed and caressing my Nellie, who was visibly enraptured. Her not-so-white paws were stretched up in the air and I could see some brown marks on the floor. Oh no! Nellie had just walked in here with mud on her feet!

"I am so sorry, um, my Nellie ran away ..." I stammered and hastily wiped the dirty spots on the floor.

"She is so cute! Thank you so much for bringing me your dog, that was the best moment of my day!"

The woman beamed at me and then, with some difficulty, lay back properly in her bed. Her bare arms were skinny and pale, but covered with pigment spots, and the blue veins on her wrinkled hands stood out thickly. Her snow-white hair was cut very short. Why wasn't she in the dining room? I asked myself. Should I help her get there? There was a wheelchair in the corner of the room. But I had no experience at all in lifting people out of bed, and the old lady looked so fragile! No, I'd better leave that to the professionals!

Once again, I bent down to wipe off a newly discovered paw print. Just as I stood up, a carer came in, pushing a rack with several trays, tea and coffee pots, water carafes, cups and pillboxes. She involuntarily gave a sharp cry and was visibly frightened. She had definitely not expected a man in the room! Her ice-blue eyes seemed to spark fire and a menacing frown appeared on her stern face. She was powerfully built and looked as if she would hit me with one of the carafes if she had to.

"What are you doing behind the bed?" she glowered at me.

"I'm sorry, but I was just looking for my dog. Hi! Um, I'm Michael, Marie's son, the new resident in the next room," I blabbered, feeling like a little schoolboy who had been caught cheating.

"Oh, I see!" The blonde carer relaxed and grinned broadly, straight away looking less intimidating. "Good to know you aren't a thief! Yes, we will certainly meet more often in the future. I'm Silvie. And this is Ruth."

She nodded to the old lady, raised the bed and helped her to sit up. "Time to eat some yummy food, Ruth!"

"Well then, bon appétit! Come on, Nellie, we have to go!" I said and snapped the leash on to my dog's collar.

"Goodbye!" Ruth looked lovingly at my dog.

On the way out, we heard beautiful music coming from a piano and a man's deep, velvety voice. My mother would like that! It was only when I was already sitting in the car and just about to leave that I remembered my mother's suitcase. I quickly took it out of the boot and went back (with Nellie in tow, as the temperature in my Toyota was far too hot), informed the lady at the reception about my new visit and stowed Mum's clothes in her flat. The singer's sonorous voice was now accompanied by a bright, crystal-clear female voice.

* * *

When I finally returned to my rental property, my garden looked desolate. The grass was almost knee-high and some weeds had taken advantage of my long absence, spreading out vigorously. Mum, the industrious amateur gardener, could run riot here! Anyway, I would have to mow the lawn immediately, because otherwise Nellie was guaranteed to turn into a grass-green dog. Somehow her fur seemed to attract seeds and sticks like a magnet, and it also matted terribly quickly. Besides, I should trim and file down her nails so that she wouldn't scratch any tender-skinned arms or legs on our next visit to the nursing home.

Nellie was rolling around on the rug in the living room, obviously happy to be at home. I, however, felt terribly weak and tired, and although I should be doing all kinds of work, I couldn't get myself to do anything at all. I filled Nellie's bowl with fresh water and made myself a strong coffee. Then I plopped down on my armchair like a wet sack. And only now did I remember that Mum didn't have an armchair in her new flat!

10

Tina made herself comfortable in front of the television, trying to distract herself from her gruelling musings about Michael and their shared possessions. She had chosen a movie that promised to be exciting. Too lazy to cook a proper meal for dinner, she had opened a bag of chips and poured herself a glass of red wine. She was startled when someone knocked loudly on her front door. Who could that be? By now it was pitch dark.

"Hello?" a familiar voice called out, and Tina opened the door with relief.

"Hello, Katja! Jeez! You scared the hell out of me! I am watching a thriller where a nasty serial killer was just sneaking up on a woman ..."

Katja smirked and dropped onto Tina's couch.

"What kind of horror stories are you watching? You're lucky I'm not a killer!"

Her expression darkened.

"But unfortunately, true events can be worse than a thriller. Have you heard the news? Just imagine, the young woman who played the guitar so beautifully in the café has been killed! Yesterday morning, at dawn, someone discovered her body while walking his dog – and here in Coolum Beach, of all places!"

A bloodcurdling scream on TV made them both flinch.

"Seriously? That's horrible!" cried Tina, putting the movie on pause.

"Yes, and we may have been sitting unsuspectingly next to the deranged murderer!"

"What?" Tina asked incredulously. "What makes you think that?" She frowned angrily. "Or are you trying to pull my leg? Don't make any stupid jokes!"

"No, I am serious! When we met in the café that Sunday morning, I noticed an old guy watching the guitar player very intensely. At first, he was looking almost grim, and then he was smiling to himself, kind of creepy!"

Katja ran a hand through her blonde hair and grinned unexpectedly.

"I bet you didn't even notice, because you only had eyes for Philip the whole time!"

Tina smiled sheepishly.

"You're right, I immediately fell for your nice colleague, it was crazy! Well, I did see the old man, but he seemed somehow familiar and rather likeable, at least completely harmless. However, another guy gave me the creeps. Namely the chubby man with the fat dog. I don't know why, but he kept staring at the musician, and my hair stood on end when he left the café right after her and brushed against me as he left. Although it happened in broad daylight and in public!"

"Really? No, I didn't pay much attention to that guy. But I remember the dog well. He was very overweight indeed, but seemed friendly. Well, read the article about this old man! So much for friendly and harmless!" Katja handed her the newspaper.

Tina put on her reading glasses and read the article.

On Monday morning, a woman had been found dead in the park near the library, lying half-naked between the spreading roots of a large tree. Her only clothing consisted of silky blue-grey brassiere and knickers in the same colour. She was later identified by an old school friend in Noosa as Maureen Collins (how and why was not clear from the article). According to this friend's statement, Maureen was a 25-year-old nurse from Sydney. She had been on a holiday and had spent two days with her. She had intended to meet various friends, travel around Queensland for several months and earn some cash from busking. Unfortunately, she had only made it as far as the Sunshine Coast, where her life abruptly ended. The cause of death was a broken neck.

Tina could hardly believe it! She went to this library all the time to borrow books and films (mostly thrillers). And only recently she had played badminton with a friend in that park. It had always seemed so quiet and peaceful there. Horror gave her goosebumps and she took a huge gulp of wine before reading on. An old man named Bryan Murphy had been arrested. He had allegedly been sitting right next to the body, singing quietly until the police surrounded him with guns drawn. He allowed himself to be taken away without resistance, but remained persistently silent. A motive for the murder was not yet known, and the investigation was underway ...

How sad! Tina's mouth felt dry. "Would you like a glass of wine?" she croaked.

"Oh no, I'd rather not, I still have to drive. But some water would be good."

Tina fetched a carafe of water from the fridge, carrying it in her left hand, while Katja took a couple of potato crisps and crunched noisily.

"Can you pour it yourself?" Tina handed Katja a drinking glass. "My wrist is hurting pretty bad, and earlier I dropped a heavy pan. I guess I'll have to see a doctor after all."

"Yes, I said so straight away!" mumbled Katja, her mouth full of chips.

"But what was the killer's motive?" asked Tina.

Secretly, she was still wondering why the old man had looked so familiar to her in the café the other day. Had she met him before, perhaps somewhere in town? Or during a walk on the beach? Was he really a dangerous, brutal person? Possibly mad – like the ghastly murderer in the movie? An icy shiver ran down her spine and she switched off the television.

Katja drank some water.

"Perhaps it wasn't murder but just involuntary manslaughter. But it's strange that the guy was crouching next to the corpse and singing – he must have been insane! And the woman was supposedly almost naked. What happened to her clothes?"

"Maybe she was raped and then killed!" Tina suggested, and the thought made her sick to her stomach.

What had the guy done to the poor woman? Had he already attacked her the night before and held her hostage for hours? He was old, but looked quite spry. Bryan Murphy – his name too seemed strangely familiar to her.

"Nah, there was no report of rape, and nothing about any other injuries. Maybe it was just an accident, which unfortunately turned out to be fatal." Katja pushed the bowl of chips away from her. "Phew, these things are addictive!"

"What kind of accident? Do you think the woman would have climbed a tree half-naked and then fallen down? Or that she could have broken her neck from a fall over a root?" Tina asked doubtfully, finishing her wine in a single draught and pouring herself another glass.

Ow! Stupid wrist! Tomorrow she would definitely go to the doctor's or at least get an appointment. She sipped her red wine and added thoughtfully:

"Why was this woman, apparently a young tourist, out and about so early in the morning? That would only make sense if she had partied the night away somewhere, wouldn't it? But where and with whom? And why was she involved with an old man? Was she drunk as a skunk? Did she piss him off so much that he got mad at her?"

Tina realised now that she had gulped down her wine far too quickly and was feeling tipsy. A handful of crisps wasn't the best basis for drinking, and she'd never been able to tolerate much alcohol anyway.

"Well, who knows!" Katja looked sadly at her friend.

"Life can end so darn quickly!"

11

I would have loved to lie down like Nellie and slumber blissfully for a while, but the thought that my mother had no comfortable place to sit in her new room gave me no peace. Should I quickly bring her my old armchair? But it really was quite shabby and much too chunky, and besides, it certainly wouldn't fit in my Toyota. So, I would have to ask Patrick if he could deliver Mum's recliner from Brisbane next weekend. After all, he and Sarah had a trailer.

As if my brother sensed I was thinking of him, he called me just at that moment.

"Hi, kiddo, is everything okay at Mum's?"

"Yes, the aged care home makes a good impression and the staff that we met so far was super nice and friendly! Only one of the carers seemed terribly grim, but that was my own fault!"

I chuckled briefly and told Patrick about my encounter with Sylvie, who had screamed in terror when I had unexpectedly appeared behind an old lady's bed. Finally, I asked him to bring certain things from Mum's unit, a few flower pots and also her beloved, familiar armchair on Saturday.

Patrick had a good idea. "Why don't you ask somebody from the nursing home if they could lend Mum an armchair until then? But make sure you don't talk to the old dragon of all people!"

I had to laugh. "Nah, actually Sylvie looked classy and not at all like a dragon once she realised I was harmless."

Just now it came to my mind how beautifully Sylvie's face had brightened when she had smiled at me, and how gentle and sweet she had been with Ruth. Sylvie's voice had a deep, pleasant sound, and her figure was a little sturdy, but greatly shaped. Her blonde hair shimmered golden ...

My brother snapped me out of my reverie.

"Hey, Michael, my lunch break is almost over. Talk to you later, and good luck! Give Mum a big hug from me tomorrow!"

"Okay, thanks! Bye, Patrick!"

I hung up the phone and noticed Nellie's curious eyes and attentively pricked ears. Apparently, she had heard her name when I had told Patrick about our experiences at the nursing home.

"Hello, my darling! Tomorrow afternoon we'll visit Mum, right? But you mustn't run away again! And now I'll try to organise something for her!"

Nellie listened, tilting her head and once again looking irresistibly cute. No wonder so many people got excited about her! And she was my best friend, to whom I could confide all my worries and even my deepest secrets at any time. I cuddled her briefly on her white-haired chest and called the aged care home. Fortunately, I got hold of Lesley, the manager, and I explained my concern. In the middle of the conversation, however, she interrupted me:

"Just a moment, Sylvie is coming over, can you please discuss this with her? I'm afraid I have to take care of something else ..."

For a while I heard nothing but a babble of voices in the background, and then the 'dragon' came to the phone and said in a rather cool tone: "Good afternoon! How can I help you?"

"Hello, Sylvie! I'm Michael, um, Marie's son ..."

"The mystery man behind Ruth's bed?" She sounded amused and already less reserved.

"Yes, exactly!" I cackled a little silly and embarrassed. "Um, I'm a bit worried about my mother because unfortunately my brother won't be able to transport her own recliner before Saturday, and so ..."

"No problem! Yolanda has just brought her a wheelchair that she can use for a while. You see, your mother wanted to carry one of the chairs from the verandah to her room, but it's more comfortable to sit on the wheelchair, isn't it?"

"Oh, thank you, that's very kind!"

It took a load off my mind. Apparently, Mum was in good hands! I would have loved to ask Sylvie how my mother was doing in general, but she was certainly very busy and had no time for chit chat.

Sylvie suddenly laughed.

"At first your mother made a big fuss, going on and on about how she didn't need a wheelchair and could still walk very well, and she even waved her cane wildly. But luckily Yolanda is very patient, and after a while she got her to try out the seat."

"Yes, my mother can be very stubborn!" I replied and sighed.

"Don't worry too much, she'll settle in over time!" said Sylvie, sounding genuinely sympathetic. "But now I have to go, work is calling. Bye!"

"See you soon!" Smiling, I turned to Nellie. "That's done! One problem solved!"

My dog wagged her reddish-brown tail, the end of which looked as if it had been dipped in white paint. I felt better in a flash and my paralysing lethargy was gone. Was it due to Nellie's faithful brown eyes or Sylvie's lovely voice? In any case, I was filled with new energy, mowed the lawn, did all sorts of tedious paperwork and then went to the sea with Nellie.

As soon as I smelled the fresh, salty air and saw the vast ocean before me, I felt magically freed of all worries. Snow-white clouds were gathering in the bright blue sky and it was quite windy. A kite surfer whizzed across the waves at lightning speed, and I heard his loud whoop when he was yanked high into the air. Nellie and I ran across the hard sand at the water's edge and played ball. She was incredibly nimble and skilled at catching the ball, and she could swim quite well too. After a while, she took a longer bath to cool down and I knew she was starting to get tired. After all, she was not the youngest any more. It was time for a break!

I was sure my mother would be happy to see the ocean again. Even if one day she could no longer walk and I had to push her around in a wheelchair, we could still enjoy the magnificent views from various vantage points and boardwalks. Maybe we would even see whales, happily spouting water!

12

On Wednesday morning, Tina finally went to the doctor's office, was sent to a medical diagnostic imaging center to get some X-rays, and was subsequently written off sick. Luckily, her wrist was only sprained and not broken, but she was supposed to take it easy for a while. Too bad it was her right wrist! She felt terribly clumsy and even the slightest wrong movement hurt. But she was happy not to have to work for the next few days. Although she usually liked her job as a hotel manager in Mooloolaba, it could be very stressful at times. The other night, there was a short power outage during a heavy thunderstorm, and some guests were fuming right away. A few weeks ago, a group of drunks, mainly tourists from Germany and England, started a fight at the hotel entrance. As one man was attacked with a knife and got badly injured, Tina rushed to his aid, while a colleague called an ambulance and the police. She had no idea how much booze those guys had drunk before, but they seemed pretty crazy, and her knees were shaking afterwards when she realized that she herself could have been hurt. It was shocking how quickly excessive drinking could lead to violence!

Unfortunately, she had been silly as well, having too much wine the day before! After Katja had left, she had gone to bed and fallen asleep straight away. But in the middle of the night, she woke up and couldn't stop brooding. At first about the dead guitar player, then about a problem with a rebellious hotel employee, later about her husband and their impending divorce. Annoying! And now she had not only a head-ache but also a guilty conscience because she hadn't called Michael for a long time.

When Tina returned home in the early afternoon, after her doctor's appointment and a snack in town, she was pretty tired. She brewed herself a coffee and enjoyed the delicious smell of the freshly ground coffee beans. While she was looking in the fridge for a dessert (maybe a piece of chocolate?), she suddenly heard a scratching noise at her back door. Immediately getting goose bumps, she shut the fridge and listened tensely. Who was sneaking up on her? Oh, she'd better not watch all those scary films anymore! It had probably just been some noise from her neighbours.

But then the door to her laundry opened with a soft squeak! She was gripped by paralysing horror, and for a moment she stood stock-still in the kitchen. Her heart was beating like mad. Was it a burglar? Or had they arrested the wrong man the other day, and the real murderer was still on the loose, now intending to kill her too? She would need a weapon! Spontaneously she reached for the heavy frying pan that she had left unused and spotless clean on the counter the evening before. She took it with her left hand quick-wittedly, as her injured right wrist would be useless for any defence. Before she could react, however, a medium-sized dog was leaping towards her, and in shock Tina almost dropped the pan again.

"Nellie! What are you doing here?" she shouted.

* * *

"Hi, Tina! Why are you here and not at work?" I asked, puzzled. "What's wrong with you?" I stared at the pan in her left hand and at her bandaged right arm.

"Hello, Michael!" croaked Tina. "What do you want?"

Realizing that she sounded harsher than intended, she managed a pathetic smile. "Sorry, I didn't mean it like that, I just got so scared!"

"I've been trying to call you all morning, but your phone seems to be switched off. I just want to get my drill from the garage, that's all! I couldn't find my house keys, but then I remembered that I have a spare key to the laundry room ... but what happened to your arm? And what are you going to do with that old pan?"

"Oh, silly me slipped on a banana peel the other day! I scraped my knees and sprained my arm. That's why I took the day off so I could go to the doctor. I just put a cold gel on it, let's see if it helps. And because I thought you were a burglar, I grabbed the pan as a weapon!"

Although I should have felt sympathy, I snorted with laughter. I had always regarded myself as a completely harmless-looking man, but the other day I had frightened Sylvie as well. She too had looked like she wanted to hit me over the head. Her eyes had been flashing menacingly!

Tina put the pan down and stroked Nellie.

"Well, I'm a bit scared after that nasty murder!"

"What murder?" I asked, astonished.

"How come you haven't heard about it? The day before yesterday, a walker with his dog discovered a dead body in the park. That sounds like a classic case, right? But he also saw the perpetrator. And it was in the middle of Coolum Beach!"

"What? Where?"

I must confess that I hadn't heard any news at all for days, completely distracted by the dealings with my mother and her new home in Coolum Beach. But not a single person at the nursing home had mentioned murder or manslaughter either. Unbelievable! I quickly poured myself a cup of coffee and filled a bowl with water for Nellie. Then we sat down in the living room, where Tina told me what she had learned so far. Finally, she handed me a newspaper article with a picture of the alleged perpetrator.

"But that's Bryan!" I exclaimed, horrified. "He wouldn't hurt a fly!"

Tina frowned. "Do you know that man?"

"Of course, he's an Irish friend of Dad's! He used to visit us in Brisbane all the time, and they already knew each other as children. We must help him! Bryan is not a murderer, that's absolute nonsense! He's a totally nice person!"

I was terribly excited. Sometime last week, Mum and I had been looking at old photos of my father and Bryan. One showed the two of them as teenagers on Rossbeigh beach in Ireland. It was a long sandy beach, and I remembered how Dad had taught my brother and me to swim there. The water had been freezing cold, but that hadn't bothered us at all …

In another picture, my father and Bryan were sitting in a pub in Glenbeigh, beaming at each other over a glass of

Guinness. And there was a photo from a later date in Brisbane, where they were having a barbecue in the garden with their wives. My mother had made a droll grimace, but looked really pretty, and Bryan's wife had smiled mischievously at the camera. When had I last seen her?

Tina tapped her forehead.

"Sure, I'd met him and Julie before, how could I forget! It had been at your parents' house, many years ago, and I think they were celebrating a milestone birthday. Or was it a special wedding anniversary? Anyway, no wonder the old man looked so familiar to me when I saw him on Sunday! But he didn't pay any attention to me at all, he just kept looking at the guitar player."

I was impressed that she remembered the name of Bryan's wife. Julie, that's right! I myself was better at remembering dog names – for whatever reason.

"You met Bryan?" I asked.

"Yes, I was in a café with Katja and Philip – um, a colleague of hers."

To my amazement, Tina blushed, nervously twiddling her hair with her left hand. Then she went on:

"Bryan was sitting at a table nearby, all alone. Apparently, he was on his way to the sea because he had a towel with him."

"Oh, that's interesting! Maybe he lives in our area now! Or maybe he's just here on a holiday. And now he's been arrested? Poor Bryan! I better don't tell Mum about that."

Taking our empty cups, I stood up and said:

"I need a cold drink. Would you like some water too?"

My wife seemed tense, quite pale but with red-flecked cheeks. She nodded without looking directly at me, and I went into the kitchen. And immediately my eyes fell on an ugly hole in a tile.

"What have you done?" I shouted and bent down to inspect the damage.

Tina followed me into the kitchen and said meekly:

"I'm sorry, but I forgot about my wrist and that's when the pan hit the floor."

Against my will, I had to laugh. "Well, you'd better hit the floor than my head! No problem, I still have some spare tiles in the garage. But what are you going to do with your arm now? Will you be all right on your own?"

That afternoon we talked for a long time. I told Tina in detail how I had spent the time with my mother in Brisbane and that she was now in an aged care facility nearby (fairly close to Tina's home and not too far away from my house). It was a very intimate conversation and I realised that I still liked Tina very much.

And then, out of the blue, she said:

"Michael, I have fallen in love with Philip!"

13

Sometimes I wondered how loyal my cute, fluffy Nellie really was. On the beach, she would often run up to strangers, dropping her ball right in front of their feet, and sometimes she would even swim to children on their boogie boards, hoping they would play with her. She loved people of all ages and was a contented, easy-going pet. She was happy if I took her for a walk at least twice a day or played ball or Frisbee with her in the garden or in a park. Otherwise, she made herself comfortable, either on the cool tiles or on one of her many dog mattresses. I liked her independence and we were a great team!

The father of a friend had once confessed to me, ashamed, that he had mourned the loss of his old dog much more than the passing of his own wife, and in a way, I could understand that. Well, Tina and I had our problems and would soon get divorced anyway. Funnily enough, after the initial shock, I was pleased that she had fallen in love with another man. What had become of me, the jealous macho? A better person? Had I really changed in the last six months, perhaps since the separation from my wife?

After we had split up, I often felt quite lonely without Tina, and I was incredibly happy and grateful that Nellie continued to live with me. I loved my dog dearly, and she was my best friend from whom I would never part! Living with her was definitely easier and more harmonious than I could currently imagine with a woman.

Of course, Nellie wasn't perfect either. She could be very stubborn, especially when I wanted her to take a shower. Although she wasn't afraid of water, she tried to get away every time, timid and with her tail between her legs. And she was easily scared. If she heard a nail gun or other loud noises coming from a construction site, she would brace her legs vigorously on the ground, refusing to go any further in that direction. Unfortunately, she completely freaked out when a thunderstorm approached. Even before I noticed any thunder or lightning, she would become agitated, running back and forth in the room, jumping onto my lap and immediately back down, or she incessantly scratched my arms with her paw, her eyes fearful and her whole body trembling. Sometimes I managed to distract her with ball games. Once I had sung loudly to lull her, even though I don't have a particularly melodic voice.

The calming drops that I had bought from her vet seemed to help a bit occasionally, but not always. No idea why that was! Patrick advised I should ignore Nellie's fear and pretend that everything was just fine. Sarah, on the other hand, recommended a special thunderstorm jacket. Or at least I should pull a tight-fitting garment over her head and neck. In my mother's wardrobe in Brisbane, I had discovered an ancient kidney warmer (was it from her youth in Ireland?), which I could try out on Nellie for that purpose. Mum certainly wouldn't wear it any more.

The very next Thursday, there was a huge thunderstorm, and I quickly pulled the blue, soft garment over Nellie's head. I had to laugh out loud. She looked very cute and funny! It fit like a glove and was tight over her ears and around her neck. But would it help? Or should I sing to her again? Maybe reading aloud would work too! Well, I decided to read my notes about Alzheimer's disease to her, which I had collected on the internet over the last few days. Since my own memory was not the best either, I had written them down in a notebook:

Alzheimer's is not contagious. The highest risk (of getting it) is old age.
Alzheimer's disease is the most common form of dementia.
The word 'dementia' comes from Latin and means 'without mind', 'being out of one's mind' or even 'madness' or 'insanity'.
Dementia is a general term for several diseases and conditions that affect the brain and the ability to perform daily activities.
The Alzheimer's disease is a gradual decline in memory and certain abilities.
Impaired are, for example:
Thinking, orientation, remembering, linking of content (the correct processing of information), language (finding words), arithmetic, judgement.
Everyday activities and even simple tasks can no longer be managed.
The disease can lead to a change of personality. Depression or aggressive behaviour may occur ...

"Oh dear, I heard Mum was waving her stick around the other day. I hope she doesn't get too wild!" I said to Nellie and then continued reading:

In the advanced stage, the affected person needs high care. He/she becomes bedridden and can hardly interact with his/her environment. Other people are no longer recognised. The control over the muscles fades more and more, and difficulties to swallow may occur.

"Terrible!" I whispered and swallowed hard.

Alzheimer's disease was named after the German doctor and psychiatrist Alois Alzheimer, who worked at the 'Städtische Heilanstalt für Irre und Epileptische' ('Hospital for the mentally ill and Epileptics') in Frankfurt (at the river Main) and at the Psychiatric Clinic in Munich, among other places. He was interested in the human brain, conducted many studies and published a number of scientific papers.
In 1906 he gave a lecture on the medical case of a patient who suffered from memory impairment, disorientation and hallucinations. After her death, an autopsy of her brain showed that the cerebral cortex was thinner than normal, and there were certain deposits (plaques) in the brain.
His superior, Dr Emil Kraepelin, later described this patient's disease in a textbook and called it 'Alzheimer's disease' to honour his pupil. In the past, 'old age madness' was not attributed to biological causes but to a 'lewd lifestyle', and Alois

Alzheimer was disappointed that his findings were not taken seriously at first ...

"But now he is famous all over the world! Anyway, I guess most people know the word 'Alzheimer's' by now, as there is so much talk and research about it."

Again, a bright flash lit up the sky and both Nellie and I flinched.

"Poor Nellie, my notes are not exactly reassuring. And who wants to talk about illness all the time? We should rather read an amusing book, or perhaps something romantic! What do you think?"

Nellie was sitting half on my lap, half on the wide armchair, actually listening to me intently. Since our return from Brisbane, I graciously allowed her this pleasure. But she was still not allowed to jump on other furniture or onto my bed. I gently pushed her aside and looked for an entertaining, relaxing book. I found a lovely story about a dog called Molly and sat down again, reading to Nellie while more lightning flashed across the sky. Many thunders cracked in rapid succession, and I hoped my mother wouldn't be frightened! And then a pelting rain broke loose.

"You know what, Nellie? I'm going to take a nice children's book to read to Mum on a rainy day."

14

I decided to keep a diary. I don't know why, but I had the feeling that it could help me to organise my thoughts and to clear up the chaos in my head. After all, a new phase of life had begun not only for my mother but also for Tina and me. I began with a description of my first impressions of the nursing home on the Sunshine Coast:

On the fourth of February, with a heavy heart, I took Mum to a nursing home called 'Puzzle House'. On my visit on Tuesday afternoon, she grumbled that she had to wait so long for her breakfast, because she is used to getting up at 6 am at the latest. But she thinks the food is delicious and the staff members seem nice. However, she was indignant when a male carer – a strange guy! – wanted to help her wash and dress. There are seniors who are already worse off than Mum, just lying helplessly in bed like a baby. I imagine it's awful not to be able to express your needs! Not to be able to tell anyone when you feel scared or lonely, thirsty or hungry, when you are cold or in pain. When others have to take you to the toilet, wash you from head to toe and change your nappies.

On top of that, the turnover of staff must be confusing. As a person with dementia, how do you cope with new faces and strange voices? How would I feel if a complete stranger washed my bum; or a young trainee fed me soup with a spoon, more or less patiently? How does my mother feel now, how will she feel later when her health will deteriorate?

Oh boy, I should try to make the best of the present and not to worry about the future. In any case, I am glad that Patrick and I have put our mother in this home – although it was a very hard decision for us. We do feel guilty and relieved at the same time.

On Wednesday morning, Mum was neither in her room nor in the dining room, and I immediately felt queasy, concerned that she had run away. But then I found her in a central garden, where she and an old gentleman were enthusiastically planting small veggies and herbs into a tall container, while a volunteer and two old ladies were busily spreading mulch in another raised bed. Everyone wore gloves, sun hats and smocks and looked cheerful. The air smelled of basil and rosemary. Because Mum seemed to be well occupied and happy, I didn't stay long. I went back to Mum's room and hung up some pictures to make it cosier.

At home, I decided to decorate my own walls as well and to finally fix a shelf that had been sitting in the corner of my living room for ages. But stupidly, my drill was still at Tina's. When I arrived there unannounced, Tina thought I was a burglar, almost hitting me with a frying pan! She was all excited about the murder of a young woman in Coolum Beach. Dad's old friend Bryan, of all people, was found with the dead body and got arrested! I have to help him and find a defence lawyer if need be!

Tina has fallen head over heels in love with another man! His name is Philip and until recently he lived in Sydney. Is he the right man for her?

Reading aloud seems to have a soothing effect on animals. Anyway, it calmed down Nellie during the last thunderstorm. She has already turned a lot of old people's heads at the aged care home. (Oops, I guess the poor woman in the park got her head turned too, but I meant it in a positive way with regards to Nellie. It's great that I get to take her to the oldies!) Last night I dreamed about Sylvie. She is a carer and incredibly attractive.

*　*　*

On Friday morning, I called the local police station. I had intended to enquire about Bryan earlier but had kept putting it off. I was a miserable coward! Even now I was terribly nervous when I made my request, and my heart was pounding. The woman on the phone sounded very friendly but was unwilling or unable to give me any information. Was Bryan in prison? Didn't it usually take forever to convict someone? Unfortunately, I knew little about criminal procedure. I hoped that they had already released the poor old man for lack of evidence, because I simply could not believe in his guilt. I would like to talk to him, but how could I get in touch with him? Had he and his wife Julie moved away from Brisbane, perhaps to the Sunshine Coast? However, when I searched the local phone book, I couldn't find their address. And how did Julie cope with Bryan's arrest? She was a few years younger than my mother and I remembered her as a happy, bubbly and loud woman. Was she still alive?

Once again, my brain was filled with question marks. It was unnerving! A glance at the clock told me that I'd better get going. I whistled for Nellie, who was in the garden, and off we went. Luckily it was only a short distance to the nursing home.

After the usual registration and hand disinfection at the reception, I marched to Mum's room. In the corridor I met Sylvie, who seemed rather tired and stressed. But she smiled at me as she hurried past me, and immediately butterflies seemed to dance in my stomach. Mum looked really chic today. She was wearing a jaunty blouse and an airy skirt, and her softly curled hair smelled of shampoo. She greeted me very formally, though. Obviously, she didn't know who I was, but she was pleased when I suggested a walk.

The pretty park surrounding the nursing home had wide, gently meandering paths that allowed the residents to comfortably navigate around, even with a wheelchair. After the thunderstorm, it had cooled down a little in the early morning, but as soon as the sun rose higher, it became unpleasantly humid. The air seemed to be steaming. Nevertheless, it was a peaceful atmosphere. The leaves of the bushes and trees glistened with wetness, and the birds were happily chirping away. After a while, we spotted a small pond and a creek with a quaint wooden bridge over it, and my mother and I stopped to look into the gently gurgling water. A group of small, silvery fish scurried among the rocks. But we saw something else shimmering.

"There's gold!"

My mother shouted so loudly that I would certainly have fallen into the water in shock if it hadn't been for the railing. We stared spellbound at the golden thing in the stream. What could that be?

"It would be great to find a treasure, hey, Mum? Although I'm sure we wouldn't be allowed to keep it."

"Oh no!" said Mum, disappointed and with her typical sweet pout, and I had to laugh.

"I'll have a look! But wait here, okay? And you, Nellie, stay here too! Sit!"

Quickly, I marched on, climbed over a low bamboo fence and then down a rocky slope. A stone came loose under my foot and I almost lost my balance. It wasn't very smart to clamber around in slippers, so I continued barefoot.

"There!" Mum called, using her walking stick to point me in the right direction.

As the bank became steeper, I carefully went into the creek, moving very slowly on the round, slippery stones. The water reached up to my knees and suddenly a bigger fish shot right through them. Mum waved her stick impatiently, but I had difficulty finding the golden object. Where was it? My little toe stubbed painfully against a rock and I cursed. And then I saw it. It was a medal! I bent down to pick it up when I slipped and fell into the cold water.

15

When I stood up again, snorting and slightly dazed, Nellie was next to me, happily splashing around in the creek. "You disobedient dog, you were supposed to stay with Mummy!" I scolded and examined my legs. My left knee was bleeding and my right ankle hurt. My mother leaned over the bridge's railing and grinned broadly.

"Have you got it, kiddo?" she asked, her eyes gleaming with amusement.

"What's he got?" someone called, and I caught sight of a gaunt, hunched man behind a walker. He joined Mum, pushed back his brown cap and gawked at us curiously.

"Gold!" my mother declared in an impressed tone.

I eyed the medal. Well, it was nicely decorated and had obviously served as a reward in some sporting competition, but it certainly wasn't worth very much. And just for that I had undertaken this silly action and was now soaking wet, had a bloody knee and a bruised ankle! As I trudged sullenly back through the creek and climbed up to the path, I saw a whole group of old people approaching. Nellie quickly ran to them and shook herself profusely in their midst, so that the drops of water sprayed all over them. How embarrassing!

"Nellie!" I shouted angrily.

"Such a cute dog!" exclaimed a fat man in a wheelchair, laughing heartily. The others seemed amused at the dripping wet sight of me.

"Marie and Michael! What are you doing here?" asked a lady with silver-grey, long hair that was braided into two plaits like Pippi Longstocking's hair. She wore a yellow floral blouse and light blue shorts and beamed at us, countless laugh lines embellishing her wrinkled face. It was Julie, hard to believe! A tentative smile spread across Mum's face. I wasn't sure if she recognised her old friend, but I was pleased and would have liked to hug Julie – as wet as I was.

"Hello, Julie, what a coincidence! Do you live here too? Mum just moved in a few days ago," I said, holding out my hand to her.

"What?" she yelled, "You'll have to speak up, otherwise I won't understand a word!" It was only on the third attempt that she understood me. She shouted: "How nice! Then we can see each other more often! Bryan and I live over there."

She pointed behind her where I saw nothing but trees. She laughed at my uncomprehending face and said to Mum and me: "Come with me, I'll show you our new house. And you can dry off at my place, Michael!"

She winked mischievously at me and I grabbed Nellie's leash before she could hop back into the creek. Fortunately, the other walkers had lost their interest in me and sauntered off. After only a few minutes we reached a residential area that looked brand-new. Julie told me that it was meant to be for elderly singles or couples who did not yet require full-time care and were relatively independent, but could use certain services of the aged care home if needed. Bryan's and Julie's house was built with solid, ivory-coloured blocks, had large windows and a tiny garden all around. A flowering bush next to a wooden bench gave off a lovely, not too intrusive scent.

As soon as we entered, Julie called out loudly:

"Bryan, look who's here!"

Hooray, Bryan wasn't in prison! I thought happily. But I was startled when he appeared in front of us. He was very haggard and wrinkled, and there were deep shadows under his eyes. His hair was even sparser than before, and he looked much older than in my mother's photos.

He grinned broadly and patted me on the shoulder. "Have you and your dog been in the pool, Mickie? You always were a cheeky rascal! I hope no one caught you at it!"

Then he turned to Mum and grabbed her hands.

"Hello, Marie! What a nice surprise!"

My mother looked at him in confusion, but didn't withdraw her hands. No one had called me 'Mickie' for a long time!

"That's Bryan!" I whispered to her and noticed the small puddle forming under Nellie, still dripping wet and yet snuggling up to Julie's legs.

Julie frowned and fetched a towel to give my dog a good rub down.

"Why don't you have a quick shower, Michael? Bryan can lend you something to wear afterwards. And I'll make us some coffee in the meantime, okay?"

"Um, oh, that's nice!" I said sheepishly.

Could I leave my mother alone for a moment? She seemed a bit intimidated in this strange environment and I didn't want her to know about the young woman's murder. Oh, nonsense, I always worried too much! After all, we were staying with old friends of my parents. And it wasn't exactly pleasant to chat in wet clothes. A hot shower sounded like a good idea! I went into the bathroom and was amazed. Wow, it was beautiful and huge! I showered much longer than I had intended, and when I came into the living room, the others were already drinking their coffee and eating biscuits. And of course, they were talking about Bryan's arrest! Mum listened spellbound while Nellie lay at Bryan's feet, hoping to catch a crumb.

Julie, who was very hard of hearing, talked loudly:

"Poor Bryan! He wanted to go swimming that morning, as he usually does every day. But then he found a half-naked woman in the car park, right next to a dumpster and partially covered with a black plastic tarp. At first, he thought she was drunk and sleeping it off, but no, she was dead as a door-nail! He could hardly believe it!"

Bryan continued in a softer tone:

"I had met this woman before, when she was playing the guitar in a café. Her music and her voice were lovely, and she looked a bit like you when you were younger, Julie. And now she was dead! I couldn't bear to see her lying there on the ground ... so undignified – almost like discarded rubbish."

He swallowed, obviously tormented by this gruesome memory.

"Therefore, I carried her to the adjoining park and placed her carefully under the big tree ..."

His watery blue-grey eyes filled with tears.

"Those bloody reporters!" Julie cried angrily. "They took heaps of photos and called him a murderer! How could they do such a mean thing?"

Mum whispered: "Murderer?"

"Yes, the police came quite quickly and arrested me. I was so confused I could hardly talk at all," Bryan muttered, wiping his eyes. "And I couldn't identify myself because I had left my wallet at home, since I was going swimming."

"What?" cried Julie.

To my surprise, my mother now squeezed Bryan's hand and said sympathetically: "How awful!"

"And then?" I asked curiously.

"Well, they asked me thousands of questions, first in the park and then in custody. I was sick with excitement and it took me a while until I could speak again. But I couldn't answer much, and even when they asked me for my address, I just couldn't remember it. After all, we only moved here three weeks ago, and I stupidly couldn't remember our new phone number either, only our previous one in Brisbane ..."

"I was sitting here at home wondering where Bryan could have been for so long. I was afraid he'd drowned in the sea!" Julie said, and her voice sounded a bit hoarse. "And then I couldn't take it anymore and called the police. That's how I finally found out they had arrested him. My poor Bryan!"

Her nose still quivered with indignation and her brown eyes sparkled. She clapped her hands unexpectedly, and Nellie jumped up in shock.

"But then they let him go!" exclaimed Julie. "After all, Bryan is completely innocent and harmless!"

My mother nodded in affirmation. "For sure!"

16

After our long conversation, I took my mother back to her room, carrying my wet clothes in a bag. This time we approached the nursing home from a different direction, and we discovered the outdoor swimming pool that Bryan had mentioned earlier. The pool was behind the main building and constructed in a natural setting. It almost looked like a large clear pond, with palm trees, grasses and other plants, rocks, gravel and a tiny waterfall, a wooden deck with benches, and a small sandy beach. The terrain was shaped in such a way that you could walk directly into the water, on a gently sloping, natural-looking surface. I liked it! Maybe Mum could go for another swim, if someone would help her. On closer inspection, I also discovered handrails on the sides of the pool. Of course, there was a fence all around so that no one could accidentally fall into the water and drown. All strangers and dogs were guaranteed not to enter!

It was about time for lunch, so I accompanied Mum to the dining room, where I promptly met Sylvie. She looked me up and down, with raised eyebrows, probably wondering about the brightly coloured Hawaiian shirt and the ill-fitting, far too tight shorts that Bryan had lent me.

Back in the car, I had to grin and said to Nellie:

"At least Sylvie doesn't know I'm wearing the clothes of a man they suspected of being a murderer. Crazy things can happen!"

The ghastly discovery of the body and his prompt arrest must have been one hell of a shock for Bryan! I sincerely hoped he (and Julie too) would get over it. In my opinion it was absolutely outrageous that a journalist had named and pictured an innocent 85-year-old man as the culprit in the newspaper, without any evidence. Was that even legal? And who was the real murderer? Despite the heat, an icy chill ran down my spine. No wonder Tina was scared the other day when I unexpectedly entered her house at the back door! Maybe she should get a dog too! But for her protection she would need a better guard dog than Nellie, who usually barked briefly at guests but then greeted them joyfully and lovingly.

The next morning Nellie was making quite a bit of noise when my brother and his girlfriend drove onto the property.

"Hello!" We all hugged and Nellie was petted extensively.

"Wow, you guys brought lots of stuff!" I marvelled when I saw the fully loaded trailer. Where was all this stuff going?

Patrick rubbed his chubby nose. "Um, we have to clear out Mum's unit anyway. And you need a new sofa and a better washing machine, don't you?"

Well, he was right, but couldn't he have discussed it with me first? I scratched my head, perplexed.

Sarah grinned at me. "I have to go to the bathroom first, but then I'll help you unload." And off she dashed into the house.

"Ken was so kind and helped us carry the sofa downstairs!" explained Patrick, untying the safety ropes he had lashed across the furniture.

"He really is a friendly and helpful person!" I replied.

How could I fit the big couch into my small living room? There was no way I was going to part with my old armchair! After some back and forth, we managed it. Finally, everything found a place, and only Mum's armchair and a small side cupboard for her were still on the trailer. Sarah was exhausted. She dropped onto the sofa and brushed her light brown, slightly sweaty hair out of her face.

"Phew, I need a break! When are we going to your mother's place?"

Her round, pretty face was red with exertion and I handed her and Patrick an iced drink.

"I'd rather wait until after lunch," I said after a glance at the clock and a sip of mineral water. "I wonder if she will recognise you both. Sometimes she clearly sees me as her son, but quite often she seems to ask herself, "Who the hell is that man?" But strangely enough, I don't find that so terrible anymore. At least she's always happy to see me and never afraid of me."

Sarah asked in surprise: "Why should she be afraid?"

"Well, now and then she gets frightened when she's meeting strange men. For example, she was utterly shocked at first when a male carer tried to wash her. And the day before yesterday she allegedly shouted loudly at a doctor who'd come to her room to introduce himself. She thought he were a thief! Because he was dressed casually, she didn't want to believe that he was a doctor!"

"Did your mother have a bad experience with a man in the past?" asked Sarah.

"No idea!" I exclaimed.

„Hopefully not! If she did, she never mentioned anything about it. And Dad was always gentle and nice!" Patrick replied.

I could see in his face that he was appalled at the thought that something bad could have happened to our mother.

"By the way, I met Bryan and Julie quite by chance!" I said. "But you know what, I'll take you out for a Thai Lunch and then I can tell you all about it."

In the restaurant, facing Patrick and Sarah, I was suddenly unspeakably happy that we got along so well. Although my brother and I sometimes had little arguments and he was a bit too dominant for me, I could always count on him, whatever happened. And I also liked Sarah. They had been together for ages and had three children, but they'd never married – much to the annoyance of my quite conservative parents.

Tina and I, on the other hand, had been separated for many months and were soon to organize our official divorce. In that regard, it was good that we had remained childless, which I sometimes regretted, though. Whenever I met a nice family, I was envious and felt I had missed out on something very important. However, when I encountered horrible teenagers or loudly whining babies, I was grateful that my life was much easier without children of my own and that I had more freedom. Tina definitely found kids too annoying and exhausting and preferred to pursue her career. Fortunately, she was very fond of animals. Long time ago, we adopted a shy dog called Teddy and shortly after his death our Nellie, who had now enriched my life for about seven years. I still sorely missed our dear Teddy, and Nellie couldn't replace him by any means, but she definitely filled my heart with new love!

Sarah's and Patrick's children were also smitten with Nellie, especially their youngest daughter, who was now already 15 years old. The siblings spent this weekend with other relatives, Sarah's sister and her family.

"Do you still see Tina from time to time?" asked Patrick after I had told him the news about Bryan and the mysterious murder case.

"Yes, but she fell in love spontaneously and we …," the last bite of my delicious Thai meal got stuck in my throat as I spotted my wife at that very moment. "Over there … there she is!" I croaked.

Across from the restaurant, separated by a small park, Tina was sitting with a man in a café known for incredibly yummy cakes. Could this be her new boyfriend? Even from here I could hear their loud laughter.

"Don't stare at her like that!" I admonished Patrick and Sarah, who were gawking open-mouthed at the people who had managed to get a shady spot in front of the café.

Patrick grinned cheekily.

"Let's have a coffee there after lunch and say hello to them. And this time I'm paying!"

"Nah!" I hissed. "That's far too embarrassing!"

"Why?" Sarah asked cheerfully. "It's a good opportunity to meet Tina's new lover!"

17

Tina laughed gleefully. She had rarely felt so carefree and comfortable in the company of a man, and she was head over heels in love with Philip. Not only did he look super and sexy, but he seemed honest and warm-hearted, had similar interests to her own, and a great sense of humour to boot. The night before they'd slept together for the first time, and that too had been wonderfully uncomplicated and erotic. She could still hardly believe it! Now, drinking her cappuccino, she was surprised to notice that her wrist hardly hurt at all anymore. Philip grinned mischievously and unexpectedly gave her an intense kiss – in the middle of the busy street café!

"You had frothy milk at your mouth!" he explained.

"Oh!" Somewhat embarrassed, she dabbed at her lips with a napkin and let her gaze wander around the park. A couple of little kids in pretty summer dresses were hopping around in a rain puddle, having a blast, while loamy water splashed around them. Then she saw three adults approaching, and she turned pale.

Philip lovingly took her hand. "What's the matter? Are you afraid again you're being followed by a nasty murderer or burglar?" he joked.

"Um, no, here comes my husband!" stammered Tina, now turning bright red.

Fortunately, she had told Philip the previous evening that she was still married. She didn't even want to imagine how embarrassing their unexpected encounter might have been otherwise. Still, she feverishly wished that Michael, Patrick and Sarah would take a different direction. But no, they were coming straight towards them. Bummer!

*   *   *

I wasn't exactly thrilled with the idea of marching up to Tina and her boyfriend. I was annoyed at my brother, who was once again getting his way, and at myself for following him like a well-behaved dachshund. Patrick unabashedly headed for Tina, who had already caught sight of us. She furrowed her brows and quickly ran her fingers through her black curls. She's still wearing her wedding ring! it flashed through my mind.

"Hi, Tina!" said Patrick and lightly kissed my wife's cheek.

Sarah hugged her briefly, but I merely said, "Hi, Tina!", nodded to the stranger and stood indecisively beside their table.

Tina cleared her throat. "Hello! What a small world, I didn't expect to see you three here! This is my friend Philip. Um, Philip, this is Michael, his brother Patrick and his partner Sarah."

"Good day!" Philip grinned at us in a friendly manner.

Admittedly, he had a very nice smile and a pleasant voice. But I had no idea how to deal with the situation. The group at the next table was leaving, and Philip said quickly:

"What a good timing, why don't you sit with us?"

"We don't want to intrude ..." I started lamely, but Sarah and Patrick were already moving the vacated table and three chairs closer.

I resigned myself to my fate and sat down next to Tina. She had put on a discreet perfume and looked smart. I hoped that I didn't smell too bad, since I hadn't showered after the sweaty business of furniture hauling, but had only changed into a clean T-shirt. But why was I worrying about things like that? More importantly, should I hide the fact that I was Tina's husband? What should we talk about? Maybe politics rather than personal affairs? I had never been very good at making polite conversation – and certainly not with my wife's lover!

Philip smiled at me disarmingly.

"Tina told me a lot about you yesterday, Michael! It's wonderful that you still get along so well despite your separation. Unfortunately, it didn't work out at all with Ronnie, my ex-wife. Um, she never wants to see me again in her life." His face twisted a little, but soon brightened again. "I think it's a great shame, but on the other hand, I've wished to move away from Sydney for years anyway, and I've finally managed to get a new job here on the Sunshine Coast. And now Ronnie can be sure not to run into me unexpectedly."

He glanced at Tina, who was sheepishly fiddling with her napkin.

"How's your wrist?" I asked her.

"Much better," she replied. "Now I could easily hit a thief with a frying pan in my right hand!"

Sarah looked at her puzzled, and we told her about our experience at Tina's house when she had mistaken me for a burglar. Then we talked about nursing homes, jobs and moving house, and Philip seemed to listen with genuine interest. Apparently, he was a likeable person. At any rate, Tina was completely blown away! Her eyes lit up whenever she looked at him and I could feel a certain sensual electricity between her and Philip. Despite a tiny twinge of jealousy, I was happy for Tina.

Patrick had ordered coffee for everyone and shared a slice of chocolate cake with Sarah.

"We should take Mum along next time, this cake is super yummy!" he said, licking his lips.

I only tried a tiny bite, as I was pretty stuffed after the delicious Thai lunch.

I asked myself if Sylvie liked Asian food and was surprised how often I thought about her. After all, I hardly knew her, and she certainly had a husband and family. I should put her out of my mind right away!

"We'd better go and visit Mum!" I urged my brother and Sarah.

"Give Marie my love," Tina said, suddenly looking a little sad. "I'm going to visit her soon, I promise."

"Yes, do that! Bye!"

18

Shortly after 2 pm, Patrick, Sarah and I arrived at the retirement village. The car park was almost full on this Saturday afternoon, and because of the trailer we had to park further away at the side of the road. As soon as we unloaded Mum's chair, Nellie jumped on it and looked at me indignantly when I shooed her off. First, we carried the armchair and the side cupboard to Mum's living area. Then we quickly returned to the car to get the flower pots and other odds and ends that Sarah and Patrick had brought from Brisbane. I was curious to see how Mum was doing today, and my brother suddenly seemed nervous. He was seeing the nursing home for the first time, and I knew that the decision to tear our mother away from her familiar surroundings had been as difficult for him as it had been for me.

Grinning encouragingly at him, I knocked on the door and called out, "Hi, Mum!"

No answer. I shouted a little louder, "Hello!?"

"Who is it?" asked a strange voice, and a dog yelped shrilly. Oops, who was that? Nellie pricked up her ears. I opened the door and saw a plump lady with snow-white curls in front of me. A tiny dog, also with snow-white curls, raced towards Nellie and barked again.

"Bella, shut up!" the woman said, smiling kindly at us.

"Hi, I'm Ann! I went to see my sister Hazel and met Marie in the corridor afterwards. She looked a bit lost, and so I asked a carer for her room and accompanied her here. Don't worry, my dog doesn't bite!"

Nellie and Bella briefly sniffed at each other's bums, but Nellie quickly lost interest and ran to my mother. Nellie generally preferred humans to dogs.

"Well, I better go. If you like, I'll come back another time, as Bella seems to like you!" Ann said to Mum and winked at us. "Bye! Come on, Bella!"

And she was gone.

Patrick and Sarah now greeted my mother.

"Hi, we've got some plants for you."

One after the other, they hugged her tenderly and Mum smiled. "That's so sweet! Such beautiful flowers!"

"We've also brought your comfortable armchair," I said and gave her a big hug as well.

She looked from one to the other in disbelief.

"You're all here?" she asked.

"Yeah, sure! It's our free weekend, and Michael took us out for lunch earlier. It was totally delicious, and next time we'll take you along," Sarah babbled on. "Today we wanted to check out the food first. But we brought you your favourite biscuits and a piece of homemade cake."

Patrick eagerly moved the wheelchair out of Mum's room and pushed her armchair into the corner instead.

"No, it's not for you!" I admonished Nellie as a precaution and carried in the little side table. It was a tight fit between the bed and the wall.

"Where shall we put the plants, Marie?" asked Sarah. "Out there by the lone geranium?"

Mum nodded. She started arranging the pots on the shelf, fetched her little watering can and eagerly watered the plants. Later, after Mum had eaten her pear cake and we'd managed, by the skin of our teeth, to get half a glass of water into her, we played a game of Ludo on the patio. We had to help her from time to time, and to her delight she won the game. Before dinner was served, we went for a little walk through the park. This time we discovered a smoking area where several old women and men were sitting together at a table, smoking profusely.

"Phew, it stinks in here!" Mum said loudly, and Sarah snorted, while Patrick groaned softly and shook his head disapprovingly. I was glad neither of us smoked.

Saying goodbye, Mum bent down to Nellie and whispered tenderly, "Bye, you sunny hog!"

"Yes, Nellie really is a funny dog!" I replied.

By now I had already got used to the fact that my mother sometimes used the wrong words, which, strangely enough, often rhymed with the words she actually meant.

"Bye, we'll be back tomorrow morning!" said Patrick and hugged her affectionately.

On the way to the car, he blew his nose and I saw tears shimmering in his blue eyes. Sarah also swallowed noisily and put her arm around his waist. It was certainly never easy to move a loved one into a nursing home, and even harder if that person didn't want to go there voluntarily. Luckily, Mum had been in a good mood today and hadn't even asked about her unit in Brisbane. Phew, we'd have to worry about that one too!

Patrick and Sarah stayed overnight. We set up an igloo tent in the garden, as my little house didn't have enough space for visitors, and prepared a simple dinner. None of us was very hungry – except for Nellie. As I went to the laundry to fill her bowl with dry dog food, I remembered that my clothes which had got wet from my fall into the creek were still in a bucket with soapy water. I quickly rinsed them out and only now realised that the medal was still in the pocket of my shorts.

"Look what I found yesterday!" I said to Sarah and Patrick and showed them my 'treasure'.

"Oh, how pretty!" exclaimed Sarah, who was cutting an onion and had to blink away some tears.

"Can I have a look?" asked Patrick. He put aside the knife he had been using to cut a yellow capsicum into strips and examined the medal more closely.

19

Katja swept the leaves and sticks off her roof that the last storm had blown onto it. Her husband Sam stood on a ladder and cleaned the gutter.

"Hey, watch it, you're sweeping the stuff in my face!" complained Sam.

They heard a door slam and looked at the neighbouring property where an elderly lady was just stepping out of the house. A small, fluffy dog followed at her heels.

"Hi, Ann!" called Katja and Sam.

"Hello, you two!"

Their neighbour waved to them and the dog barked excitedly.

"I'm sorry it's been so noisy at our place the last few nights, but our guests left yesterday," Katja said, leaning on her broom.

"Thank God!" muttered Sam.

"Would you like to come over for a tea, in twenty minutes or so?" Katja asked the neighbour.

"Okay, see you in a bit! Shh, be quiet, Bella!"

"Time for a break, Sam!" Katja smiled at her husband and waited until the ladder was free so she could climb down.

Together they quickly picked up the leaf litter from the path and lawn and took it to their compost heap, and then they went into the house to freshen up and have a second breakfast. After all, today was Sunday!

A few months ago, they converted parts of their house to rent out to holiday guests when they were not using it for their own friends or relatives. Their 25-year-old daughter had been living in Adelaide for six years and their 20-year-old son had recently moved to Darwin, so that the house was getting too big for them. Besides, renting out the holiday home was a lucrative extra income, and they also liked meeting new people. Unfortunately, their last guests had caused them a lot of grief. A young American couple had stayed with them for a total of four days, and from Thursday afternoon to Saturday morning they had thrown a party with some Australian friends. They didn't care that Sam had explicitly stated in the house rules that parties and loud music were not allowed.

Katja was still a bit tired after all the excitement, but she whistled happily to herself as she now put the water on. And in came Ann, holding a plate with nicely arranged grapes and mango slices.

"Oh, you didn't have to bring anything! But that's sweet of you! Go ahead and sit down on the terrace! Would you like tea or coffee?" asked Katja.

"Black coffee, please," said Ann. "Without sugar."

„Okay! "Katja brought tea, coffee and a vegan nut cake outside and smiled apologetically at the neighbour.

"Well, we'd thought it would be a great idea to rent out our flat. And in the meantime, we've indeed met very nice and interesting people from all over the world. But the last couple was just awful, so loud and annoying! Sam was furious, and he almost called the police on Friday night."

"What are you talking about me?" her husband inquired and sat down with them.

"That you were terribly enraged! I don't think I'd ever seen you so angry before."

Sam grinned sheepishly, ran a hand through his short, wispy brown hair and was startled when his fingers came across an insect. Disgusted, he shook it off and said to Katja:

"It's true, those guests drove me mad! But I was impressed how calm and level-headed you spoke to them. And that you made them turn down the music, although they were pretty drunk."

He looked admiringly at his petite yet energetic wife and then turned to Ann. "Did they disturb you too?"

"Nah, it wasn't that bad, because my bedroom is on the other side, and during the day I was mostly away. Only on Thursday I woke up from a terrible noise some might call music, just before midnight, but after that I slept like a log," Ann replied and took a bite of the cake. "Oh, it's delicious!"

Then she giggled. "For a tiny moment, though, I toyed with the idea of going to your meter box to turn off the power." She ate her piece of cake with obvious pleasure and took another one without being asked. Katja was amazed at both her appetite and her words. The old lady was shrewd!

Ann continued: "By the way, last week I had a chat over the garden fence with your previous guest, the young German. What was his name again? Peter? Anyway, he seemed quite nice. Do you actually know that the poor guy almost drowned in the sea?"

"What?" asked Sam, furrowing his bushy eyebrows.

"Yeah, he'd had a barbecue and a few beers with a bunch of other tourists in the Tickle Park. Later that afternoon, he jumped into the sea, all by himself, and got right into a dangerous rip. But luckily, he was rescued. However, he was so drunk that he insulted his rescuers and never even thanked them properly. Afterwards he was quite embarrassed! I advised him to track down the lifeguards to apologise to them and possibly give them a little something for their great services."

"Good idea!" Katja said. "Some time ago there was a bad fight among some drunken tourists in front of the hotel where my friend Tina works. It's shocking how some people behave!"

"Maybe that Maureen from Sydney was murdered by a brutal drunk," Sam said, his brown eyes taking on a troubled expression. "Such a terrible story! Just to think about it makes me sick to my stomach! She was so young, the same age as our daughter ..."

Ann plucked thoughtfully at her pink blouse. "Peter told me something about the dead woman in the park. What was it again? I'm afraid my memory is dwindling."

Katja and Sam looked at her curiously.

"Ah, now it comes back to me. He had met her on the train from Brisbane to Nambour and had a long conversation with her. She had been employed as a nurse in a Sydney hospital and took an unpaid leave because she had got into trouble with a doctor and couldn't stand to keep working there. Anyway, she wanted to take a break and figure out what to do, whether to quit and move somewhere else or ..."

Ann paused to sip her coffee.

"Yes, and?" asked Katja tensely.

"Um, it was about the death of a patient. An old lady had been in her ward for a long time and she had grown very fond of her."

Ann took off her glasses and carefully cleaned them with a corner of her blouse. Then her grey-blue eyes widened and she exclaimed: "How could I forget? That Maureen woman allegedly accused the head physician of killing the old lady."

"What?" Sam looked at her, aghast.

Ann nodded. "Yes, that's what Peter told me. But they couldn't prove anything, I guess, and all the other staff at the hospital – just except Maureen – claimed the patient died of natural causes. After all, she was already 92 years old."

Katja blanched. "Then Maureen may have been killed to shut her up forever!?"

Sam grunted disapprovingly. "That doesn't make any sense if there was no evidence to support her accusations anyway. And we're a long way from Sydney."

"True! But Peter should still discuss everything with the police, don't you think? I'll call him right away." Katja said and rushed into the house.

Ann took another sip of coffee and Sam noticed that her chubby hands were shaking. They were silent for a while, looking into the garden, until Ann cleared her throat and said very quietly: "Who knows, maybe that doctor just wanted to do the old woman a favour and euthanize her? Because there was no hope left and she was suffering too much? My sister Hazel has also indicated several times that she doesn't want to live any more. She is mentally fit, but she can hardly move and can't get out of bed without help. Yet she used to be so sporty and active."

Sam squeezed her hand. "I'm so sorry to hear that! But at least she has you around! And you visit her quite often."

Ann's sad face brightened. "Yes, and she loves Bella. No wonder, because the little one used to be hers before she had to move to a nursing home and that's why I adopted her dog."

Katja returned and said glumly, "I couldn't reach Peter."

At that moment Bella started yapping at the top of her lungs in the house next door and Ann hastily jumped up.

"I'd better go, thank you so much for the delicious coffee and cake! See you soon!"

20

Very early on Sunday morning, Patrick, Sarah, Nellie and I drove to Coolum Beach. We parked in an almost empty car park and followed a narrow sandy trail through the wooded dunes. A whipbird closeby emitted a whistle and a 'whip crack song', and another one answered with a soft tune. It only took us a few minutes to reach the end of the forest, where we stopped to take a deep breath of fresh air and to admire the beautiful scenery. Currently, the roaring waves came close to the dunes, leaving only a narrow strip of sand to walk on. The sun seemed to emerge directly from the sea – it was very picturesque! It quickly rose higher, and its glistening light and the breeze dispelled the last dark wisps of clouds. At the sight of the golden sky and the shimmering water, I was involuntarily filled with deep joy and optimism. Life went on, every day anew, despite all changes and hard times!

However, Patrick and I were both pretty tired. The night before, we had watched a thriller after Sarah had already crawled into the tent, and now we were yawning heartily.

After a while, Sarah admonished us mockingly:

"Hey, stop it, your loud yawning is spoiling the peaceful atmosphere!"

Nellie was jumping around us, becoming impatient, so now we marched off and dipped our bare feet into the surprisingly warm sea water. Sarah waited until the waves receded a little and then threw a ball for Nellie, who instantly took off in pursuit. At that moment we heard a shrill scream that made us turn around in an instant.

"You murderer!" a young, stocky woman shouted at a slim senior, while a bald guy with a huge beer belly stood menacingly in front of him.

That slim man who was wearing only shorts and a bath towel around his shoulders was Bryan! And now the younger man was punching him in the jaw, sending him reeling. Before I could think, I was running towards them, desperate to help my father's old friend.

"How dare you?" I shouted indignantly at the assassin. "Leave him alone!"

The thug stared at me hatefully. "What's it to you?"

"This man killed a young nurse!" the woman clamoured. Her face was already heavily made up at this early hour. "He belongs in jail and shouldn't be happily walking around here!"

"How can you attack an old, harmless man?" my brother interfered.

Bryan rubbed his chin in a daze and Sarah grabbed his arm sympathetically.

"He's completely innocent!" I said angrily. "The stupid newspaper falsely accused him and should never have mentioned him by name and photo."

"What do you know?" the guy sneered and punched me in the eye completely unexpectedly.

I screamed out in pain and surprise, and Sarah screamed even louder in shock. My brother grabbed the mean guy by his arms and hissed softly but threateningly: "Now piss off, or ...!"

The bald man smiled in amusement. "Or what?"

His face contorted into an ugly grimace as Nellie came close to us, dropped her ball and shook the water proficiently out of her fur.

"You fucking dog!" he swore and tried to kick her, but Patrick jerked him around so that he hit his partner's knee instead of Nellie.

Her sharp cry mingled with the guttural growl of my dog and the man's howl of rage, who had obviously underestimated Patrick and could not free himself from his grip. I blinked and struggled to keep my aching eye open. A particularly high wave rolled in and almost knocked me over, and Nellie disappeared entirely in the churning water. Panic-stricken, I grabbed her by the collar to save her from the wild undertow. But as soon as she reappeared, she began to growl at the nasty man again, not taking her eyes off him. Her gaze was no longer friendly and gentle as usual, but fixed and intense. Surely it would have put many sheep or cattle to flight. In a way I was pleased with her protective instinct, although I couldn't imagine her ever biting a person, no matter what. Or would she?

Bryan said calmly, "I didn't kill anyone."

Then he turned to me. "Oh, Mickie, I'm sorry ..."

"Yeah, you should be sorry!" the woman roared and also lunged for a punch, but in an instant her arm was held back by a stranger.

It was a young puny man with a large short-haired dog by his side. The skinny guy would probably lose a fight against this strong woman, and yet she lowered her arm and took a step back.

The newcomer asked in a soft and shy voice,

"What's going on here?"

Bryan grinned. "Hi! We seem to keep running into each other. This time, though, there's no banana and no dead body."

What? Was he completely mad? Had he gone bananas after the hit to his chin? I was stunned.

The skinny guy chuckled and patted his dog on the ear.

"Yes, my cheeky Onyx loves bananas."

Then he became serious again and said to Bryan:

"I have to apologise for my naughty dog trying to grab a piece of your banana – twice already! And I am very sorry for all your trouble in the park that day! After I'd seen you sitting next to the dead woman, I quickly called the police. Then another man came by with his dog, and I warned him not to go near you. But he did it anyway and took many photos, and only afterwards did I realise that this guy was a reporter. It was outrageous that he called you a murderer! I have since learned that you are completely innocent."

Patrick finally let go of the fat man who was sullenly rubbing his tattooed arms. Nellie relaxed, grabbed her ball and looked at Sarah, while the other dog sniffed at Bryan expectantly.

Bryan petted him and smiled mischievously.

"No banana for you today. But next time!"

His owner laughed and said goodbye.

"Come on, let's go!" the woman said to her partner, giving us another venomous look.

They marched off briskly, and a load fell off my mind.

"What a nasty couple!" scolded Sarah. "Actually, we should report those two idiots to the police! And the dopey journalist should be punished too, because basically it's all his fault."

Patrick held out his hand to Bryan. "How nice to see you again after all these years – even if it's not exactly the best morning for you! And with these high waves, I'd rather not go swimming."

Bryan shook hands with him and Sarah, rubbed his chin again and groaned. "You're right, and I've lost the desire to swim anyway. Phew, no one has hit me like that in a long time. But Mickie, you should quickly cool your eye! It's already swollen shut!"

Sarah looked at us both pityingly, but I grinned and replied:

"Never mind! Let's go for a walk and enjoy the beautiful sunrise! Are you coming along, Bryan? If you want, we'll give you a ride home afterwards."

With both hands I scooped up some seawater and washed my face, but this brought little relief. We then walked on together, Bryan and Patrick talking animatedly. Fortunately, the aggressive pair turned off to the next path through the dunes and disappeared from our sight. Poor Bryan! For years he had dreamed of moving back to the sea, and no sooner had he fulfilled this wish than he came across a corpse and was falsely accused of murder. And now he met such villains and was attacked by them! Hopefully his future would be brighter!

21

When I looked in the mirror at home, I was shocked at the sight of myself. I was looking like a monster! Therefore, I asked Patrick and Sarah to visit my mother without me. Besides, getting to see not too many guests at a time might be better for Mum anyway. After breakfast they left, and I lay down on a blanket in the garden, cooled my eye with a cold pack and let my mind wander. It was pleasant in the shade under the tree and I tried to relax. Nellie kept me company and snuggled up to me, still quite damp and sandy, and we quickly dozed off.

At some point, an ant crawled over my arm. Still quite drowsy, I wiped it away and continued to doze off. It was so peaceful here, and once again I was grateful that I had found this place for Nellie and me. In our region it was very difficult to find a place to rent, and more and more people were giving their pets to animal welfare organisations, as many landlords preferred tenants without pets. Some pet owners were certainly completely desperate and I felt sincere sympathy for them, but unfortunately there were also people who cruelly abandoned their dogs or cats.

"I'll never give you away, Nellie!" I promised my dog, and with my eyes closed, I groped to stroke her. But instead of fuzzy fur, I felt a human arm! Horrified, I opened my eyes – at least the one that wasn't injured – and saw my wife kneeling beside me.

Tina smiled at me. "Hello, Michael! You've been sleeping like a log! I was just about to wake you up and tickle your nose. But what's wrong with your eye? Have you been in a fight?"

I rose and felt a slight headache. The cold pack had gotten too warm and the sun was shining hot on my face.

"Yeah, some jerk took a swing at Bryan and at me," I said.

We got a drink and sat down on the shaded verandah, and then I told her the whole story while Nellie ran around the garden, looking for a stick or a ball to play with. Strange that she hadn't barked at Tina's arrival this time. She really wasn't a reliable watchdog if she allowed a person to sneak up on me. At least it was only my wife and not an assassin!

Tina was upset when she heard about the horrible couple on the beach.

"How could they be so brutal to poor old Bryan?" she exclaimed. "And both the journalist and the editor from that newspaper who accused Bryan should apologise and publish a huge article about Bryan's innocence."

"Yes, that would be good, but I fear the damage is irreparable. Even if someone is wrongly suspected, I guess some suspicion will always linger. Besides, some people don't read the newspaper every day. And often fake news spread quicker than real news!"

I carefully touched the uncomfortable swelling in my face.

"Anyway, I feel so sorry for Bryan! At first glance he seems quite fit and energetic, but I've noticed that he gets a bit confused from time to time. And Julie repeatedly asked about Nellie's name and age the other day, and she probably forgets about a lot of things. At least that's what Bryan said this morning. Well, they're no spring chickens anymore."

"And how is your mother doing?" asked Tina.

"Quite well, actually. Patrick and Sarah are with her right now. They can give you the latest news later."

"Um, no, I don't want to stay that long. I just wanted to ask you something ..." Tina hesitated.

"What is it?"

"Philip had an idea. He suggested I move in with him, as a trial, so to speak, to see if we really get along that well. And then you could move back into our house ..."

"Are you serious? You hardly know each other!" I blurted out. "And if it goes wrong, I'll have to move out again? And then what?" I became downright angry. "The rents these days are expensive as hell and it's getting harder and harder to find a place to live. Nah, I'm staying here!"

My eyes fell on the small igloo tent in the garden and I continued icily, "I don't fancy living in a tent or in a car."

Tina's eyes gleamed angrily. "It's impossible to talk to you! You always get upset right away!"

I could hardly believe Tina wanted to move in with Philip, whom she had just met!

I took a deep breath and tried to stay calm. "Where is he living?"

"He's renting a house in Marcoola," Tina replied. "At first he had problems finding anything and even considered moving into Katja's and Sam's holiday flat for a while." She grinned a little wryly. "But I don't think Katja would have liked that.

After all, they are colleagues and see each other all the time anyway."

"And where exactly is the house, isn't it terribly noisy there? I wouldn't want to live too close to the airport. Do you remember when we were at a garage sale in that area and for a moment we couldn't understand a word because a plane was flying directly overhead? And later when we got into the car, another plane was just taking off and it felt as if the whole car was shaking. Nellie was really scared!"

"You and your Nellie!", Tina hissed at me. "I think you love her much more than you ever loved me."

"What a nonsense! Of course I love Nellie, but that has nothing whatsoever to do with my feelings for you."

It was incomprehensible! How could she be jealous of my dog? Nellie came up to us, tail wagging, and placed half of an old, worn tennis ball at our feet. Since we didn't feel like playing, we ignored her. But as Nellie threw the dirty, wet thing directly onto Tina's lap, Tina angrily pushed her away.

Again, I felt cold anger rise up inside me, and in a bitter voice I said:

"I thought you loved Nellie too. However, now that I think about it, you just liked to cuddle with her. But loving also means taking good care of someone. All these years you rarely put fresh water into her bowl. You almost never brushed her fur or took her for long walks. Whenever Nellie was injured or sick, it was me who took her to the vet. You were never a very caring person, Tina! Just as an example, you never asked about my mother when I was in Brisbane to look after her, not once! And quite often in the past, when I was sick in bed, you didn't care for me but rather avoided me as you were afraid of catching a disease."

I snorted contemptuously.

"When I had the car accident and was in hospital for a fortnight, you even took a fancy to another man and had sex with him in our own bed of all places! You always want to have fun..."

Tina stared at me, startled, and burst into tears. Then she jumped up and ran away.

Helplessly I looked at Nellie.

"Come here, my darling! Well, now I've given Tina a piece of my mind. But was that so clever?"

I stroked her tenderly and my head hummed even more than before. I had never forgiven Tina for her fling that she had confessed to me shortly afterwards. Three years ago, she had met a tourist from New York in the hotel in Mooloolaba where she worked, and a little flirtation had turned into a hot love affair – while I was recovering from my injuries in the Nambour hospital. Of course, the guy had returned to America, and Tina had confessed everything to me, deeply ashamed. Since then, we had slept in separate beds. However, our mutual physical attraction had worn off long before that anyway, and I hadn't had sex for about five years.

22

After Tina had stormed off, sobbing and with her hair blowing, I remained sitting on the verandah, with the scent of her perfume still lingering in the air. I was sad and annoyed at my emotional outburst, but somehow also relieved. Finally, I'd told her what was bothering me! I had to admit that I had always trouble speaking my mind, and I couldn't blame Tina alone for our failed marriage – despite her infidelity. We had different expectations, and it was time for both of us to break new ground and become happier. For far too long I had tried to please Tina and to adapt – often concealing my own feelings and suppressing many desires. To be honest, I didn't particularly like any of her friends apart from Katja and Sam, and Tina had never got on well with my best friend Lucas. The two of them were like cats and dogs. Unfortunately, she had often quarrelled with my mother, too. Luckily, I found Tina's parents very nice and never had any problems with them. However, I rarely saw them as they lived in Melbourne. Tina didn't have any siblings, and in my opinion, she had been spoiled too much in the past and had quickly learned to wrap others around her little finger.

Thoughtfully, I watched a small lizard scurry nimbly to a low stone wall and then sit motionless on it. How should I organise my life to feel more satisfied? In no way did I want to regret my past in the future, grouchily saying,

"If only I had ....".

Anyway, I now firmly resolved to meet my own friends more frequently than before. And I intended to cheer up my mother's life somehow. We could make little trips to the countryside and to cafés and restaurants as long as possible. Why shouldn't we treat ourselves more often to something special? I would probably have to postpone travelling to distant countries for the time being, but there were beautiful areas close by, many of which I had not even explored yet. I was also determined to do more sports, for example cycling and swimming, badminton and pickleball, and gain new experiences – and maybe have sex? Would I ever have a lover again? At my age? I didn't think I was terribly ugly, but not super attractive either …

Nellie nudged me impatiently with her nose.

"Nah, we're not playing with this scrap of ball, it's rubbish. Come on, we'd better go to the kitchen and prepare something for lunch!"

I was slicing a cucumber when Sarah and Patrick came back. They were in a good mood, and their genuine, cheerful smiles brightened up my day that hadn't started so well.

"Hi, Mickie! Mum giggled a lot today!" my brother told me and ate a piece of cucumber.

I grinned. After we'd met Bryan again, my brother also called me 'Mickie' occasionally. I didn't mind.

"Yeah, most of the time we didn't even understand what she was laughing about, but it was so great to see! And we went for a nice walk in the park." Sarah smiled at me. "Can I help?"

"Yes, you could set the table. The salad will be ready in a minute, and I've baked some bread – fresh from the bread machine."

"Mm, it smells enticing!" said Sarah.

At lunch I told them about Tina's visit and her plans for the future.

"Wow!" said Patrick with his mouth full. "She must be madly in love with Philip! It's hard to believe she wants to move out, as she always seemed so rooted to your house and garden!"

Sarah furrowed her brows. "Maybe she's just scared of living alone."

"You think so?" I asked.

"Well, the other day she grabbed a frying pan to defend herself against a supposed burglar. And since that murder occurred in her own home town, it wouldn't be surprising if she was scared." Sarah shook herself.

"So, what's your solution for your shared house?" Patrick asked me. "Are you going to sell it?"

"Um, we still haven't really decided what to do. I would love to move back in there myself. But only if I can live there permanently and won't suddenly have to leave because Tina doesn't want to stay with her new lover after all."

I noticed that I sounded bitter again. I forced myself to smile and added: "You know what? Strangely enough, I am glad that she has a new boyfriend. Somehow it makes the thought of the official divorce easier, and besides, she hasn't been happy for a long time. Unfortunately, today I made her cry, and she's ..." I faltered.

"Why? What happened?" asked Patrick.

"I accused her of all sorts of things! Um, I was sort of implying that she's selfish and only has her own welfare in mind."

"Well, that's true!" said Patrick. "Tina is always chirpy when everything goes her way, but grouchy if anything doesn't suit her. She gets offended too easily, although she herself can be quite candid and spiteful. And she's far too interested in money, success and career, I think."

Sarah nodded affirmatively and I gazed at them in amazement.

Patrick laughed aloud. "You look awful, Michael! You won't find a new wife with a face like that, even if it's going to be gloriously colourful tomorrow!"

"How can you joke about that?" his girlfriend scolded.

"Maybe some lovely, warm-hearted woman will take pity on me and then develop tender feelings for me!" I retorted with a grin. Sarah suddenly snorted with laughter.

"Anyway, you've got a nice butt, Michael!"

"What?" I asked her, gobsmacked.

Amid more fits of laughter, she explained:

"When we came to your mum's room today, a blonde, middle-aged woman was with her. They were both giggling mischievously. I only understood the last part of the woman's chat who said: «your son was wearing very tight-fitting shorts the other day. But he looked good in them, because he has such beautiful legs and a nice firm butt!» So, Michael, you might have a chance with this woman! And she seemed a very friendly and kind person."

I turned bright red.

"Oh, um, that must have been Sylvie!" I stammered. "She saw me after I'd squeezed into Bryan's tight shorts."

My brother was grinning from ear to ear, but Sarah quickly became serious again and said:

"Poor Bryan! I hope he'll recover quickly from the new shock this morning! It was such a mean punch to the chin! And that horrible woman almost hit him too! I don't want to imagine what would have happened to Bryan without your guys' help! I really wish the police would solve the murder mystery soon so that no one will believe in Bryan's guilt anymore."

"So do I! Who could have killed this young woman? And why?" I mused. "In many cases, the murderer allegedly is the victim's own partner, an acquaintance or relative. But Maureen was only here on holiday and lived in Sydney."

"Maybe it was Tina's new boyfriend who killed her! He's from Sydney too!" Patrick joked.

Sarah rolled her eyes. "You always have crazy ideas!"

I speared a piece of Feta cheese on my fork and said:

"Apparently, Maureen did have some friends here on the Sunshine Coast, and she was identified by a friend in Noosa. Otherwise, it would have taken much longer to find out her name, as she was found in the park half naked and without any possessions."

"Yes, where did all her luggage, her purse and the guitar go? It looks like a robbery, doesn't it?" asked Sarah.

"Just awful!" I sighed.

Patrick was grinning cheekily again.

"Maybe someone couldn't stand her music any longer and that's why he snapped her neck!"

Sarah choked on a breadcrumb, coughed, gasped briefly and then croaked: "You have quite a wry sense of humour today!"

* * *

Later, we were playing a game of Brändi Dog on the verandah when my old friend Lucas came by for a surprise visit. I jumped up to greet him. "Hi, Lucas, great to see you! I was just thinking this morning that we should meet more often again!"

Lucas, however, didn't return my smile but stared at me in horror. "What's the matter with you? Did your wife beat you up?"

"Are you crazy? Tina would never do anything like that! Nah, I had a run-in with a terribly aggressive couple earlier today, and I'm glad I had my big brother supporting me!" I grinned at Patrick. "But we'll tell you later, let's just finish our game quickly, okay?"

"Well, good luck then!" Lucas peered curiously at our board game, while he gave Nellie a pat.

"What are you playing?"

"It's similar to Ludo, but it's played with cards and marbles and quite a lot of rules, and it's much more interesting and exciting," Sarah explained.

"You can also play it with four people. Would you like to join in the next game?" I offered.

"Sabotage!" shouted Patrick gleefully, moving my fourth and final red marble to another spot to prevent me from my expected win.

Originally, he and Sarah had learned this game from a friend who'd added some own rules to the proper ones, and we all had happily adopted those rules such as the 'Sabotage'.

"You are so mean!" I groaned.

But immediately I took my revenge and removed one of his yellow marbles. "Ha, I killed you again!"

Lucas laughed bemusedly. "Can you kill someone more than once?"

Sarah shouted delightedly: "You weren't paying attention, Michael! You should have attacked me instead!"

And swiftly she put her last blue marble into the goal, winning the game.

During a short break with tea, coffee and some snacks, we told Lucas in more detail about the unpleasant incident on the beach, and his sympathetic, open face took on a grim expression. He was normally an easy-going person who liked to laugh a lot, but he could get furious if someone was treated unfairly. He could not stand violent bullies at all.

Then we explained the Brändi Dog game to him as he was keen to try it out. Sarah had printed out the main rules to make it easier for a beginner. With four players, the people sitting across each other team up, and Sarah, who knew Lucas quite well, wanted to be his partner. Her cheeks were still glowing with joy from the previous victory, and Patrick winked at me good-naturedly. We both knew she was very competitive. But unlike Tina, she was also a good loser. My brother really had a lovely girlfriend, I thought and winked back.

"Hey, are you giving each other secret signs? That's not allowed!" Lucas complained jovially.

As soon as we started the game, he was on fire, catching on to the rules surprisingly fast. However, at one point he made a silly mistake and ran his hand contritely over his short salt and pepper hair.

"Oh, Sarah, forgive me!" he cried theatrically, and we all had to laugh out loud. In the end, he and Sarah won the game, both beaming like little children.

"And what do we get as a reward?" Lucas asked jokingly.

"I could give you a gold medal, but I'll have to hand it in at the nursing home, since I discovered it there," I said, showing him my find from the creek.

"Is this real gold?" Lucas took the medal and looked at it from both sides.

Surprised, he exclaimed: "My father once won a medal like this in a triathlon! He was as proud as a peacock and couldn't stop bragging about his win."

His blue eyes glittered somewhat mockingly yet lovingly. "Yep, better return it quickly, Michael! Perhaps the owner will come forward."

"Too bad you didn't find a valuable gold treasure that you could keep and use to buy a new house," Sarah said. Then she spontaneously suggested, "Maybe the four of us should play the lottery together sometime, just for fun?"

"I've never done that in my life!" I replied.

"Me neither!" said Lucas. "But we could try it out. Sometimes you can win enormous sums!"

My brother made a snide grimace but finally agreed. Despite the nasty incident in the morning, we were all in a cheerful, optimistic and somewhat silly mood at the moment – perhaps due to the Brändi Dog game?

23

The next morning, I was still in a good mood, although my face was indeed glowing in different colours and still a bit swollen. I really didn't look very handsome! Fortunately, Nellie didn't mind and greeted me as lovingly as any other day. After our walk, I treated myself to a delicious breakfast of fresh croissants and homemade jam that I'd got as a gift from Melissa, my landlady. Over the last few weeks, she had occasionally turned up at my front door to chat with me and to give me limes or tomatoes from her garden. I had an inkling she felt a bit sorry for me, the 'hermit', after I'd told her about the break-up with Tina.

Melissa was a motherly old lady with apple cheeks and kind brown eyes. Jim, her husband, was also a nice guy. He was almost as short and roundish as Melissa and had similar curly grey hair. From afar it was hard to tell them apart as Melissa rarely wore a dress or skirt and they both usually put on a straw hat when being outdoors. The saying 'birds of a feather flock together' seemed to apply to them.

Even though the rental costs for my little house seemed quite high, they were lower than the ones for comparable other houses or flats in the area, and I felt comfortable here and shouldn't complain. However, I didn't know what to do with all my mother's belongings. She had accumulated so much stuff!

Patrick, Sarah and I planned to start clearing out her household next Saturday, and I was already dreading it. Wasn't it unfair to sort through Mum's possessions in her absence? Wasn't it wrong to throw away things that might have been dear to her? But what else could we do?

My eyes fell again on the sparkling medal on my table and I quickly put it in my pocket so that I wouldn't forget to take it to the nursing home.

Later in the morning, I handed the medal to a young receptionist I had never seen before. She was wearing a turquoise and blue patterned uniform with the home's logo, had a light blonde pageboy hair-cut, a narrow, elongated nose, dark brown eyes and long, probably false eyelashes. There was a name tag attached to her blouse, and as I read it, I caught a glimpse of her huge breasts. Her name was Leah, and she eyed me critically as I explained my request.

At that moment Ann, the white-haired lady I had once met in Mum's room, stepped next to me and called out:

"You found the medal? Hazel will be so pleased!"

She continued eagerly: "My sister is often frustrated because she can hardly move. And yesterday she told me, very embarrassed, about a tantrum that she had last week. When a volunteer put her into a wheelchair and took her out into the park, Hazel was suddenly seized with an enormous rage about her own disability, and she hurled her medal into the creek. She had won it in a triathlon a long time ago. She had always carried it with her proudly all these years, first as a pendant on a gold chain around her neck and later in her bathrobe pocket."

Ann sighed sorrowfully. "Poor Hazel! She could always run much faster than I could. But now her legs give her so much grief, and she is more and more dependent on assistance from others. Surely, she will be happy to get that medal back, even though she'd thrown it away in her burst of anger!"

She promptly held out her hand. "I'll return it to her straight away!"

Leah frowned, saying in a cool, almost stern tone:

"Well, first I'd like to ask Hazel herself about this incident before I'll give away the gold medal. It seems strange to me that your sister didn't tell anyone about it. And which volunteer was with her in the park that day? What's her name?"

Unexpectedly, Ann became so grim that I almost felt frightened.

She hissed at Leah, "Don't you believe me?"

She propped her chubby hands on the rather high reception counter, stretched and pushed her face very close to Leah's. The receptionist instinctively backed away and batted her eyelashes nervously. At the same time, I heard a low, warning growl from Nellie, who was apparently getting tired of the curious attention by Bella, Ann's little dog. Despite the tense atmosphere, the situation suddenly seemed funny, almost like a bad comedy, and I had to laugh.

Ann turned to me as swiftly as I would hardly have expected from an old woman, and she scolded me:

"That's not funny at all!"

"Good morning!" Yolanda crooned.

She was pushing a senior in a wheelchair, who gave us a toothless smile and then beamed at the two dogs. Just behind them Lesley, the manager of the nursing home, appeared. She was a tall, stocky woman with a dashing short haircut. She too wore the typical uniform of the aged care facility as well as a name tag on her blouse.

"Morning!" replied Ann and I.

Then I noticed how Ann's ugly grimace, distorted with anger just a moment ago, changed into the rather pretty face of a harmless, nice woman. It was scary and yet fascinating! She obviously had the talent of an actress or was prone to enormous mood swings!

Leah uttered a small sound of relief and turned to Lesley. "Can you help me find the right owner of this medal?" In a whisper she told her what it was about.

"No problem!" Lesley replied. "I'll ask Hazel right away."

She took the medal and motioned Ann and me to follow her. On the way we met Sylvie, who looked a bit puzzled at our little procession. Ann's sister was living in a different ward from my mother, but the arrangement of the individual rooms and the communal dining and lounge areas was exactly the same. Three women and two men were sitting at a table with a male staff member playing some game with huge cards. Great idea when you can't see very well!

Lesley knocked on Hazel's room and after her reply "Come in!" she opened the door. I caught sight of a white-haired woman lying in bed, looking amazingly like Ann, but frighteningly pale. Bella jumped joyfully to her, and the old lady bent down to pet her. Of course, Nellie got jealous and also ran to Hazel, who patted her as well with a kind smile. An old feature film was playing on the television.

"Sorry to disturb you, Hazel, but I want to ask you something. Did you throw a medal into the creek last week? And if so, can you describe it? This nice man here found it by chance, on a walk with his mother."

She smiled fleetingly at me.

Hazel turned down the sound of the TV, kneaded her wrinkled hands and said:

"No way! Recently someone stole my pretty medal! I always had it in my pocket and suddenly it was gone. But I already told you, Ann!"

Ann had red spots on her cheeks, and I detected a new hint of anger in her face.

Yet she said calmly: "Apparently you've forgotten that you threw it away in a fit of rage. Never mind, we got it back."

"What did the medal look like?" Lesley asked impatiently.

"I won it in a triathlon when I was 30!" declared Hazel proudly, giving a detailed description.

"That's exactly right!" Lesley exclaimed delightedly and handed her the gold medal.

"Yes, that's mine!" Hazel beamed, and she looked really cute. Her blue eyes lit up as she squeezed my hand. "Thank you so much!"

"I'm glad my jump in the water paid off!" I said with a grin.

"Well then, all the best! I'm going to visit my mother now. Come on, Nellie! Goodbye!"

"But where is my golden necklace?" I heard Hazel ask as I was leaving and immediately turned around again. What necklace?

"Oh nonsense, you lost that a long time ago!" Ann replied in a firm voice. "You've always had that medal loose in the pocket of your dressing gown since you've been here."

Hazel looked at her doubtfully. "Well," she murmured, "the main thing is that my medal is back. I was so happy about my victory back then, and besides, I met my husband that day!"

Tenderly and with a dreamy expression, she kissed the medal and placed it on a side table. I suspected that her husband was no longer alive. Lesley was looking irritated, and I too wondered about the sisters' completely different statements. Why had Ann made up the story about the tantrum in the park? Or was Hazel not so clear-headed after all? Who was to be believed? I should find out the name of the volunteer who, according to Ann, had been there when Hazel had allegedly thrown away the medal.

Lesley gazed at me sharply for a moment and then turned to Hazel:

"If anything goes missing again in the future, please let me know immediately! Recently, some jewellery and money were stolen from two residents in the neighbouring wing. We already notified the police, and we will keep our eyes open. But now I'll leave you alone. Have a nice time with your sister and little Bella!"

She gave Ann a curt nod. "Bye!"

"Bye!" I said as well and walked to Mum's room, deep in thought and with Nellie at my heels, while Lesley hurried back to reception.

I was glad that no one accused me of stealing Hazel's golden necklace! But her sister Ann seemed very suspicious to me. Had she possibly stolen the item? Had she kept the necklace, presumably made from real gold and very expensive? Had she chucked the medal, which was of no value for herself, into the creek? That would be outrageous!

It was just as well that my mother didn't have any valuable treasures in her room! She hadn't been able to handle money for a long time, and therefore I also kept her purse. Luckily, Patrick and I already got the power of attorney for her bank account a few months ago. It was great that I could trust my brother one hundred percent!

24

My mother was dozing off on the patio. It hurt me to see her so tired, thin and fragile, whereas before she had always been hyperactive and quite strong. One day she would surely become bedridden like Hazel. But it wasn't that time yet! I gave myself a jolt and tried to put myself in a more positive mood.

"Hi, Mum!" I said cheerfully and sat down next to her, and Nellie squatted down expectantly right at her feet.

Mum blinked a little in confusion, but widened her eyes when she noticed my swollen face.

"What happened to you?" she asked in dismay.

"Oh, some dorky guy punched me on the beach yesterday, but it's not painful anymore," I explained, feeling relieved when she didn't inquire further.

She lovingly stroked Nellie, mumbling something into her ears.

"Shall we go for a walk?" I suggested. "But first you must have a drink."

I filled a glass with water and handed it to her. Mum pinched her lips together and shook her head grimly.

"Come on, at least a tiny bit!" I insisted. "One sip for Nellie, one for me ..." Patiently I waited, but she only drank half a glass. "You'd prefer a schnapps or liqueur, wouldn't you?" I joked, eliciting a grin from her.

After a visit to the toilet, I helped Mum put on her sturdy shoes and tie the laces, handed her the walking stick, took Nellie on the leash, and then we walked off. Although the smell in the nursing home was not unpleasant, I breathed in the fresh air in the park with relish. Mum was soon waving her stick around to draw my attention to various things. A tiny bird was nibbling on a Grevillea, a Tibouchina tree was resplendent in purple blossom, and a gardener in a straw hat was expertly pruning a tall Lilly Pilly hedge. After a while, we entered an area that looked like a natural rainforest, providing soothing shade, and we marvelled on the rich greens of the plants and the light-flooded palm fronds. For a few minutes, we sat down on a bench and watched some ducks in a pond, and Nellie was disappointed that she was not allowed to go swimming.

I chattered away, telling my mother about Hazel's joy at our discovery of her medal, about Patrick, Sarah and Lucas, and the latest news from all over the world that was not too negative. On the way back, we passed the beautifully landscaped pool again. Looking over the fence, my heart seemed to stop. There was a corpse! A woman in a blue swimming costume was floating in the clear water, face down, with her arms stretched out wide. Her blonde hair was spread out like a fan. Oh no, that was ... that was Sylvie! I was seized with icy horror and felt sick to the stomach.

Hastily, I pressed Nellie's leash into Mum's hand and shouted to her: "Stay here!"

With clammy hands, I fumbled awkwardly with the gate's safety catch, opened it and rushed to the pool. I tore my trainers off my feet and jumped in the water. As fast as I could,

I swam to Sylvie, fervently hoping to get there in time to save her! When I was almost by her side, she turned over on her back and gasped for air. She rubbed her eyes and asked incredulously:

"Michael, what the ..."

Before she could say any more, I impulsively embraced and kissed her deeply. Sylvie was alive! I was so happy!

Sylvie pushed me away gently and took another deep breath.

"What's wrong with you? Why do you keep jumping into the water in your full gear?" she asked, grinning at me.

"I thought you were dead!" I stammered.

She snorted with laughter.

"I was just relaxing for a while, and at the same time I wanted to check how long I could hold my breath!"

I felt completely stupid. But Sylvie surprisingly pulled my head towards her and gave me another kiss.

"Thank you for coming to my rescue!" she said, now noticing my mother standing stock-still beside the gate, watching us.

"Hello, Marie! It's all right!" Sylvie called out to her and stuck her thumb up in the air.

Then she swam with powerful strokes to the end of the pool and stepped out of the water ahead of me. I admired her smooth, wet, shiny skin and the tight muscles and would have liked to pull her back into my arms again. And I felt feelings stirring inside me that I hadn't felt to this extent in a long time.

Sylvie turned to me.

"Will you wait here for a moment? I'll just change quickly and then I'll take your mother to her room so you don't have to walk around the hallways soaking wet!"

She sighed exaggeratedly. "What I do for others! All I wanted was go for a swim after work ..."

Mum giggled gleefully.

"You do have an interesting son!" said Sylvie, winking at her.

She disappeared into the change room and rejoined us a moment later, dressed in her work uniform, and with her hair rubbed dry and dishevelled.

"You better get out of here before you run into Lesley in your wet state!" she said to me. "Because she can get furious sometimes. And besides, you're probably causing too much of a stir with your black eye anyway! Have you been in a fight?"

"Nah! But that's a long story."

Embarrassed, I tugged at my wet shorts.

"You know what? I'll buy you lunch and then you can tell me everything in detail! After all, you just tried to save my life, that has to be rewarded!" Sylvie beamed at me. "How about a Thai restaurant? I know one that offers quite inexpensive and yet very tasty dishes at lunchtime. You don't have to dress up, but please come in dry clothes!"

"Great!"

Now I was beaming too. I said goodbye to Mum and made an appointment with Sylvie for noon, hardly believing I was about to meet her in private. My heart was beating like crazy.

25

After a hot shower, I put on my favourite light blue shirt, sand-coloured shorts and new sandals and drove to the restaurant Sylvie had suggested. My heart still seemed to be beating faster than usual, there was a gurgling in my stomach and my palms were a little damp. When I arrived at the restaurant, Sylvie was already sitting outside at a table next to a long planter with a palm tree, various small shrubs and low grasses. She had on a sky-blue, airy dress and was grinning mischievously at me.

"Hello, Michael! I am glad you're on time, because I always get a ravenous appetite from swimming!"

"Hi, Sylvie!" I sat down opposite her and smiled shyly at her. "Have you ordered anything yet? By the way, there's no need for you to pay, I'm happy to ..."

"Nah, nah, my brave saviour, I'm paying, don't you argue!"

"All right! But I have no idea if I would have succeeded in resuscitating you, because my first aid course was ages ago!"

Sylvie laughed heartily. "Even so, I'd like to reward your great effort."

A young waitress appeared, filled two glasses with water and handed us the menus. Sylvie and I both chose a meal recommended by the chef, which was offered at a reasonable price at lunchtime.

"Mm, I already smell a tantalizing aroma coming from the kitchen! I totally love Thai food!" I said.

"Me too!" Sylvie took a sip of water. "By the way, my husband had liked to emigrate to Thailand for a while, but that idea never really appealed to me. I enjoyed our holiday there, but otherwise I'd rather live in Australia."

"So, you're married?" I asked, trying not to sound disappointed.

Sylvie shook her head. "Not any more. Harry, my husband, passed away five years ago. He had a lung disease that he'd probably caught at work." Her eyes were sad.

"From working with asbestos?" I asked sympathetically.

"No, Harry worked with artificial rock and inhaled too much silica dust," Sylvie explained. "He had suffered from coughing and shortness of breath, and later he was diagnosed with silicosis. He was employed by a company that made kitchen bench-tops, and by now there are stricter precautions. At least I hope so! But unfortunately, no doctor could help my Harry any more, and he ..." Her voice failed.

"I'm so sorry!" Spontaneously I took her hand and squeezed it briefly.

"Yes, I miss him very much! And of course, my two daughters were also completely distraught."

At that moment the waitress who looked rather Philippine than Thai served us the steaming meals, and only now did I realise that I was quite hungry too.

"Enjoy your meal!" said Sylvie.

"Thanks, you too! And how often do you see your daughters? Do they live nearby?"

"Yes, Lucy lives in Noosa and Jacqueline in Yandina. Both of them were – and still are – a huge comfort to me, and I don't know how I would have got my life back on track without them!" Sylvie's eyes lit up warmly while she talked about her daughters. Finally, she asked, "And you? Are you married?"

I almost choked on the hot vegetables. It was the first time in many years that I was seeing a woman, and despite the break-up with Tina, I suddenly felt guilty. Nuts, right?

I looked at Sylvie, saying frankly: "Yes, I am. However, we are in the process of getting a divorce. Tina and I split up about half a year ago, and we've been living apart from each other for quite a while."

Sylvie poked around in the food on her plate for a few seconds and then put her spoon to the side. "Hmm. I'd met someone before who supposedly wanted a divorce." Her voice sounded bitter now. "And stupidly, I fell in love with the guy. But after a year, I finally realised he'd only made empty promises, and he's still with his wife – even today."

"Well, it's not exactly easy to end a long and intense relationship," I said hesitantly. "But I've come to regret putting up with Tina for so long. I still like her and would like to keep her as a friend, but we argued far too often. Somehow, we are not a good match ..."

Hastily, I took a sip of water to hide my embarrassment. At the next table, a woman laughed shrilly, making me wince. When I reached for the water bottle to fill our glasses again, I touched Sylvie's hand, as she had just been about to do the same. Exactly as described in so many cheesy romance novels, I felt the electricity spark between our fingers and I felt a hot wave of affection for Sylvie. I was falling more and more for her! And she was so beautiful!

"You look pretty!" it bubbled out of me, and I blushed.

Sylvie smirked. "So do you! That shirt suits you perfectly and goes so well with your blue eyes!"

After lunch, I spontaneously invited Sylvie to my house and to my surprise she agreed without hesitation. Nellie greeted us both with joy, and to my delight Sylvie was obviously quite fond of her too. Over coffee in the garden, I told Sylvie more about Tina and also about her new flame Philip. Gradually, I was becoming more confident and relaxed. We exchanged information about our jobs, and at some point, we got to talk about Hazel and Ann.

"Do you actually know all the volunteers from the aged care home?" I asked. "I have the impression that Ann made up the story about her sister's tantrum and that she herself hurled the sports medal into the creek. But why? Had she stolen the golden necklace and tried to get rid of the medal that way? Not very clever, hey? She could have just thrown it into a bin."

Sylvie frowned. "Strange indeed! I should check out if anyone has taken Hazel into the park lately. Currently there are only two women who go for walks with certain residents on a regular basis. Our other volunteers usually help with the weekly bus tours, or they help out at parties or other special events. And then there is a painting and craft session, gardening and various games. All other activities, such as sports exercises and fitness training for the brain, are led by suitably trained staff members. Professionals are also always present for swimming and water gymnastics – after all, we don't want anyone to drown!"

Sylvie grinned at me mischievously, stroked Nellie and said:

"By the way, you should also keep dogs mentally on their toes, like teaching them new skills or assigning tasks to them. What have you learned, Nellie?"

Nellie wagged her tail eagerly and ran off to search for a ball. That was her favourite game! However, I did like the idea of teaching her some new tricks and making her life more interesting.

Sylvie continued: "We don't have many male volunteers. But occasionally a very nice man from Fiji comes to sing and play music. You should see – or hear – how beautifully the old folks can suddenly sing again! Some even dance or at least sway enthusiastically!" She giggled. "One lady in a wheelchair moved so ecstatically once that I was afraid she would fall off! And a man who's almost 90 showed off some quick dance moves the other day, it was amazing!"

"Fantastic! I'm sure my mother will also enjoy such musical performances. She was actually singing an old Irish song to me this morning, and she could remember the whole lyrics, even though she usually has a lot of difficulties finding the right words. I was perplexed!"

"Yes, music is special! And your mother has been busy gardening too." Sylvie smiled. "I like your Mum, she seems so warm-hearted, honest and nature-loving!"

Sadly, I replied, "She was always very socially minded, energetic and engaged, but she's gone downhill since my father died. He was a great singer, by the way! His voice was just wonderful!"

Sylvie got up, sat on my lap and hugged me lovingly. Astonished, I froze for a second, but then I pressed her against me and could hardly believe my luck! The fabric of her dress felt silky as I gently stroked her back. Her blonde hair smelled wonderful. Her skin was warm and smooth, and I felt her soft yet firm bosom and her excited heartbeat against my chest. We caressed each other, gently and tenderly, and I felt downright intoxicated. Then she gave me a long kiss that triggered long-forgotten emotions in me and made me forget everything except Sylvie – until Nellie jumped up at us.

"No!" I exclaimed, and Sylvie giggled.

"Your dog is quite jealous, isn't it?"

"And absolutely addicted to games!" I retorted, as Nellie now brought us a ball.

In the evening, a soft rain began to fall. I wrote in my diary:

I had a wonderful day with Sylvie, and I am totally in love! And the best thing is: she also has a crush on me! She admitted it although she had sworn never again to start a love affair with a married man, after having a bad experience with such a guy. Tragically, her husband has passed away at the age of 51. She is 46 years old and has two daughters aged 25 and 22. It was indescribably lovely to cuddle with Sylvie and I can't wait to see her again. I feel like an excited teenager!

And some other good news:

My nephew would like to move into Mum's unit in Brisbane and the landlord has already agreed. So, we don't have to clear out everything! Furthermore, we intend to give some of Mum's belongings that she no longer needs to Sarah's and Patrick's other two children. It's still very, very sad and yet a huge relief.

26

The next morning I arrived at the nursing home at half past nine. The sun was shining, and a light breeze chased off the last few clouds. Mum was not in her room. Where was she? I quickly took Nellie to the common room where an employee was mopping the floor.

"Do you happen to know where Marie, my mother, is?" I asked her.

"Oh, she's probably on the bus tour. They are going to have a picnic in a park in Noosa today!" the woman said, busily continuing to clean without paying any further attention to me.

"Thank you! Then I'll come back this afternoon," I replied and was about to head back to the car park when I had a spontaneous idea.

"Come, Nellie, let's visit Ruth if she's home!"

My mother's neighbour had been so happy to see Nellie the other day, and she certainly was too frail for an outing by bus. Why shouldn't we give her some joy? And indeed, the white-haired lady was all smiles when we came to her bedside.

"How cute!" she exclaimed. "Such a beautiful doggie! And what an interesting colour! What's his name?"

Apparently, she had forgotten that we had already met before. But just as eagerly as the last time, she bent down to Nellie and stroked her fuzzy fur.

"That's Nellie, and she's a girl," I explained with a grin.

The next moment my smile faded as Lesley stood in the open doorway. She snapped at me, "What are you doing here?"

"I came to see my mother, but she's not here at the moment. And because Ruth is such a dog-loving ..."

"Would you please come to my office?" Lesley interrupted me gruffly, "I want to discuss something with you."

But her features softened as she watched the old lady who tenderly rubbed Nellie's chest and had eyes only for her.

"Such a pretty dog, and so friendly!" Lesley said.

"Yes, Nellie loves cuddles!" I replied. "If she were a cat, I'm sure she'd be purring now."

Ruth was visibly delighted and thanked me profusely for my visit with Nellie, even though I didn't stay very long at all. Her joy was heart-warming! Unfortunately, my mood was dampened again shortly afterwards when I spoke to the manager in her office.

Lesley gave me a severe telling off:

"Michael, I can't allow you to enter the rooms of our residents other than your mother's, at least not without notifying the staff! Even our volunteers have to indicate each time which seniors they are going to visit. You might have seen the computer by the door at the reception, where they have to register their visiting times. By the way, no one is allowed to distribute food in our home without the approval of the nursing staff either, as some residents have to follow strict diets."

She fiddled with the collar of her uniform and looked at me sternly.

"In the meantime, we have found out that Ann's story is not true. Hazel hasn't been to the creek in our compound for a very long time. She continues to claim that her necklace with the medal was stolen. Are you sure you didn't find a necklace?"

"Of course, otherwise I would've handed it in as well! It was just the medal!" I replied indignantly. "What does Hazel's sister say about this story?"

"Well, I'm not allowed to give you any details. But there has been another theft! This time at Henry's, a nice old gentleman on your mother's ward. Someone has stolen his wedding ring, a precious watch, and money from his bedside table. It can't go on like this! Fortunately, he'd hardly had any cash in his wallet, but he is quite heartbroken about the disappearance of his ring. It has been a special memento of his wife who already passed away."

"That's terrible!" I groaned. "Good thing I haven't brought my mother's jewellery box from Brisbane yet! But who'd steal from the old folks so brazenly?"

"I would like to know that too! This was now the third incident in our home. If we don't find the thief soon, we'll have to install surveillance equipment."

"Sounds good! But surely only in the hallway and the common rooms, and not in the individual rooms, right? Otherwise, you wouldn't have any privacy at all!"

A horrible idea that someone could secretly watch me in my own room! While I was eating, sleeping, reading or even while I was having sex? Involuntarily I imagined a loving, erotic scene with Sylvie and blushed at the thought.

"We'll see!" Lesley said in a cool tone, quickly bringing me back to reality.

"But Ruth seems so pleased when she sees Nellie. Can't I visit her now and then?" I asked.

Lesley thrust her chin forward energetically.

Before she could say anything, I blathered on:

"I'm definitely not a thief! And getting visitors would be a nice change for her, as she's usually all alone."

I could be very persistent (had I inherited that from my mother?) and didn't want to give up so easily. Somehow, I had liked Ruth straight away. I think she reminded me of my dad's mother.

Lesley played indecisively with a pen for a while and tidied a slightly out-of-place pile of papers on her desk.

"You could become a volunteer. Then you are welcome to visit all residents who'd agree. But we would need a police clearance certificate from you, at our expense of course, and you would have to pass a little test."

"A test?" I asked, puzzled.

"Yes, you would need to study the floor plan of the nursing home to be able to find the nearest emergency exit, fire alarm or emergency switch in case of an emergency. If you're interested, you can discuss this in more detail with Tessa, our volunteer coordinator."

"Okay, I'll think about it," I replied a little hesitantly.

Lesley was smiling at me now.

"That's very kind of you! Unfortunately, our caregivers almost never have enough time for the residents, and many seniors are quite lonely and would certainly enjoy a visit with your cute dog! And it would be nice to have more male volunteers as we mainly get female ones."

27

In the afternoon, I returned to the nursing home. But again, my mother was not in her room, and I was a bit startled at the sight of her empty, neatly made bed. Where could she be? I set out to find her. Marching through the hallways, I almost felt like an intruder after my morning conversation with Lesley. Some doors were wide open, allowing me glimpses of residents sleeping, reading or watching TV. In one room, a man and a woman were lying together on the bed (fully clothed) holding hands. How lovely! I wondered if my old mother would also find a new boyfriend.

At this instant, I heard her loud voice. She sounded completely upset! What was going on?

"Come quickly!" I shouted to Nellie, and we raced through the common room and around a corner to another corridor. And there was my mother, with her back to me, raising her walking stick. This time, however, she didn't use it to point at something joyfully, but rather in a threatening manner. Was she about to fight someone?

"Hey you ... you nasty crook!" she shouted at a white-haired lady.

It was Ann! Her little dog Bella was hiding behind her, with its tail between its legs. Ann's eyes blazed with anger, but when she saw me, she quickly turned around, intending to escape. At that moment Sylvie came running and blocked her way, and a terribly loud alarm was blaring into our ears. Nellie wanted to flee in panic, but I held her tightly by the leash.

"What's wrong?" I asked my mother.

"That ... scoundrel!" she cried angrily.

Ann roughly pushed Sylvie away and ran with Bella to a glass door leading into the garden. Bella yelped excitedly, made an unexpected leap to the side, and the dog leash tangled around Ann's legs. With a sharp cry, Ann tumbled to the ground and landed hard on her hands and knees. Both Sylvie and I rushed to her aid. Sylvie bent down to her in concern, and quickly backed away as Ann struck at her furiously with a handbag.

"That's enough!" I said grimly, clutching the old lady's chubby arm.

What a malicious bitch! Fortunately, more employees approached and finally Ann gave up her resistance. To my further relief, the annoying alarm stopped.

Mum said eagerly, "Thief!", pointing her walking stick towards Ann.

"What's actually happened, Mum?" I asked her.

Eventually, we found out that my mother had been restlessly walking around. Quite by chance, she had caught Ann stealing a handbag from the wheelchair of a woman who was slumbering deeply and blissfully in her bed, right next to it. Despite her increasing dementia, my mother had immediately grasped the situation and tried to intervene.

"Super, Mum! You are the heroine of the day!" I praised her and she beamed at me.

Ann, however, stared at us hatefully. If looks could kill we would be dead!

A tiny but wiry old gentleman had raised the alarm as soon as he'd heard the shouting in the hallway. The lady who had been robbed had woken up from all that noise. She was blissful for getting back her pretty leather handbag with her purse, reading glasses, a comb and other utensils. Lesley had quickly called the police, and Ann became quite meek when they arrived. Stammering and red-faced, she made a confession. She had indeed stolen her own sister's necklace with the sports medal some time ago, and afterwards she developed a taste for stealing. With a cheerful face and Bella in tow, she had walked around and taken every opportunity to look for an easy prey. It was hard to believe how brazenly this old lady, who at first glance seemed quite likeable, had acted! It was lucky that my mother had caught her red-handed! But sadly, because of Ann's thefts, many residents and staff members in this aged care facility would probably be more suspicious of visitors now – as Lesley had been earlier today when she'd seen me in Ruth's room.

Later on, I called my brother to tell him the whole story, finishing with the words: "You should have seen how boldly Mum planted herself before the thief!"

Patrick chuckled. "I can hear how impressed you are, Mickie!" Then he said thoughtfully: "Our parents have always been absolutely honest and fair. They couldn't stand it when someone was treated poorly. It's no wonder that Mum was so upset and wanted to help the sleeping lady!"

"That's right! By the way, you'd met Ann yourself very briefly in Mum's room, remember? Who knows, maybe she had been spying on her too, and just pretended to be so helpful that day. Back then, she also suggested to visit Mum again because Bella had taken a liking to her. That sneaky bitch! I don't mean Bella, of course, but Ann!"

Patrick guffawed. "The older they are, the wilder they get!"

I heard Sarah's voice in the background. Patrick told me, now in a grave tone: "Sarah just reminded me of a terrible TV report. A few days ago, a young nurse in another old folks' home – somewhere in West Australia – could be seen beating an old, skinny man! That nasty nurse hadn't known about the secret camera in his room!"

Now Sarah shouted: "It was all recorded, so now the whole world could see her giving the poor old man a severe slap for no reason at all, and she was laughing spitefully!"

"That's ghastly!" I exclaimed indignantly. "I hope that nurse was immediately dismissed."

"I hope so too! I felt so sorry for the man!" Patrick said. "He was just lying in his bed completely helpless and petrified! Sarah and I were almost in tears at the report. And it's absolutely sickening to think that someone could slap Mum or treat her roughly in whatever way!"

What a horrible thought indeed! I swallowed uneasily before saying: "I guess surveillance cameras aren't so bad after all. On the other hand, it seems wrong to me ..."

"That's a difficult subject!" Patrick cut in. "I'd rather have my privacy, too. And there are already so many cameras everywhere. Actually, you're being watched all the time, it's scary!"

"Big brother is watching you!" Sarah joked.

"And yet so many crimes never get solved. Strange that no one seems to have noticed anything when the dead Maureen was dumped like a rubbish bag in the car park behind the shops," I pondered and involuntarily got goose bumps thinking of Bryan's gruesome find.

"Aren't there any surveillance systems installed?"

"No idea! Maybe there was a power outage that night. After all, we had some pretty wild thunderstorms here in the week of the murder."

"Or the murderer quite cleverly disabled the CCTV system or removed the relevant film," Patrick replied. "Um, I have to admit I don't know much about these cameras."

"I could ask Tina. She might know, as the car park of the hotel where she works is guaranteed to be under surveillance."

"If she still talks to you after your last argument," Patrick said doubtfully. "But now I have to go, because Sarah and I are about to visit a friend. See you soon! Take care, little brother!"

"Bye, big brother! Bye, Sarah!"

Shortly after our conversation, it struck me that we always spoke of a murderer in the masculine form. Couldn't it have been a woman who killed Maureen? Maybe a harmless-looking but fairly strong woman like Ann? And again, my hair stood up on end.

28

Tina was pretty tired after work. Nevertheless, she listened spellbound to her friend on the phone, surprised to hear about the evil deeds of Katja's neighbour Ann. Tina knew the old lady from occasional chats over the garden fence, having found her quite nice, even though a bit overbearing. Now the police had arrested Ann and already searched her entire house. It was hard to fathom!

Excitedly, Katja gushed out: "Ann always seemed so helpful and cheerful. I don't want to believe she's a sneaky thief! Maybe she's already stolen something from us too!"

"You think so? Are you missing anything?" asked Tina in dismay.

"Well, I can't prove it, of course, but I had a fifty-dollar note in a kitchen drawer, and now it's gone. And Sam swears he didn't take the money. But no one but Ann was here to visit us recently."

"Did you spend some time together in your kitchen that day?"

"Nah, we were sitting outside. But she had to go to the bathroom at some point and was in the house for quite a while. So, theoretically she could have stolen the fifty bucks."

"That would be mean! I'm glad my neighbours are so honest and reliable! They always watered the plants in our garden when Michael and I went away for a longer period, like on a holiday. And we even gave them a key to our house so they could check on things in case of an emergency. One long weekend they also babysat Nellie and the house for us. They're lovely people!"

Katja sighed. "Well, who would have expected something like that from Ann! Anyway, I don't trust her anymore."

"Will she have to go to prison now? And what will happen to her little dog?" asked Tina.

"I don't know! Bella actually belongs to Ann's sister, but Hazel can't look after her anymore. So, someone else would have to adopt Bella."

"How sad this whole story must be for Hazel! A ghastly idea, to be robbed by your own sister!" Tina frowned.

"Yes, and she supposedly was always so happy about Ann's and Bella's visits. But now Ann is guaranteed to be banned from the nursing home, even if she doesn't go to jail and only gets a fine. By the way, have you visited your mother-in-law in the meantime?"

"Um, nah ..." Tina blushed. How could she explain it to Katja?

Finally, she shouted, "I hate old folks' homes! It's so frustrating to see people age and I can't stand to observe ..."

"You're mean, Tina!" Katja snapped at her unexpectedly. "Imagine yourself as an old woman! Would you like to sit alone in a tiny room all the time, completely lonely and forgotten by the world?"

"Marie has got her sons! Michael is with her every day, I think. And recently, Patrick and Sarah visited her and ..."

"That's no excuse! Sometimes you are very selfish, Tina!" snorted Katja.

Tina blanched. Only the other day Michael had accused her of all sorts of things, and now her best friend was turning on her. She wanted to reply snottily, but burst into tears.

"You're right!" she muttered, feeling ashamed.

"Now, now, don't cry!" Katja tried to cheer her up again. "Why don't you go to Marie's at the weekend and give her some delicious chocolates or a pretty bouquet of flowers? I'm sure she'll be happy!"

Tina felt miserable. All her life, she had detested hospitals and aged care facilities, the sterile walls, the strange smells and especially the sight of old people just staring into space, drooling or talking nonsense. As a child, she had found it very oppressive to visit her mentally confused grandfather in the nursing home, although she had always liked him very much. He had constantly asked about his wife who hadn't been alive anymore; and in addition, plaintive sounds or even hoarse screams had come from an adjoining room from time to time, giving her the creeps. But Katja and Michael had been right to scold her. She was far too selfish! Even at work, she kept trying to impose onerous tasks that she was supposed to do herself on others. Energetically, she blew her nose, washed her face with cool water and decided to change. And to do it straight away!

* * *

I had just washed my dishes and was about to make myself comfortable on the couch, planning to read a crime novel, when the phone rang. Could it be Sylvie? My heart was beating wildly at the thought, and I felt warm and cold at the same time. But it was my wife.

"Hello, Tina! What's up?" I asked, not very friendly.

To my horror, I heard desperate sobs. Well, I hadn't been that harsh, had I?

"Hey, Tina! What's the matter?"

Did she have a fight with her new lover?

"Oh, Michael! I ..."

Again, all I heard was her howling and a gasp.

"Yes? What is it?"

Gradually, I became concerned. Nellie, who was sitting opposite me in my old armchair, pricked up her ears and looked at me attentively.

"I want to apologise to you! I'm terribly selfish and self-centred, I'm an idiot and I do everything wrong!" Tina groaned and blew her nose noisily.

"Why?" I asked perplexed.

"I avoid everything that could be unpleasant, and I treat my colleagues like dirt if they don't dance to my tune right away. It's true that I always want to have my fun and be the boss. And besides, I was just scared to visit your mother. I find old folks' homes totally creepy, but it's so unfair of me to completely ignore Marie!" Tina gushed.

Before I could reply, she continued:

"And I often treated you in a mean way too. Yet you were always so good-natured and even let me stay in our house ..." Tina's voice went hoarse. "Please forgive me, Michael!"

What could I say to that? I was quite flabbergasted.

Finally, I replied:

"Oh, Tina, you're not quite so dominant and horrible, otherwise I certainly wouldn't have put up with you for so long! And normally you get along well with your colleagues."

I cleared my throat briefly.

"In a way, I also understand why you haven't visited my mother in her new home yet. After all, you've never got along very well, and it's really not always easy to deal with her dementia. Even some of her best friends have turned their backs on her since her Alzheimer's disease has worsened."

However, at this thought bitter bile rose in my throat and I laughed derisively.

"Great friendship, when you turn your back on someone just because he or she gets sick!"

Tina was sobbing away again. "I too abandoned Marie instead of helping her! But I'll go and see her on Saturday, I promise!"

"That would be nice! Would you like my company? If so, we could meet at the nursing home at half past nine."

"Okay! Thank you, Michael! And sleep well!" Tina said and hung up.

I had mixed feelings about the upcoming meeting. How would my mother react to Tina, whom she hadn't seen for a long time? Was it smart to visit her together, even though Tina and I had grown apart and still argued from time to time?

I realised that I continued to hold a grudge against certain parts of Tina's behaviour. I still couldn't forgive her for everything. But at least she had apologised now, which certainly hadn't been easy for her.

I watched Nellie, who was sleeping blissfully under the table. Could dogs get dementia as well? To distract myself from my pondering about Tina, I reached for my smartphone and googled the subject. Yes, apparently dogs could also become forgetful, anxious and disoriented in old age!

It wasn't until I was in bed that I remembered something. Oh no, I had forgotten that I was going to drive to Brisbane on Saturday! I quickly texted Tina to cancel my appointment with her. She would have to visit my mother without me this time. Somehow, I felt relieved.

29

Tina felt uneasy when she arrived at the nursing home on Saturday morning. Michael had asked her not to tell his mother about the household clearance in Brisbane and not to mention that Simon was going to move into his grandmother's unit. Hopefully she wouldn't blab! She took a deep breath before knocking on her mother-in-law's door. Stepping into the room, she was surprised to see two other visitors there: Bryan and Julie. They all gazed at her, baffled and obviously without a clue who she could be.

Tina was startled at how pale and thin Marie looked, but she said in a cheerful tone: "Good morning! Hello, Marie!" and gave her mother-in-law a light kiss on the cheek. Then she handed her a pretty potted plant.

"Michael told me you have a shelf for plants. Can you find a place for this one?"

"Yes, thank you!" beamed Marie, clutching the pot with both hands.

Bryan watched Tina with a furrowed brow. "We know each other, don't we?"

"Of course, I'm Michael's wife!" Quickly she babbled on: "By the way, Bryan, I saw you in a café the other day, but I didn't recognise you back then. How nice that you're living here now, so close to Marie! When did you actually move to the Sunshine Coast?"

Julie asked: "What? Can you talk louder?"

"That's Tina, Mickie's wife!" roared Bryan. "Or nope, his ex!"

Tina grinned sheepishly.

"Well, we're not officially divorced yet. But we've been living apart for a while."

"Oh, what a pity!" Julie shouted.

Marie seemed a bit puzzled and went outside with her new plant. Tina followed her, looked around, sniffed at a flowering shrub and said admiringly:

"What a nice place! Great that you have a garden and can sit outside!"

Julie suggested: "Tina, we actually just came to pick up Marie and have a second breakfast at our house. Would you like to come with us, to see where we are living now?"

"Oh, with pleasure!" agreed Tina.

Although she liked the nursing home much more than expected, she was still glad to leave.

On the way through the park, Julie hooked up with Marie and chatted cheerfully to her, and after a while they both sang a children's song. A bird in a tree joined in.

Bryan grinned bemusedly and said quietly to Tina:

"My wife has become a bit deaf, but she still loves to sing. Often too loudly, though, and I wonder what our neighbours think of it."

Tina laughed. "Maybe they don't hear so well anymore either. Or they are happy about the music. After all, Julie has a beautiful, melodic voice!"

"Yes, she has! Even if she sounds a bit hoarse by now. And she still plays the guitar now and then."

Bryan's tanned, gaunt face suddenly took on a sad expression. "You must have heard about the murdered guitar player, right?"

Tina nodded. "Yes, poor Maureen, such a terrible story! And crazy that you, of all people, came under suspicion!"

A fresh breeze made her shiver, although it was a warm, sunny morning. There was a rustling in the bushes beside her, and then she saw a large lizard scurry away.

"Who'd have thought I'd become infamous!" Bryan joked with a forced smile. "Unfortunately, the latest newspaper article reporting my innocence was much smaller than the first one accusing me of being a murderer." Involuntarily, he touched his chin. The unexpected attack on the beach had instilled more fear and terror in him than he cared to admit.

"Do you think it was a robbery?" asked Tina. "Just ghastly that a tourist had to die in our town! Since then, I haven't been feeling as safe here as I used to. And yesterday my friend Katja told me that two young women from China had cancelled the booking of her holiday unit. They'd prefer to spend their vacation on the Gold Coast now."

"Well, that's rubbish!" said Bryan. "After all, you can have the misfortune of running into the wrong people anywhere."

The two women in front of them stepped aside to make way for a man in a wheelchair, who exchanged a few friendly words with them before driving on. Shortly afterwards they arrived at Julie's and Bryan's house. Tina and Marie were warmly entertained and pampered. Julie, who was obviously a bit forgetful, told a funny story twice, but made everyone laugh again the second time.

30

Katja was angry and cleaned the windows with more force than necessary. She was annoyed about the cancellation of the two Chinese women who had originally wanted to stay in her holiday flat for a whole week. She had been looking forward to learning a bit about their home country, as she and Sam had never had visitors from China before. She had even bought chopsticks and a new teapot. When the phone rang, she flung her rag into the bucket so hard that some water sloshed out.

"Crap!" she muttered, wiping her wet hands briefly on her jeans and grabbing the phone.

"Hello, Katja! It's Tina!" her friend gushed out. "Could you accommodate some new guests? Our hotel is completely booked at the moment, and I just got a call from a family who is planning to have a special mourning ceremony in Coolum Beach. They are already quite frustrated as nothing seems to be vacant at the moment. They are Maureen's parents and sister."

"Maureen? You mean the young lady who was killed?" Katja asked in surprise.

"Yes, exactly!"

"When do they want to come and how long do they intend to stay?"

"Um, I got their mobile number, do you have something to write?" Tina rattled off a number and continued: "Can you discuss everything with them yourself? I have to go and quickly clean a clogged toilet! It stinks awfully! Bye!"

Katja grinned. Tina could be a bit bossy at times, but she had real talent in organising and was certainly a good hotel manager. But since when did she take care of clogged toilets herself?

She looked thoughtfully at her sparkling clean window and then dialled the number she had hastily scribbled on a newspaper. After the third ring, a tired-sounding woman called Judith answered. She made a booking for three nights and three people, planning to arrive the following Thursday morning. What a sad occasion to travel to our idyllic Sunshine Coast! Katja thought pitifully. Later, when she told Sam about her new guests, he said succinctly:

"At least they won't be having a loud party!"

* * *

When I arrived at Mum's unit in Brisbane, my brother and his family were already gathered for breakfast in the small kitchen. I felt rather queasy, and I had to force myself to eat a roll with honey. Simon was obviously looking forward to moving in here soon – for the first time he would be leaving his parents' house! It was really a good timing, as he could directly take over the furniture, and many other items from his grandmother, which she could no longer use in the nursing home. Simon's two younger siblings picked out a few things for themselves, such as books and all kinds of knick-knacks. All of them were rather modest than demanding, almost timid to touch my Mum's belongings, and there were no arguments.

Patrick and I started clearing out the wardrobe in the bedroom, while Sarah and the children rummaged around in the living room. We packed some clothes for Mum into a big suitcase and sorted out many others for a second-hand shop. To our amazement, we found some of our father's shirts, socks and shoes, an old bobble hat from Patrick, and a worn teddy bear that had belonged to me. As I pressed the stuffed animal against me, hot tears came to my eyes, and then I burst out sobbing. Patrick cried with me and we hugged each other for a moment.

Shortly afterwards, we had to smile when Nellie dropped a football at our feet that must have been from our childhood. Some items were ancient, others looked brand new. We found so many towels that were still unused and wonderfully soft that I had the idea of filling bags for other relatives and our best friends, collecting things they might like. For Sylvie I chose a pretty, unusual wooden bowl, for Tina a chic vase, for my kind landlords preserving jars and a bottle of liqueur. We also found gifts for Mum's neighbours. We all rummaged around, sorted and packed in peaceful harmony.

This way it was a tiny bit easier for us to deal with Mum's household, although we shed many tears throughout the day – even Simon. Nellie licked Sarah's wet face, making her squeal, and later we roared with laughter when my dog expectantly brought us a noodle roll. Our laughter was a little hysterical, but liberating nonetheless.

In the evening we were completely knackered (except for Nellie). It had been a very emotional day! And I must confess that Patrick, Sarah and I had too much wine after dinner. They spent the night in my parents' double bed, the three teenagers slept on some mats in the living room, and Nellie and I laid down on a thin mattress in the hallway.

The next morning my head was buzzing, my hips were aching and I felt quite old. But Nellie was already nudging me impatiently – life went on.

31

Katja looked around contentedly. The place was tidy, the beds freshly made, and there was an unobtrusive smell of honey and fresh lemons. She had even put a bouquet of flowers on the table in the guest living room to make it extra cosy. Still, she felt uneasy because this time she and Sam would not be hosting carefree holiday guests, but a family in great mourning. What could she say in greeting? Should she offer her sincere sympathy or rather avoid all topics related to the horrific murder? For a second, she almost regretted that Tina had sent her these people, but then she pulled herself together. What a nonsense! Tina only meant well, she thought and smiled. Lately, her friend had been unusually attentive and helpful anyway. Apparently, she had taken her criticism to heart. Or was it Philip's influence? In any case, Katja was pleased that Tina had finally visited her mother-in-law in the nursing home.

The sound of a rattling motorbike told her of the postman's arrival. After one last critical look, she left the holiday unit and was walking to their mailbox in the front garden when a green car pulled up into their driveway. Their new visitors arrived.

"Hi! Welcome to Coolum Beach!" she said spontaneously, shaking everyone's hands. Judith, a relatively small woman with slightly greying reddish curls, appeared pale and haggard, but had a surprisingly firm handshake. Her husband David was a lean, tall man with warm brown eyes and short dark hair. Their daughter Hannah looked so much like the murdered Maureen that it gave Katja a twinge. Were they twins? it flashed through her mind.

"Come on in, I'll show you the unit right away!" she said, leading the guests into the house.

"It looks very cosy!" said Judith appreciatively, and her husband nodded in agreement and put his hand on her shoulder.

"Who is that?" asked Hannah, pointing to a picture in a wooden frame on the living room wall. It was painted with watercolours and showed a young woman playing the guitar on the beach. She was smiling dreamily, and her blonde hair seemed to be blowing in the wind.

Katja blushed. Oh no, why hadn't she exchanged the picture with another one?

Quickly, she replied: "Sam, my husband, painted it a few years ago, using a photo of our daughter as a reference, but she doesn't like it very much, saying her nose would appear too big in his painting. But I think it's such a beautiful, peaceful mood with the delicate, wispy clouds at dawn."

To her relief, Hannah smiled. "My stepfather is an artist too! He paints impressive landscapes, but his portraits usually look nothing like real people!"

Stepfather? thought Katja.

David grinned. "Well, I only paint as a hobby, and my portraits are just a new attempt."

"Practice makes perfect!" said Katja. "Would you like some tea or coffee? You'll find everything next to the kettle, and there are also some biscuits for you."

"Thank you very much!" said Judith. "But we've just been to the café where Maureen apparently played her guitar in public for the last time, and there ..." Her blue eyes filled with tears and her voice died away.

Her husband pulled her lovingly into his arms. His eyes moistened too, while Hannah let out a dry sob and her hands flew to her mouth.

Hot anger rose in Katja. She had seen and heard the guitar player herself back then, when she had been chatting and laughing cheerfully with Tina and Philip, even if only from a distance. Who had killed Maureen, and why? Such a young, likeable woman!

"I do hope the murderer will be caught soon!" she said grimly. Then she added more gently:

"But now get some rest, because you must be exhausted after your long journey. Just knock on my door if you need anything, I'll be home all day today."

She quietly closed the door behind her.

32

On Thursday evening, I wrote into my diary:

Last Sunday, after our cars had been loaded and we'd locked Mum's front door, we said goodbye to the neighbours. Linda and Ken waved at us as we left, and their children threw us kisses. Nellie whined softly and I felt miserable, like I had lost a piece of home myself.

Never again would I visit my parents in this house where they had lived for many years; never again would my mother open the door for me with her bra over her jumper; never again would she stand next to me early in the morning, watching me; never again would we work in her garden in unison or cry together at a maudlin movie in the evening.

And yet I am unspeakably happy that Simon and not a stranger will move into her unit. It's an exciting new start for him, and I'll report back to my mother at some point that her grandson is now living there and taking good care of everything. (In any case, I hope that the young brat won't throw too wild a party).

So far, Mum has never once asked about her unit, her neighbours or her friends in Brisbane, and her thoughts seem to wander mostly to her own childhood.

The other day, I finally found out why the nursing home was named 'Puzzle House'. It was the idea of a man whose wife had got dementia. In her early stages of Alzheimer's disease, she had explained to him that it felt as if her brain was made up of puzzle pieces, and that she was having more and more trouble putting them together. Unfortunately, she would no longer be able to fill in some of the gaps.

But according to Lesley, the name 'Puzzle House' is supposed to remind us of good times and fun puzzles. I like that idea, although I was never very good at jigsaw puzzles! That had been more Tina's thing. Tina visited me yesterday and told me about her meeting with Mum, Bryan and Julie. She was delighted with the vase that I gave her, saying it would always remind her of my mum's love of nature and flowers. And later she hugged me and said:

"It's great that you get along so well with your brother and his family! Some family members argue terribly or even commit murder when it comes to an inheritance!"

This made me think of Ann, the old lady who had stolen from her own sister. To my astonishment, Tina already knew the whole story from her friend Katja, who's a neighbour of Ann. It's a small world!

I put the pen aside. Tina had also mentioned that she and Philip could possibly move into Ann's house. They'd look after her dog if Ann would have to go to prison for a long time. Was that supposed to be a joke? I sighed as I thought of all the paperwork I still had to do. My brother wanted to help me as much as he could with regards to our mother's finances and all the legal stuff, but I also had to take care of my impending divorce. Should Tina and I really sell our house? I sighed again and Nellie looked at me questioningly.

"Okay, let's go for a walk!" I suggested, and immediately Nellie jumped up enthusiastically and pranced around me like a playful puppy. Since I had to go back to work, Nellie was alone during the day and was especially happy about each outing.

It was already dark when we left the house. A bat flew overhead and a dog barked in the distance. After a while, a soft drizzle started and I quickly opened my umbrella. At the same moment, the rain intensified. You have to be lucky! Nevertheless, I decided to take a shortcut and turned into a different road than originally planned. A long time ago, a row of trees had been planted here. They had constantly been trimmed on one side only because of the overhead power lines, and had thus developed a strange shape. Several times my umbrella brushed against the lowest branches, and once I even had to duck. Obviously, nobody had thought of the pedestrians under the trees when they'd done the last pruning.

"Do you know that it was frowned upon when men used an umbrella in the past?" I asked my dog. "Tina's mother told me that."

Nellie ignored me and jumped blithely through a puddle.

"Pretty stupid, isn't it? Anyway, I'm glad I'm not getting soaking wet again."

I blathered on, grinning as I remembered the scene in the swimming pool. With all my clothes on, I had jumped in the water to save Sylvie, and had kissed her for the first time. How wonderful that she had returned my kiss! While my heart leapt joyfully and Nellie sniffed excitedly at a tree trunk, my umbrella got caught again on a low-hanging branch. I shook it a little, looked up and froze. Nellie started to bark at the top of her lungs. I felt like my blood was freezing in my veins and my mouth went dry. A human arm was dangling in front of my nose! In the dim light of the street lamps, it looked very pale and lifeless. With trembling fingers, I turned on my torch and held my breath, fearing something terrible.

But I merely discovered a doll's face that seemed to stare at me with a slightly amused expression. The life-size, bald and naked mannequin was hanging from a branch like a monkey, with only its left arm dangling down. The next moment I heard a suppressed giggle and saw two children running away. Oh boy, had they scared me! What kind of children were they, doing such shenanigans in this lousy weather and at this hour?

"Kim! Daniel! Where are you?" a woman shouted nearby.

The voice sounded familiar. Nellie barked again, but this time she sounded downright ecstatic. We walked on and soon met Yolanda, who was also equipped with an umbrella and a flashlight.

"Yolanda! What are you doing here?" I asked her.

"Hello, Michael! I'm looking for my sister's children. They've run away again. Those cheeky kids are driving me mad!" she snorted. Then she grinned mischievously. "I'd rather babysit old people, somehow I get along better with them!"

She gave me a fright when she suddenly whistled loudly on her fingers. Nellie pricked up her ears expectantly, and the children returned.

"You're not supposed to go out alone at night!" Yolanda scolded, sounding more relieved than angry.

The girl and the boy, who were certainly not yet ten years old and looked rather dirty and soaked, looked at me curiously.

I smiled. "Hello, I'm Michael! Did you put the doll up there in the tree? You seem to be good climbers!"

Daniel, whose dark curls were almost as long as his sister's, pointed at Kim.

"My sister climbed up and I helped her!"

Kim eagerly recounted: "We discovered the doll on a rickety wooden chair by the side of the road, where that shabby old house was demolished the other day. There are many more things. Do you want to go and have a look?"

Daniel gently stroked Nellie's back and said: "There was a guitar too!"

Yolanda ran a hand through her reddish mane of hair and replied:

"All right, you're all wet and dirty anyway! But just for a little while, and then we'll go home and have a hot shower, okay? Quick, quick!"

"Quick, quick!" repeated Daniel and laughed merrily.

The children dashed ahead and Yolanda groaned. "I'm always far too good-natured! My sister is much stricter."

I winked at her. "Well, they seem to be nice kids! Does your sister live in this street?"

"Yes, for about two months, in that new house over there!"

Yolanda pointed to a building that I had already noticed before. It had an unusual façade and a beautifully designed front garden. I liked it a lot!

"Then we are almost neighbours. I live just around the corner."

"Maybe I should introduce you to my sister Debbie so that you can take over the babysitting for me next time!" Yolanda joked.

Kim and Daniel stopped in front of a collection of junk, spread out on the verge. We saw various pieces of furniture, a tattered carpet, a box of books and some flower pots and kitchen utensils.

"Why don't people donate their unwanted belongings to a second-hand shop instead of ruining them in the rain?" I exclaimed angrily.

The books, of course, were already completely soaked, which hurt my soul as an avid reader. But I bent down to inspect a pretty pot. I could plant it and give it to my mother!

Yolanda took the guitar. "I wonder if it still works?"

The little siblings tugged at a black tarp to sneak a peek underneath.

"There's another big doll!" cried Kim.

Yolanda directed the beam of her flashlight at the mannequin that was lying on the ground. It was dirty, had strangely contorted limbs and already lost an arm. And all of a sudden it reminded me of Bryan who had found Maureen's dead, half-naked body under a plastic tarp. It gave me the creeps!

Yolanda said matter-of-factly: "I didn't even know that there's a kerb side collection again. My brother-in-law will be happy. He's not a poor guy by any means, but he always likes to drive around to collect things. His whole garage is already full of stuff he can't use most of the time."

"Good thing he has a big house!" I retorted, thinking of my tiny home.

"Yes, he inherited a chunk of money and used it to get their new house built! You have to be lucky!"

A light was switched on in a house across the street and Yolanda now said:

"Well, I am taking the guitar. It would just rot here in the rain anyway. Let's go, kids, hurry up! Hey, Michael, would you like to come in for a chat and a hot tea?"

"Yes, why not?"

Somewhat embarrassed, I grabbed the flower pot and asked the children to spread the tarp over all the stuff again for protection. Maybe others would find their personal treasure the next day. On the way back, I remembered the mannequin in the tree. We'd better remove it to prevent anybody getting a heart attack from fright! So, I pulled it down and Kim and Daniel carried it home together. It wasn't until we stepped inside that I noticed a rubber ball in Nellie's mouth. She was indeed a successful collector of balls! I rubbed her down with a towel and Yolanda accompanied the children to the bathroom.

"Make yourself at home!" she called to me. "I'll be right there!"

"She's really nice, isn't she?" I murmured to Nellie and took the ball off her.

Should I go into the kitchen and make some tea? Hesitantly, I opened several cupboard doors to look for cups and tea. The kitchen was super modern and spotless, and I was feeling uncomfortable in my damp clothes, with my still quite wet dog in tow. I had just found various kinds of tea when a deep voice addressed me:

"Good evening!"

I quickly turned around and saw a medium-sized young man, slim yet muscular, with a hooked nose and thinning light brown hair, eyeing me curiously.

"Hi, I'm Michael!" I introduced myself.

"Are you Yolanda's boyfriend?" the guy asked bluntly.

"No, I'm just..." I paused when Yolanda came into the kitchen. She stiffened for a moment and then she hugged the man stormily.

"I thought you weren't coming back until next month!" she exclaimed.

"So did I, Sis!" The man grinned broadly and held out his hand to me. "Hi, I'm Tony!" Turning to Yolanda, he continued: "Debbie and Mark picked me up at the airport, but we wanted to surprise you and the kids."

Yolanda beamed. "Great! And I'm off work this weekend and also on Monday, so it's good timing!"

"Yes, I know! Debbie and Mark have already told me heaps on the way. Also, that you recently got a new boyfriend, and that you ..."

With a reluctant grimace, Yolanda interrupted him and hurriedly explained:

"Michael, this is my brother. He's been living in Alaska for a whole year."

"Really? Wow, that must have been freezing cold!" I said, dumbfounded and not particularly witty.

Tony laughed. "Yeah, it was!"

"Would you like some herbal tea, Tony?" asked Yolanda.

"Sure! I always get terribly thirsty from the thin air on the plane!"

Yolanda put tea bags and boiling water into the four cups I had already fetched from the cupboard and added three more.

"Uncle Tony!" The children rushed to him excitedly. Both were dressed in colourful pyjamas, though neither looked at all sleepy. Tony hugged them one by one and swung Daniel high into the air. Putting him back down on the floor, he gave an exaggerated moan. "You've gotten way too heavy! A year ago, you were a featherweight!"

He winked at Kim and she grinned. And then more voices rang out:

"Hello, we're back! Phew, what a lousy weather! And there was a ghastly long traffic jam on the motorway!"

A couple now appeared at the kitchen door, and I immediately recognised that the woman had to be Yolanda's sister. Although Debbie was slightly taller and slimmer and more flat-chested, she had the same friendly smile and similar wavy reddish hair.

"Wasn't it a nice surprise?" her husband asked, smiling at Yolanda and the kids.

He was quite tall and portly, with a shock of blond hair and grey-blue eyes. He set down two huge boxes of pizza on the kitchen counter, and the smell was enticing.

"Yes, it was!" said Yolanda. "By the way, this is Michael, whom I met at the nursing home. His mother is in our care."

"Good evening! Maybe I'd better go!" I said sheepishly. "After all, I don't want to interrupt the family reunion!"

"Oh nonsense!" said Mark, bending down to Nellie and giving her a pat. "Yolanda's friends are always welcome here! And such a cute dog for sure!"

"Yeah, stay for dinner. We've bought some pizzas, and I guarantee it'll be enough for all of us," Debbie offered.

"No, thanks!" I replied. "I've already eaten at home, and besides, I'm a vegetarian."

"So is Mum!" exclaimed Daniel. "And we already had some weird soup, but ..."

Yolanda protested: "My soup was delicious and not weird at all!"

Daniel continued his sentence: "... but you can always eat pizza."

"No wonder you've become such a fat boy!" Tony joked.

In reality, Daniel was skinny as a rail. But he obviously had a good appetite, and I stayed after all and ate a slice of pizza as well. Sitting in the cosy living room, I soon felt cheerful and upbeat and not at all like I was among strangers. Tony told very vividly about his life in Alaska, where he had worked as a dentist. The children listened with rapt attention, asking countless questions. Daniel wanted to know how many moose he had seen, and his uncle had to describe exactly what the animals looked like.

"And why did you return to Australia earlier than planned?" Yolanda asked.

"Did you pull the wrong tooth of some poor devil and had to run away because of that?" Kim asked, laughing aloud about her own joke.

Her mother rolled her eyes and pushed an old shabby teddy bear aside. In contrast to the neat kitchen, the living room was cluttered. The sofa was full of cushions, stuffed animals and dolls, a side table was piled high with magazines and books, and on the floor were various board games like Backgammon and Monopoly. Nellie sniffed curiously at the TV table for a while and then stretched out on a runner.

Tony laughed bemusedly and pinched Kim's cheek lightly. "Nah, luckily not! But I've got a new job as a dentist and I'm supposed to start there soon. And guess where?"

"In Alaska?" Daniel asked.

"You fool!" exclaimed Kim. "Then he wouldn't be here with us!"

"In Coolum Beach! Another dentist recently moved with her boyfriend to Western Australia and I'm going to take her place in the practice." Tony winked at the children. "So, I guess you'll be seeing a lot of me soon!"

"That's wonderful!" cheered Yolanda, and her blue eyes sparkled.

She was obviously very fond of her brother. Debbie also seemed content. She smiled lovingly at her siblings and her greenish eyes seemed warm and kind. However, I caught her husband turning the corners of his mouth, very briefly and almost contemptuously. I wondered if Mark didn't get on so well with his brother-in-law.

Tony yawned loudly and unabashedly.

"Kids, I have to go to bed! And tomorrow morning I'm going to start house-hunting."

With a sideways glance at Mark, he added: "But don't worry! I won't be a burden for you as I already booked a temporary accommodation from Monday on."

"Where?" asked Debbie in amazement. "I thought you were going to stay in our spare room until you'd find a place to live."

"No, I found some furnished accommodation near the practice on the internet. It belongs to a couple called Katja and Sam. Normally they only take holiday guests for a few days, or at most a week, but I spoke to the woman on the phone for a long time, and apparently she couldn't resist my charm." He laughed merrily and in such a way that I couldn't help laughing too. "Anyway, I get to rent their unit for a whole month."

"What a coincidence! Katja and Sam are friends of mine!" I blurted out. "They're really nice, I'm sure you'll like it there!"

Tony and his sisters smiled, but Mark stared with a strange expression at the guitar from the kerb side collection that was leaning against a cupboard.

33

It was a sunny morning, and Sam had already left for work. Katja finished her second coffee and winced when she heard a shrill yelp. Ann and Bella were back home. Katja had found out from another neighbour that Ann had had to pay a fine and had been living with relatives in the hinterland for a while. Despite her mean thefts, Katja felt sorry for the old lady. She and her husband had liked her in the past. But how should they face her now? Could they ever trust her again? Should they pretend nothing had happened?

Katja sighed and decided to postpone her planned house cleaning for another day and mow the lawn instead. The sun was shining bright today, but rain showers were forecast for the next few days. Her guests Judith, David and Hannah had gone back to Sydney, and Katja felt close to tears every time she thought about the reason for their trip. The three family members had performed a special mourning ceremony in the park where Maureen's dead body had been found, and afterwards Katja had met them in her front garden. They had seemed so miserable and grief-stricken that it had cut deep into her heart. And it had been terribly quiet in the house.

Now she longed for new guests and merry laughter. Unfortunately, she and Sam had not received any enquiries about their holiday unit for a long time. She wondered if the gruesome murder case in her town had scared away not only the two Chinese women but other tourists as well. Should she and Sam just wait and see, or rather improve their advertisement? Maybe Tina had an idea! In the middle of her musings, a young man from Alaska called, asking to rent their unit for a whole month. He sounded so nice and funny that she quickly agreed and even spontaneously offered him a discount.

* * *

On Monday morning, it was pouring rain as Yolanda drove her brother to his new accommodation.

"Good thing we don't have to carry any furniture in this bad weather!" said Yolanda, setting the windscreen wipers to full blast.

Tony replied: "Yeah, that would be terrible. And I'm gradually getting used to renting furnished flats. However, it will be the first time for me that the owners are squatting right next door. I just hope Katja and Sam aren't absolute control freaks or people who want to chat with me all the time!"

Yolanda chuckled. "They're friends of Michael, so I'm sure they'll be fine."

"At first I thought Michael was your lover, although he seemed much too old for you. But now tell me more about your new boyfriend! When will I get to meet him?"

Yolanda furrowed her eyebrows, not taking her eyes off the windscreen. "Oh, that's over already. That guy really was a freak! Somehow I have no luck with men."

They drove through a deep puddle, causing the water to splash onto the windows of the car.

Yolanda giggled.

"My colleague Sylvie is dating Michael, and she's totally in love with him! I'm so happy because I know how sad she was after her husband died. She never talked much about him, but I often felt she missed him a lot and was lonely."

A few minutes later, they arrived at their destination, and no sooner had they parked than Katja rushed towards them with a huge umbrella.

Tony whispered: "See, she'd apparently already been lying in wait for us!"

Yolanda, however, looked at the neighbour's house, where a white-curled woman with a small dog on a leash was just stepping out of the door. That was Ann, who had stolen from her own sister! She lived here? With a forced smile she waved at the old lady. Should she warn her brother about the thief?

Katja beamed at Tony. "Good morning! We'd never had visitors from Alaska before!"

Tony smiled.

"Well, I was only there for one year! Originally, I'm from Brisbane. And later I've lived in Townsville for a while. But now I'm happy to be back in Australia and to live so close to my siblings. This here is my little sister Yolanda."

"Hello, Yolanda! Come in quickly, it's raining cats and dogs!"

The petite Katja took Yolanda energetically by the arm, held her umbrella high above her and led her into the house. Tony took his heavy suitcase out of the car and followed a little slower. Ann watched them curiously and Bella barked excitedly.

* * *

When I woke up, it was still quite dark and the rain was pelting down on the tin roof. I wondered about the unusual, loud noise until I realised where I was. Sylvie was lying next to me, blissfully asleep, on her side and with the duvet up over her ears. I stretched out and painfully bumped my head. Ouch! I still had to get used to Sylvie's bed! It was huge and super comfortable, but last night, in the middle of having sex, I had bumped my head on the solid wood headboard and screamed out loud in shock. Sylvie and I had laughed heartily and kissed and embraced more intimately than ever before. Our lovemaking had been wonderful, gentle and careful at first, then more and more eager and wild, and finally very gentle, harmonious and tender again. I had completely let myself go, forgetting everything around me, simply enjoying Sylvie's warm, soft body and our touch. Never before had I felt so erotic, ecstatic and at the same time so free, so natural, and completely accepted.

I love you, Sylvie! I thought happily and full of wonder.

As if Nellie had sensed my thoughts, she possessively put a paw on my arm.

"I love you too, Nellie!" I whispered, patting her on the chin. "You will always be my best friend, little sweetie!"

Sylvie turned and moaned softly. "Are you two always up so terribly early?" she murmured sleepily.

Nellie ran briskly to her side of the bed to greet her and then back to her dog bed in the corner of the room. Sylvie snuggled against my back, put a hand on my bare chest and began to stroke me. And soon I was floating on cloud nine again.

Sylvie lived in an old stone house surrounded by tall trees and thick bushes. The building looked smaller from the outside than it was. It was spacious and cosy but could do with some repairs. The tiles in the kitchen and dining room were drummy, the walls in the living room and the door to the laundry room needed painting, the garage roof had holes, the mailbox hung crookedly from a post, and a paved garden path was bumpy and full of weeds. But right from the start, I felt very comfortable in Sylvie's home.

This Monday, Sylvie took off time in lieu of her many overtime hours, and I had managed to take half of the day off work. After a long walk with Nellie, we had a hearty breakfast on the patio. We were joking and laughing boisterously when my mobile rang. Hearing Lesley's voice, I immediately feared the worst. Something must have happened to my mother! A thick lump seemed to fill my stomach as I listened to the manager of the nursing home. I ran my fingers through my hair, only now realising that I had caught a bump on my head in the night.

As soon as I finished the short phone call with Lesley, I looked frantically at Sylvie and gushed out:

"I have to go to the hospital right away! My mother had a fall! But today of all days I have an important meeting at work and I have to prepare a room for a seminar and ..."

"Where is she? And what happened?" Sylvie interrupted my hectic torrent of words.

"My mum was walking all alone in the park and had a fall! She couldn't get up by herself, but luckily Henry found her and helped her."

"Poor Marie! Is she badly injured?"

"I am not sure! At least it seems she hasn't broken any bones, but apparently, she was very confused. I guess she has to be examined more closely."

Sylvie squeezed my hand sympathetically. "I'm sure it was a shock for her to find herself lying helplessly on the floor. But just call the hospital to find out more. Maybe it's not so bad."

"Yes, good idea!"

Sylvie lovingly stroked my back and started carrying the breakfast dishes into the house. Nellie snuggled against my legs while I talked on the phone, looking up at the grey sky with trepidation. The rain had stopped shortly after dawn, but there were still single thick drops falling from the old trees and from a leak in the gutter. It took forever before I was connected to a person who could tell me something.

After the conversation, I sighed with relief and called out to Sylvie:

"You were right! Mum is due to be discharged from hospital this afternoon, and at the moment she is snoozing. She had circulation problems and was a bit dehydrated, but overall, she is said to be doing quite well. She just has a few scrapes on her knees."

"That's a relief! Marie was lucky!" Sylvie's blue eyes sparkled. "And great that she doesn't have to stay in hospital any longer. Otherwise, I would have gone straight to her."

"You would have done that? On your day off?"

"Well, of course! After all, she's almost my mother-in-law now, hey?"

She grinned at me mischievously.

34

Katja leaned back comfortably and closed her eyes for a moment. After Tony had moved in, she had gone shopping in Maroochydore. Now she was dog-tired from all the walking around, looking at items and trying on clothes. In the end she had only managed to get a T-shirt for her husband, a pair of smart trousers for herself and a few goodies. She switched on the television and was instantly wide awake again. There was a picture of Peter on the news! She could hardly believe her eyes. Peter was reported missing!

"Sam!" she called out to her husband, who was fiddling around in the kitchen. "Peter has disappeared without a trace!"

"Who is Peter?" her husband asked, handing her a glass of beer.

"The friendly German tourist who was our guest for a while!" Katja was upset. "I hope nothing bad has happened to him! He was such a cheerful, outgoing guy!"

"Maybe he went swimming drunk again and didn't have any rescuers around this time," Sam replied unkindly. He had been arguing with a colleague at work and was still angry. That arrogant fool!

"Shhh!" hissed Katja, listening intently to the report on TV. According to the testimony of two German friends, Peter had intended to meet them at the railway station in Nambour after his working holiday in North Queensland. However, they had waited for him in vain and finally called the police the next day. They got worried because his parents and siblings in Germany hadn't heard from Peter for a long time either.

"Peter had a lot of nonsense in his head! He probably just changed his plans on the spur of the moment. I bet he's travelling around, without a care in the world. Maybe he likes the tropics and is still in Cairns." Sam sighed and was about to sit down when the doorbell rang.

Bella, the little dog from next door, immediately barked at the top of her lungs. They heard someone opening and closing their garden gate.

"Who's coming to visit now?" Sam grumbled, shuffling sullenly to the door.

"Hello, Sam!" said a young man with a tousled blond mane and a huge backpack on his back.

"Peter!" marvelled Sam and shook his hand.

"Peter?" Katja jumped up as if stung by a tarantula and ran to the unexpected guest. She hugged him stormily and called out:

"Hey, I thought you were dead! I feared you had an accident or you were murdered!"

"What? But why?"

"Well, you're reported missing! We just saw the news!"

"Really? Oh dear!" Peter slapped his forehead.

"Come on in!" suggested Sam, forgetting his bad mood.

"Um, I was wondering if I could possibly stay over for two nights," Peter said.

"Oh! Nah, that's not possible! We've rented out the holiday unit for a whole month," Tina explained.

"I see! Um, well ... I hardly have any money left anyway and ...", the German stammered and looked embarrassedly at his worn trainers.

"Now sit down first. Would you like a beer and something to eat?" asked Sam. "We have leftovers from dinner."

"Yes, please!" Peter smiled gratefully.

Sam quickly warmed up the pasta dish while Katja opened a beer bottle and handed it to Peter. Afterwards they watched with amusement at the appetite with which the young man devoured his food. Peter told them in detail about his long journey. At first he had worked on a farm near Bundaberg for a while, later he had been to Mackay, Magnetic Island and Cairns among other places. He enthusiastically chatted away about pretty turtles, blue crabs, dangerous-looking crocodiles, beautiful rainforests, thundering waterfalls, and picturesque beaches. He had met many nice tourists and lovely locals, thoroughly enjoying his holiday. But then a streak of bad luck began. Out of the blue, his girlfriend Kathrin called him from Germany and admitted that she had fallen in love with someone else. Out of sheer grief, he got senselessly drunk, fell into a ditch and injured his leg. The next evening, he lost a large sum of money in a card game. Only a few days later, his mobile phone went overboard during a boat trip.

"And therefore, I couldn't reach anyone," Peter said finally, taking a sip of beer.

"I don't understand that!" said Katja. "You could have borrowed some mobile phone or used an internet café to contact your friends and relatives!"

Sam frowned and eyed Peter thoughtfully. He was a slender yet muscular, tall man next to whom the petite Katja seemed like a dwarf. But still, he looked almost like a little schoolboy at the moment, with vulnerable features, tousled hair and sad blue eyes.

"Somehow, I was completely off track after Kathrin had broken up with me. I didn't want to talk to anyone at all, especially not to my relatives or friends. I was terribly depressed, and for a while I even had suicidal thoughts."

After a short pause, he continued:

"Well, at some point I pulled myself together and decided to enjoy my last week in Australia. Actually, I wanted to meet two friends from my school days anyway. I just found out by chance that they had also planned a trip to Australia and had recently landed in Brisbane. But silly me, I fell asleep on the train and only woke up again in some town behind Nambour. And – bloody hell! – I discovered that someone had stolen my little backpack with my wallet! Luckily, my passport was in my big backpack, and some money and also my driver's licence were hidden in a belly strap, otherwise it would have been much worse. But now I had to hitchhike to Nambour, which took ages. And my friends were long gone, of course! I was pissed off! Finally, I decided to go to Coolum Beach. However, I ended up in Maroochydore and spent a night there as a couch-surfer."

"Your German friends were terribly worried and called the police!" said Katja gruffly. She still didn't understand why he hadn't contacted them.

"I tried to call them! But I didn't have their Australian mobile numbers written down anywhere and couldn't remember them properly. And my mobile phone was gone!" Peter defended himself.

Sam had to laugh. "What a story! But I think we should tell the police that you're alive and well!"

Katja said in a firm voice: "Exactly! And right away!"

"Yeah, okay!" Peter grinned a little wryly.

"And also ask them for the mobile number of your friends who reported you missing. Or give them our number!" suggested Sam eagerly.

"Good idea!" Peter smiled, but seemed rather meek during the phone call to the police. Afterwards he said: "They want me to come to the police station in the morning and identify myself!"

"The one in Coolum Beach? No problem! I can drive you there," Katja said.

"Did you get your friends' phone numbers?" asked Sam.

"Yeah, the policeman was really nice. At first, he refused because of privacy and stuff, but then he gave me the information anyway. I'd better call them right away!"

Katja and Sam went into the kitchen so Peter could talk on the phone, undisturbed.

"It's a pity Peter can't stay in our holiday unit. What shall we do?" whispered Katja.

"He could sleep on our couch for one night," suggested Sam. "But let's wait and see what he's up to."

"Anyway, I'm glad Peter has turned up!" said Katja. "But he should also notify his family in Germany!"

After several text messages and three long phone calls, Peter declared:

"That's done! Luckily, I was able to reach my mother and she is totally relieved! Even my father was in sheer panic, although he is usually very calm. And my little sister almost wanted to fly to Australia to look for me herself, she's really sweet! My two friends are in Noosa at the moment, but they want to go to Coolum Beach tomorrow. I'll spend the next few days with them before flying back to Germany."

"Super!" Katja beamed. "If you like, you are welcome to sleep in our living room this night."

"Really? Oh, that's great, thank you so much!"

"Shall we have another beer? We have to celebrate your return, after all!" Sam smiled mischievously.

"Maybe Tony would like to join us too?" Katja mused.

And off she went to the holiday unit, knocking on the door of her new guest.

35

Tony liked his temporary accommodation. It was practically furnished and spotless clean. He had just started reading the autobiography of a psychologist in South America when Katja knocked on his door. He was surprised and even a bit annoyed about her invitation, because he didn't feel like talking at all. Nevertheless, he quickly agreed, as he hadn't met Sam yet and found Katja quite nice – even though she was a bit hectic and too motherly.

As soon as he entered his hosts' living room, he was greeted warmly by Sam. Katja introduced him to Peter and smiled at both of them, and Tony inwardly admired her almost perfect white teeth. Being a dentist, he automatically peered into people's mouths. He thought Katja was decidedly pretty, while Sam was rather average looking in his opinion. He had very bushy eyebrows and a rather thick knobby nose. However, his brown eyes seemed friendly and kind-hearted. The young tourist from Germany was tanned and athletic-looking, but had deep shadows under his eyes. His sand-coloured shorts and blue T-shirt were slightly stained.

Katja offered Tony beer, wine or juice, but he preferred a glass of water. She put a small bowl of peanuts and a larger one of chips on the table and then turned to Peter:

"I tried to call you some time ago but couldn't reach you. Do you remember Ann, our neighbour? She told us that you'd met Maureen on the train from Brisbane to Nambour. You must have heard that the young woman was murdered, right?"

Peter nodded. "Yeah, unbelievable! She was such a nice girl! Why on earth was she killed? By the way, I met her again by chance in Coolum Beach, when she was playing guitar on the beach with another young woman. I was with some acquaintances, though, and just gave her a quick wave."

He thoughtfully turned his half-full beer glass in his hands and put it down again without drinking. "Oh yes, I noticed a man sitting nearby with an overweight dog listening to them at the time."

Katja almost choked on her beer. "What did he look like?" she croaked.

"Why do you care?" asked Sam in wonder.

"I'm sure it's nonsense, but Tina and I once heard Maureen playing guitar in a café. Later Tina mentioned a rotund man with a fat dog who was also there. And ... well, he appeared kind of creepy to her as he kept staring at Maureen. And what's more, he left the café right after her."

Peter scratched his head.

"Well, how should I describe the guy on the beach? He was in his early or mid-forties, I guess, quite tall and strong, with fair hair. I wouldn't have noticed him at all, if he hadn't been staring at the two women like that. But maybe he just liked their music. They played blues songs and sang along."

Grinning, he continued: "I remember the dog better because it came up to us, wagging its tail and wanting to be petted. It was a mix of a Labrador and a Bulldog, rather ugly actually, yet really cute!"

Tony was about to take a handful of chips and now paused.

"That's exactly the kind of mongrel I know! My brother-in-law often looks after a friend's dog when he has to go away on business. Ernie is a lovely animal, but such a heavy lump! Mark has also looked after his friend's house several times, once even for a fortnight. That's when Debbie, my sister, got a bit upset." He laughed. "Because her kids are pretty rebellious sometimes, and she believes that Mark leaves way too much of the housework and parenting to her anyway. She would have preferred to take the dog to live with them, but the owner didn't want that. Ernie just prefers to be in his familiar surroundings. I guess he's being pampered quite a bit."

"Ernie? Yes, that's it! That must be the same dog! I remember the man calling him back after a while, when that friendly dog was cuddling with all of us!" exclaimed Peter.

"And what does Ernie's owner look like?" Sam wanted to know from Tony.

"John? He's a tiny, spindly man," Tony replied. "He's an old school friend of Mark, and in the past, their classmates often made fun of them because they just looked funny next to each other. You see, my brother-in-law was always quite powerfully built, even as a kid ..."

Tony stroked his narrow nose, lost in thought. To be honest, he had often wondered about Debbie's taste and didn't particularly like her husband. He could be funny and jovial, but unfortunately, he was also often cynical and opinionated. Suddenly his heart grew heavy. Had it been Mark who had gawked at Maureen, in such a way that others had noticed, and more than once? But why? His brother-in-law despised blues! Had he found her attractive and stalked her? Or – could he have something to do with her murder? But no, that was a ridiculous idea!

Sam thought of his own daughter, who used to play the guitar on the beach from time to time. He murmured in sorrow:

"What a gruesome ending! Why was Maureen killed? In our peaceful neighbourhood of all places, it's hard to believe! I'm sure it was a huge shock to this other musician too. I wonder if she was an old friend or a new acquaintance of Maureen's?"

"Who knows?" Katja shrugged and turned back to Peter.

"Are you going to make ends meet? Do you have enough money for the rest of your holiday? Or would you like us to lend you some?"

"Oh! Um, would you?" asked Peter, befuddled.

He twirled a strand of hair nervously. He was already embarrassed anyway that he had just turned up at the nice couple's house and asked for accommodation. After all, he hardly knew them. On top of that, he was aware that he was a bit smelly and all his clothes were pretty dirty. What a bummer that someone had robbed him! His friends could lend him some money, but they still had most of their holidays ahead of them and weren't exactly well-off themselves. They hadn't reckoned with how expensive everything was in Australia.

Sam suggested: "Can't you just transfer money from your account in Germany to ours? It will probably take a while, but never mind. And we'll give you some cash tomorrow."

"Awesome! I didn't even think of a bank transfer!" Peter laughed merrily.

All at once, he couldn't wait to see his old friends from Germany. It would be great to catch up with them!

Katja looked at her two guests, thinking of Maureen's family who had also lived in their house for a short time. The three of them would probably never get over the brutal, seemingly senseless murder. How terrible to lose a beloved daughter and sister in this way! Who had killed Maureen? Would the case ever be solved? Had Maureen actually had a boyfriend? All her friends must be shaken up! Katja sighed softly.

Sam yawned loudly. "I'm going to bed! Peter, I'll give you a pillow and a sheet for the sofa. You have your own sleeping bag, right?"

"Yeah, great, thanks a lot!" replied Peter.

Tony stood up and said goodbye.

But then he abruptly turned around. "You know what? Peter could sleep in the spare room of my holiday unit this night. I guess a real bed is much more comfortable than the sofa!"

Katja asked in a doubtful voice: "Is that really okay with you?"

"Of course, no problem!"

In the middle of the night, Tony woke up. He was drenched in sweat and his heart was racing. Had he eaten too many chips? Only vaguely could he remember a nasty dream. His sister Yolanda had been in terrible danger, but his hands were tied and his brother-in-law had laughed boomingly. Mark's wide-open mouth had seemed to him like a yawning black hole threatening to swallow him up ...

Tony switched on the pleasantly bright reading lamp beside his bed and looked at the clock. It was 3 am. Far too early to get up! What's more, he didn't want to wake up Peter in the adjoining room. The young fellow had looked a bit rough and certainly needed his sleep. Tony threw the covers off himself and thought about their hosts. They were such a nice couple, and so friendly and helpful! He'd noticed how they'd exchanged tender glances from time to time. So cute! They seemed to be happily in love with each other!

Did Debbie still love her husband? He hoped so, both for her and Mark and their children. He had actually missed Kim and Daniel, the cheeky rascals, when he had been in Alaska. Would he ever have children of his own? Just like his younger sister Yolanda, he'd had little luck in love so far. He shivered and quickly covered himself up again, and shortly afterwards he fell asleep.

36

My heart was filled with love and happiness every time I thought of Sylvie. And I admired how well she mastered her hard job. Working in a nursing home was definitely no walk in the park. Nevertheless, Sylvie was always wonderfully gentle and patient with everybody in her care. Some of the residents were very ungrateful, bitter, stubborn or even aggressive, others were depressed and introverted. My frequent visits gave me a good insight into the usual routine in the 'Puzzle House'. To my amazement, my mother had become the favourite of several employees, although she too had her moods and quirks and – fortunately only rarely – even downright tantrums. Not only Sylvie and Yolanda, but also Leah (the receptionist with the mighty bosom) and a doctor called Adam (a young man with a huge Adam's apple) were particularly fond of her.

Henry, the old gentleman who had helped Mum after her fall, seemed to like her too, and from time to time they went for a little walk around the nursing home. Unfortunately, communication was a big problem. He was a bit hard of hearing, and my mother's speech difficulties due to her Alzheimer's disease were constantly increasing.

Tina too came to see Mum occasionally. She never stayed long, but I gave her credit for her visits and all her generous gifts like flowers and healthy snacks. Sometimes she was reading to Mum. I think both of them enjoyed that.

As promised, Linda and Ken visited my mother several times with their children, and once they brought along an old friend from Brisbane. Did Mum recognise them all? I don't think so. But it was always nice when someone made her smile. As far as I knew, everyone made an effort to speak clearly and slowly, everyone treated my mother with warmth and respect. Nobody talked about her in her presence as if she were a baby or couldn't hear anymore.

On a rainy evening, I wrote into my diary:

Mum has been in the nursing home for about seven months now. Although she is well cared for, there are also devastating experiences, and quite a few upsets. I am very glad and thankful for the support of Sylvie, Patrick and Sarah (and Yolanda and others too).

Mum had to be taken to hospital twice but recovered quickly both times. Once she had a fall, another day she had terrible stomach aches. I have become a volunteer visiting various residents in the nursing home, sometimes just chatting with them, sometimes doing some gardening with them, or taking them for short walks. Unfortunately, my spare time for the seniors is quite limited due to my 'real job', but I always enjoy their delight in cuddling my cute dog. Mum's neighbour Ruth had always been thrilled to see Nellie, but she passed away recently. I was really sad!

A fortnight ago, there was a costume party where children from a kindergarten performed singing and dancing, and afterwards I helped serve drinks and cakes to the whole troupe. Both the children and the seniors had an incredible time and so much fun! Some of the oldies had a boisterous ball game with the kids (with some very soft balls), laughing like crazy! Even one senior who's always grim and reserved joined in and smiled.

Last weekend, Sylvie and I started to renovate her house. And what a nice surprise: we can work super well together! (Unlike Tina and me! When we'd done some repairs together, she'd constantly accused me of working too slowly. But I want to do everything properly and thoroughly).

Finally, Tina and I are officially divorced! That evening, we both celebrated with Sylvie and Philip. Crazy, isn't it? Tina is staying in her house, paying me a certain amount every month until she has paid me my rightful share. Although I absolutely trust her, we've put everything in writing in a contract and the house is now in her name. Philip wants to move in with her soon.

I folded the diary shut, glanced around the room and then at Nellie, who was sleeping on the carpet. It had been a hard decision to give up the house I'd shared with Tina. But now I felt unspeakably relieved. At last, we had settled this! Despite all the differences of opinion, I was still fond of Tina and genuinely wished her to be happy with Philip. And I liked my rental property! What more did I want? I leaned back and closed my eyes. The sound of the gentle rain lulled me to sleep.

"Hello!" A familiar voice roused me from my snooze. I quickly walked to the door, almost tripping over Nellie who had also jumped up.

"Hello, Michael!"

Standing in front of me were Melissa and Jim, my landlords, who looked kind of taken aback.

"Are you free right now? We need to discuss something with you," Jim said in a grave voice, taking his rather sodden hat off his head and twirling it nervously between his hands that were crippled by arthritis.

"Of course! Come in, sit down!"

Why did they look so sad? Had something bad happened? Melissa remained standing beside the door while Jim dropped into a chair and sighed.

"Michael, we have bad news! We're very unhappy. Um, we've decided not to renew your lease because our niece Arya wants to move in here. You see, she broke up with her boyfriend the other day and needs a place to live."

"We deliberated over this decision for a long time, but Arya is quite desperate and doesn't know where to go. At the moment she's staying with a friend, and later she's going to look after someone's house and dog. But that will be limited to two weeks, and therefore ... um, well, your contract is up in November ... and ..." Melissa swallowed.

"Oh!" I uttered, too shocked to say anything clever.

"Arya is prone to severe depression as it is, and that's why we'd like to help her. Otherwise, we'd love to keep you as our tenant!" said Jim, obviously quite distressed.

Melissa leaned over to Nellie. "We'll miss you!" she whispered, kissing the top of her head.

I mumbled: "Yeah, it was totally nice here with you guys! But don't worry, I'll find something."

"We'll ask around too and let you know if we spot anything suitable!" Jim promised and stood up.

"Good night, Michael!" Both Jim and Melissa squeezed my hand.

As soon as they were gone, I said despondently to my dog:

"Oh, Nellie, life is too complicated! Where are we going to go? There are so few vacant flats or houses in this area, and everything's expensive as hell!"

My stomach suddenly felt really queasy. Sure, I had my income plus Tina's repayments, but the housing market was looking lousy. More and more people, and not just poor or unemployed folks, were becoming homeless. Some were living in tents in the bushland by the sea, others tried to find shelter under the roofs of shops. A few weeks ago, I read an article in the local paper, reporting about a desperate widow who had to spend the nights in her small car with her three children. Terrible!

The rain was now intensifying, whipping against the window panes on the side of the house facing the wind. I felt like crying. Nellie snuggled up to me and I stroked her tenderly.

37

The next morning I had a throbbing headache. For a while I toyed with the idea of staying in bed. But playing hooky had never been my thing, so after walking the dog I swallowed a painkiller and forced myself to eat breakfast. However, the coffee tasted disgustingly bitter and the muesli like sawdust. The news on TV reported about wars, natural disasters, accidents and poverty – it was not exactly cheering, and I lost the last bit of my appetite. Nellie, on the other hand, licked her bowl with relish and begged for more.

"Nah, there's no more, you've become too chubby anyway!" I said and gave her fresh water.

On the way to work, it was raining very gently. I saw Debbie just stepping out of her house and I waved at her, but she didn't notice. When the radio played one of my favourite songs, I hummed along, softly at first, and then louder and louder. In the end, I sang at the top of my lungs, and my mood improved considerably. The working day was quite normal and without stress. Nevertheless, I glanced at my watch more often than usual. My colleague Karen grinned mischievously at me and whispered:

"You can't wait to meet your new girlfriend, can you?"

A little embarrassed, I smiled back.

"Are you both going to Lisa's party?" Karen asked in a louder voice, immediately earning a disapproving look from

Maya, our boss. After all, the library was supposed to be a 'quiet and pleasant place to read, study and work', as Maya kept saying.

I nodded and grinned. Lisa was an older colleague who was going to retire soon, planning to have a farewell party on Saturday. Sylvie wanted to come along too. She had already joked about me being the 'cock of the walk' at work, because I was the only man there, and she was looking forward to meeting my colleagues.

When Sylvie and I arrived at the garden party on Saturday afternoon, it was pretty busy, and loud voices mingled with the sounds of an old hit song. Most of the guests were seated at small tables under umbrellas, some were chatting and eating on the paved patio underneath a skillion roof. There were stunning bouquets of flowers and two huge cakes on a long table, and there were also various salads, bread, all kinds of finger food and drinks. The air was smelling of grilled sausages, stewed vegetables, beer and flowers.

"Wow! I didn't expect such a big party and so much food," whispered Sylvie.

"Me neither!" I replied.

"Hi, Michael!" cried Karen, jumping up from her chair and giving me a big kiss on the cheek. Looking curiously at Sylvie, she said cheerfully: "And you must be Michael's girlfriend!"

"Hello!" Lisa greeted us warmly as well. She was wearing a burgundy, long, elegantly cut dress that contrasted beautifully with her light grey hair.

I handed her our gifts, home-baked honey biscuits and a bottle of wine, and eyed her in surprise. "I'd never seen you in a dress before!"

Lisa grinned mischievously. "At sixty-six, I thought I'd dress up a bit!"

"Happy Birthday, Lisa!" exclaimed a new guest with a mane of snow-white hair.

"It's your birthday today? I didn't know!" I said and hugged her. "Happy Birthday!"

Sylvie shook Lisa's hand. My girlfriend looked especially pretty today, I thought, smitten with her warm smile, her blonde curls and a new dark blue blouse. Since we had come by bicycle, we were both wearing shorts and hadn't dressed up much.

"Help yourselves!" said Lisa, pointing to the buffet. "And Michael, could you perhaps help with the barbecue afterwards to give George a break?"

"Oh!" I looked sheepishly at George, her husband.

For whatever reason, many men enthusiastically take over the barbecue at parties, but I, as a vegetarian, dreaded flabby sausages and bloody steaks.

The next moment, Lisa laughed bemusedly. "Don't you worry, Michael, I know you! I was just pulling your leg, and George loves his work. So come on, you two, eat heartily, there's plenty of vegetarian food!" She winked at Sylvie.

"Thanks, Lisa!" I said with relief, handing Sylvie a plate. "Mm, it's looking totally delicious!"

"These food labels are a great idea!" An older lady was leaning over to one of the cakes, adjusting her glasses and reading aloud: "Gluten-free chocolate cake with cherries."

Sylvie took a slice of vegetable quiche and a few other savoury bites and replied with a grin: "I'll try that cake for dessert later."

"If there's anything left by then!" said Maya, heaping two rather large pieces of cake onto her plate at once.

My colleagues and I already knew that our boss liked sweets and was not exactly modest. I briefly introduced her to my girlfriend before Sylvie and I moved to a group in the corner of the garden. We sat down on some folding chairs close to a small creek, which banks were covered with grasses, tree ferns, palms and various trees, some of them indigenous and gnarled.

"How picturesque!" enthused Sylvie.

A chubby man with a bushy beard and a beige floppy hat smiled at us, but the woman next to him, a middle-aged lady with unusually long brown hair and a white cap, was visibly distressed. She spoke in a raised voice to a younger-looking woman with a short blonde haircut:

"The guy touched my mother indecently and kissed her, but no one believed her! Even the young geriatric nurse, who always seemed so nice to me, just shrugged her shoulders, saying my mother would forget about it anyway. What a stupid comment! Even though my poor old mum suffers from dementia, you still have to take her seriously and respect her!"

She pushed her cap out of her forehead and her blue eyes flashed angrily.

"Now, don't shout so loudly, Noelene!" the man in the floppy hat admonished her in a firm yet friendly voice. "It was terrible, but we are here to celebrate Lisa's birthday." He put a hand on her arm sympathetically.

Noelene shook him off and hissed at him: "And you didn't do anything about it either!"

"What was I supposed to do? I did speak to the manager!" he protested. I guess he was her husband.

Sylvie asked Noelene in a soft voice:

"Is your mother in a nursing home? I work as a carer in the fairly new one in town. What exactly happened?"

Noelene explained: "My mother has been in a nursing home in Brisbane for a few weeks. Recently she was deeply upset and crying when I visited her. Another resident ... that old bastard! ... approached her, pushed her roughly into a corner, groped her and kissed her! Can you imagine? And she's such a petite, frail lady! She's already 85 years old!"

Only with difficulty did she suppress a sob. "And I don't know if she can forget it so easily. Maybe she relives that moment over and over again – and is now constantly afraid!"

"That's ghastly!" I blurted out.

"Unfortunately, there are more sexual assaults than most would like to believe, and even old age doesn't protect you!" Sylvie looked at me sadly.

Then she asked the couple: "How did the manager react?"

Noelene was cleaning her nose, and the man quickly replied: "She promised to look into it and talk to the guy. But I wonder if it will do any good."

"What are we going to do? We won't find another home for Mum so soon!" wailed Noelene.

Sylvie squeezed her hand compassionately.

"If you like, I'll ask our manager if she can give you some advice. By the way, I just attended a webinar about sexual abuse the other day – a subject that still is a big taboo. Although I've been a carer for years, I didn't realise how often it happens in aged care homes. Mentally handicapped people are especially at risk because they often can't speak properly anymore."

She sighed.

"Unfortunately, it is very difficult to improve the situation. In many cases, even relatives, staff members and police officers are not willing to listen to those affected. They don't give them faith and respect! If there are no visible injuries, it's hard to prove an abuse. Often the victims are not even capable to complain, or they are far too scared or ashamed to speak out. All of us – staff, relatives and residents – can only try to be attentive. We must investigate if someone behaves differently than usual, or if someone has got suspicious bruises or other injuries." Sylvie took a little sip from her wine glass and added:

"Depending on the case, it could be helpful to contact an organisation such as Dementia Australia or the OPAN, or perhaps Lifeline or the Salvation Army."

"The OPA... what?" the bearded man asked, frowning.

"OPAN! That's short for 'Older Persons Advocacy Network', an organisation that aims to help the elderly. Not only in terms of sexual and physical assault, but also psychological abuse, financial exploitation or neglect ..."

"Yes, I've heard about that too!" said the short-haired woman who hadn't uttered a word since Sylvie and I had joined the group.

"Who wants another sausage?"

George, Lisa's husband, came to our table with a plate full of sausages.

"Oh yes, thanks!" the blonde woman took one.

George beamed at us.

"I hope you're having a good time! Somehow you all look so sad. Maybe I should open a jar of pickles."

"Pickles?" The bearded man was as puzzled as everybody else.

"Gherkins are good for the mood! Didn't you know that, Richard?" joked George.

Sylvie laughed. "I'd better go and see if there's any cake left! Shall I bring some for all of you?"

"Yes!" they all shouted in chorus.

Sylvie grabbed enough pieces of both the chocolate cake and the nut cake for our group. A tall tree nearby was buzzing with countless bats, making a noisy spectacle. My head was buzzing with countless thoughts, and once again, I was concerned about my mother. But I tried to block out my worries and to enjoy the party.

38

Late in the evening, Sylvie and I arrived at my cottage slightly tipsy. Everything was quiet as a mouse. This time there was no joyful barking of welcome, as Nellie would spend the whole weekend with Tina and Philip. They had kindly offered to look after her whenever I wanted. Sylvie and I put the bicycles into the shed and were walking towards the entrance when I heard a low moan. Oh no, had something happened to Tina or Nellie? Or who else could be in my house?

Sylvie was giggling. Obviously, she hadn't heard a thing.

"It was quite a sight to see you dancing with your boss! I didn't know what a good dancer you are, and Maya seemed enraptured! And yet you always ..."

"Shh!" I hissed. "Something's wrong!"

I tiptoed to the door and found it wasn't firmly secured. Had I forgotten to lock it in the afternoon? I waited for a second, then opened it swiftly.

"Hello!" I called loudly and flicked on the light.

"What the hell – who are you?" I shouted.

Crouched on my armchair was a young woman with dark, tousled short hair. She startled, rubbed her eyes and said sheepishly:

"I'm Arya. Um, this house belongs to relatives of mine, and I ... I ..." In the next instant, she was sobbing away. "I didn't know where to go! And my Aunt Melissa and Uncle Jim weren't home. I felt really sick with fear!"

Sylvie asked sympathetically: "What happened?"

I frowned in surprise. Strange, Melissa and Jim were always at home at this time of day. I stood rooted to the door, while Sylvie sat down on the couch after a moment's hesitation. Arya didn't say a peep, and her auburn, tear-veiled eyes seemed to me like those of a timid deer.

"Who were you afraid of?" Sylvie and I asked in unison.

Arya wiped her eyes and said: "I killed someone! Yet she was already dead before!"

"Bullshit!" I blurted out.

"What?" asked Sylvie, horrified.

I stared at the woman, not knowing what to do. Call the police? Stand protectively before Sylvie? Look for a weapon to defend my friend and myself? Was this woman deranged?

Arya was sobbing away again. "It was no intention! But ... but ..." Her voice failed.

Sylvie handed her a pack of tissues.

"Here, blow your nose! You can cry later. First, tell us exactly what's happened. Where have you been?"

Sylvie could be very resolute! As if in a trance, Arya took the tissues and blew her nose vigorously. Sylvie sat back down and I filled three glasses with water before settling down on the sofa, close to my girlfriend.

Arya inhaled and exhaled deeply several times, and only now did I notice her alcoholic breath and an unpleasant sour smell. She drank greedily from her water glass.

Finally, she told us:

"I was at a man's house in Marcoola. I'd applied for the position of a house-sitter where I was to look after a dog for a fortnight, in exchange for free accommodation. John had invited me to dinner so that we could discuss everything in more detail. In particular, I was to meet Ernie, his dog, who ..." Arya paused and blew her nose again.

"Well, the dog is really cute, and John seems to adore him. That actually made me like him. On the other hand, he was a strange guy. I think he was trying to get me drunk. Anyway, he kept refilling my wine glass, while he just sipped a little from his glass. But I only noticed that later, and on the way here I threw up. I'm such a fool to drink so much!" she suddenly shouted and jumped up.

I was startled by her outburst and her grim face, but Sylvie remained calm.

"What did John do?" she asked.

Arya stood in front of the armchair and grabbed the edge of the table as if looking for support. In a hoarse voice she continued:

"John showed me all the rooms in the house to explain where I could turn off the water in case of an emergency, where to turn off the electricity and so on. He chatted away like crazy and often chuckled in an awkward way. He's a weirdo! I thought. However, I found him more funny than scary, and besides, John is very thin and relatively small, so he doesn't seem threatening at all. But when we went into the bedroom ..."

Her nostrils quivered and she plopped into the armchair like a wet sack.

"When we ..." she croaked.

"Did he do something to you?" I asked pityingly.

Arya's eyes snapped open. "Nah, but ... there was a woman standing there pointing a gun at us!"

"What?" asked Sylvie incredulously.

"You've got to be kidding!" I exclaimed.

Arya said tonelessly: "I killed her!"

"What? How?" I felt like being in a bad movie.

"Everything happened so fast and yet it felt like slow motion. John immediately turned off the lights and it was pitch black. He gave me a violent shove and then a gunshot went off ..." Arya swallowed hard. "I fell down and somehow flicked on a floor lamp. John screamed and I saw he was lying next to me, bleeding from the arm. The woman took another step coming closer to us, again aiming her gun at John ... and ... you can't believe how hateful she looked! Ernie whimpered piteously and then began to growl loudly. And that's when the woman suddenly seemed undecided whether to shoot the dog or John. So, I jumped up, grabbed the floor lamp in a flash and smashed it over her head!" Arya let out a sob. "She fell down and was dead as a door-nail!"

"Are you sure she was dead?" asked Sylvie doubtfully.

"And then?" I asked tensely.

"Only now did I realise who she was. I felt sick to my stomach because it was ... it was ... the murdered Maureen! I recognised her because she had once played guitar in a café where I was employed as a waitress at the time."

"Nonsense!" Sylvie said vehemently.

Arya's eyes flashed with anger, and again I detected a strong whiff of alcohol. How much had she drunk? And had she taken some other drugs as well? She seemed pretty crazy to me!

"It was Maureen! Or her ghost! And that's when I absolutely panicked and ran!" Arya blurted out in a shrill voice.

"We definitely have to call the police!" Sylvie said.

"Yes, and an ambulance too! I hope John isn't too badly hurt!" I said worriedly.

Arya suddenly whimpered. "Oh, I just abandoned John! I should have taken care of him. But I don't want to go to prison!" And she began to cry profusely again.

Only with difficulty did Sylvie manage to get John's address out of her.

After I had phoned the ambulance and the police, we sat there in silence. And then I suddenly remembered what Tina had told me a short while ago.

"I've got the solution! It must have been Hannah, Maureen's older sister!" I exclaimed. "Katja mentioned that the siblings almost looked like twins."

Seeing Arya's uncomprehending face, I quickly explained:

"Katja and Sam are friends of mine. They met Hannah as they rented out their holiday flat to Maureen's family, just for a few days. But I thought they'd all left long ago."

"Interesting idea! But how did that woman, whoever she might be, get a rifle? We don't live in America!" Sylvie remarked.

Arya burst into hysterical laughter. I was feeling helpless and a little panicky. What should we do about this young woman who had invaded our house and was visibly disturbed?

How long would we have to wait for the police officers to come and interrogate her? I nervously ran my fingers through my hair, and my stomach and intestines were rumbling suspiciously.

Sylvie smiled reassuringly at me.

"I'll make us some tea!"

At that moment someone knocked on the door. It was not the police, however, but my landlords Melissa and Jim. Immediately Arya embraced her aunt, crying like a baby.

"Oh, my child!" said Melissa. "What happened to you? We were at a birthday party and only now discovered your message on the answering machine. Of course you can spend the night with us! But who are you afraid of?"

While Arya was telling them everything, several police officers came to my little house. They looked very serious, almost grim, and refused a cup of tea.

It was close to dawn when Sylvie and I were finally alone again and we fell into a fitful sleep.

39

Feeling dizzy, John had difficulty wrapping a bandage around his injured arm. Although being a pharmacist, he always felt a little sick seeing blood, especially if it was his own. He anxiously watched the woman still lying motionless on the floor. He had treated her wound to the head as best he could manage. For safety's sake, he had quickly tied her hands together with a dog leash and locked the rifle in a cupboard. There he had discovered an old clothesline which he wrapped around her ankles and then fastened to a bedpost. He was completely stunned, hardly believing what had happened. Who was this woman? What a blessing that her shot hadn't hit his heart! But why had she shot him? And how had she got into his bedroom, unnoticed even by his dog?

Ernie was now licking his hand compassionately and John stroked him tenderly.

"Good that nothing happened to you and Arya!" he whispered.

He could totally understand Arya's panicked flight and was infinitely grateful that she had saved him and Ernie. But what had she shouted at the end? Something like: "Now she's been killed for the second time!" What could that mean? Had Arya been drunk as a skunk, just talking nonsense? Admittedly, he had poured her too much wine at dinner. But she had seemed a bit uptight and shy at first, and he had only meant well. She made a nice impression, and Ernie had liked her right away, too. John would like to hire her as a house sitter as planned, but after that crazy assassination attempt, she was guaranteed never to set foot over his threshold again.

Impatiently, he looked at his watch. When would the police finally arrive? He had already called them fifteen minutes ago!

The bound woman moved and opened her eyes. At first her vision was blurred and she moaned. But then she glared at John and he was startled by the unbridled hatred in her expression. What did she have against him? She looked vaguely familiar, and yet he was quite sure he had never seen her before. It was incomprehensible! Could she have mistaken him for someone else? Or could his profession be the reason for her attack? Recently, a group of animal rights activists had broken into a laboratory, setting free many animals. An acquaintance of his, whom he had known since his student days, had been injured in the process. However, that had happened in another city, and he himself was not a researcher and had nothing to do with animal experiments.

His mind was racing. He worked as a pharmaceutical representative. Could her attack be related to the medicine that he had exuberantly promoted for a while – that drug that was later taken off the market because of its terrible side effects? It had not only caused shortness of breath and heart problems in small children, but even some deaths! Could that be the connection to this young woman? Had her own child died because of that medicine, making her wish to take revenge on him? But how had she got his address? Nothing made sense!

The woman was now trying to get up in vain, realising that her legs were tied to the wooden bedpost.

"Let me go!" she screeched, trying to wriggle out of her bonds.

Ernie growled menacingly.

John warned her: "Be careful! You have a nasty head wound that needs stitches! Why did you shoot me?"

"Because you killed my sister, you rotten bastard!" she shouted.

"Your sister? Who's that supposed to be?"

"You lying prick! She told a friend that she wanted to live here in Marcoola as a house-sitter for a while, in this very street! She was supposed to introduce herself to someone in person that evening. Although she didn't even know yet whether her application would be successful, she was already raving in advance about her free accommodation so close to the sea. But the next morning she was lying dead in the park! Under a shabby plastic tarp! Murdered!" she sobbed.

John was perplexed. His arm was hurting like hell and he was feeling nauseous.

"Ah, that was your sister? I'm so sorry to hear this! Yes, I heard about the murder back then. It was in Coolum Beach, wasn't it? What a terrible tragedy! However, I never met her and I haven't had any house-sitters besides a good friend here for a long time!"

"You bloody liar!" the woman screamed, vehemently struggling against the restraints. "I saw your last ad on the internet. And just now there was another young woman here for an introduction. Did you want to kill her too? Oh, I wish I had aimed better at you!"

She reared up and wriggled so wildly on the ground that John instinctively backed away. He had never been particularly brave and had always hidden behind his burly friend Mark, even as a child. Mark! He had often looked after his beloved dog Ernie. Did he have any idea what this story might be about? Should he give him a quick call?

"What a nonsense!" he grumbled. To his relief, he now heard police sirens nearby, and the next moment he fainted.

When John regained consciousness, he was in hospital. He still was very nauseous and dizzy and had trouble thinking straight. Had a complete stranger actually tried to shoot him? In his own bedroom? Or was he stuck in a bad dream?

"Hello, John!" a plump young nurse fluted cheerfully. "Just lie still, you have to take it easy for a while. But don't worry, the arm will heal fine!"

"Ernie ... where's my Ernie?" replied John anxiously.

"Who's Ernie? I don't know where he's! However, there's someone waiting impatiently in the corridor, perhaps he has got an idea. I'll go and get him!"

John had almost expected to see his friend Mark, but instead, a policeman came to his bed. The older man made a move to shake his hand and changed his mind when his gaze fell on his bandaged arm. He politely introduced himself, sat down on a chair and began to quiz him. Every now and then he scribbled notes in a notebook. In the end, John learned that the woman with the rifle was called Hannah. She had climbed through an open bedroom window with the intention to kill him. When the police arrived, she immediately made a full confession and was arrested. The other woman named Arya had also already been questioned. She was currently staying with relatives.

"I have to look after my dog!" croaked John tearfully.

The policeman smiled at him reassuringly. "Don't worry! Your neighbour Wayne is taking care of it. He was just coming home when we took you to the ambulance, after finding you unconscious on the ground in your house, and your dog ran joyfully towards him straight away."

"Ernie is always far too friendly to everyone. He would even lick the feet of a burglar." John grinned wryly. "At least he growled at Hannah when she tried to shoot me the second time. But if it hadn't been for Arya, I'm sure it would have ended badly!"

"Yes, you were lucky indeed!"

The policeman said goodbye as a female doctor marched into the sickroom, chasing him away with her grim expression alone. Due to the high blood loss and the shock of the unexpected attack, John was very weakened and soon fell asleep again.

It was not until the next morning that he called his neighbour to thank him. Wayne, a middle-aged man, had separated from his wife a few months ago. Since then, he often went to a pub to forget his loneliness. Wayne now affirmed that it would be no problem at all to look after Ernie. It just so happened that he was on holiday. And his father, who had come to visit for a week, was also totally fond of animals. John was happy. He had been toying with the idea of asking Mark to look after Ernie while he was in hospital. But apparently his dog was in good hands.

Relieved, he lay down again when he suddenly felt hot and cold at the same time. If he remembered correctly, he had been on a business trip at the time of Maureen's murder, and Mark had been living in his house as a dog sitter for a fortnight. Upon his return, John had discovered a guitar in his garage, quite a beautiful one though not brand-new. When he'd inquired about it, Mark had claimed to have bought it for his daughter, with the intention to keep it there until her birthday. Allegedly, he had forgotten to tell him. But he had seemed strangely nervous about it. Now John was wondering: could it be Maureen's guitar? Did Mark have something to do with her death?

John turned white as a sheet.

40

When I woke up, it was already 10 o'clock. I hadn't slept that long for ages! In the bathroom mirror I saw a pale face with deep shadows under the eyes, quite ugly. I had a horrible taste in my mouth and a slight muscle ache in my legs. Brushing my teeth, I decided to take a long, hot shower.

"Good morning!" Sylvie called out to me. "I've already made coffee!"

"Great!" I mumbled, my mouth full of toothpaste.

I had just lathered my hair with shampoo when I heard voices. Oops, who's come to visit again? I pricked up my ears, but I couldn't hear anything over the loud rush of water. Suddenly the water became ice cold. Bummer! Apparently, the gas cylinder was empty! I had never liked cold showers.

"Sylvie!" I called out. "Can you quickly connect the other gas bottle?"

Unfortunately, she didn't seem to hear me.

Disgruntled but refreshed, I finally stepped into the living room and grumbled:

"I wish my landlords would heat the water with solar energy, because ..."

I faltered when I caught sight of Sylvie and Yolanda on the couch, in a tight embrace and crying. At once I was gripped by panic. Something must have happened to my mum! She had not been well in the last week.

"Did my mother die?" I blurted out.

They both looked at me in utter confusion.

"What? No, Tony disappeared!" said Yolanda in a shaky voice.

"Really, since when? And where ..." I stammered.

Inwardly, I felt relieved that they weren't crying about my mother! But poor Yolanda was all upset! I had noticed before that she was very fond of her brother. And Sylvie must have been crying out of sympathy for her younger colleague. She was sitting there like a heap of misery, looking very peaky and tired. No wonder after last night!

Both women wiped their noses and Yolanda explained:

"We had a family party at Debbie's and Mark's last night, and Tony wanted to join us, of course. But he didn't show up, and we couldn't reach him on his mobile. Kim in particular was extremely disappointed because it was her birthday, and after a while we were all totally worried. Where could he possibly be?"

"Have you called Katja and Sam?"

"I even went there earlier today, but no sign of Tony. Allegedly, he left their house yesterday morning and they didn't see him after that. They don't know anything about his disappearance."

Yolanda sniffled loudly.

"And on top of that, the kids escaped early this morning! Debbie and Mark are absolutely frantic, and we've already searched the surrounding streets! At some point I got the idea to ask you, Michael, if you noticed anything, since you're living nearby."

I scratched my head, perplexed. "That's terrible! And surely it's too early to alert the police, isn't it?"

Yolanda put on a forced smile. "Debbie has already done that. But she only reported Tony as missing. We're sure the kids are looking for him and will soon return. But where's Tony? Oh, that jerk! Maybe he just picked up a nice woman somewhere and completely forgot about us!"

"Is he that unreliable?" Sylvie asked.

"Nah, not at all!" Yolanda sobbed out.

Suddenly I thought of Arya, John and his dog Ernie, and the woman with the rifle. We'd better not tell Yolanda about that drama, or she'd worry even more. It was hard to believe anyway! The whole story sounded like the Wild West! Where did Hannah – if it really was her, Maureen's sister – get the weapon? And why had she shot John?

Sylvie groaned. "What a mad weekend! First a wildly shooting woman and now several missing persons!"

"What?" asked Yolanda in surprise.

And Sylvie told her everything we had learned from Arya the day before. I rolled my eyes.

"I'll make us some breakfast, okay?" I suggested. "How about toast and honey? Or homemade jam from Melissa?"

Yolanda stayed, and I marvelled at her unbridled appetite. After one last sip of tea, she was about to leave when her mobile phone rang. Debbie reported that her children were back at home, safe and sound. Tony, however, had vanished without a trace.

41

Katja had been startled when Yolanda rang their doorbell, at the crack of dawn on a Sunday, to ask about Tony. Later at breakfast, she said to her husband:

"Shall we drive around and look for his car? Maybe Tony went swimming and drowned, or maybe he had an accident! That old car he bought the other day looks rickety! And yet, he's a dentist and should surely have enough money to afford something better!"

Sam was shaking his head. "Come on, Tony's car is pretty sturdy. He'll be okay! After all, Peter too went missing and showed up again. You always worry too much!"

Katja grinned a little wryly. "Yes, you're right! However, Tony wanted to buy a present for his niece yesterday morning, didn't he? And then he doesn't go to her birthday party?"

Sam rubbed his nose. "That's really weird! But maybe there was some emergency in his circle of friends or something like that. Or perhaps he was called to a patient in Woop Woop."

"In that case he would have called his family! Anyway, I'm going to the beach right now to search for his car!" said Katja resolutely.

Sam sighed. "Okay, I'll come with you!"

As Katja drove the car out of the garage, Ann came running from her garden and shouted: "Hello, wait a minute! Are you going to the market? Could you buy some potatoes for me?"

Sam rolled down the window and replied: "Nah, sorry, we are not going shopping. We're looking for Tony!"

"Tony? But why? He's out of town!" Ann leaned on the low fence of her front garden, breathing heavily. She was wearing a pink dress and her cheeks were glowing a deep pink too.

"Out of town? What makes you think that?" exclaimed Katja in amazement.

"Well, I saw him yesterday, packing a suitcase in his boot!"

"What?" asked Katja.

"You've got to be kidding!" said Sam angrily. "Tony's rented our unit for a whole month. He hasn't mentioned anything about moving out sooner."

"Did he at least pay in advance?" Ann wanted to know.

Katja had to grin. The old lady was shrewd indeed!

"Yes, he did!"

"What time exactly did you see Tony yesterday, Ann?" Sam asked.

"Yeah, well, it was around 1 pm, I think. I had just finished my lunch when I heard a loud beeping noise. So, I went to see what was going on. It was just some van reversing. And then I saw Tony on his way to his old car, which he had parked on the street."

"Nosy bugger!" Sam whispered to his wife.

"He's such a nice man!" Ann said with an admiring smile. "And he's so strong, because he had no trouble at all carrying that huge suitcase."

Katja frowned. She couldn't imagine Tony just leaving, without saying goodbye to them or to his family. Furthermore, he had only recently returned from Alaska and had already started his new job as a dentist. Nah, something must have happened to him!

"We'll let you know if we find out anything! Bye!" she said to Ann.

Katja and Sam went to check out the car parks of various beaches without spotting Tony's car. The whole area was already bustling, as it was a Sunday with glorious weather. Lots of tourists and locals were flitting around, many half-naked and barefoot, with children, dogs and balls, towels, sun hats and boogie boards. Loud music and laughter rang out from a hotel they were passing. Sam suddenly craved for a cold beer and fretted about driving around wasting petrol.

"There's no point in that!" he grumbled.

"Well, it was just an idea. Unfortunately, it happens all too often that someone drowns in the sea, and Peter also had to be rescued from a strong current," Katja murmured.

"Tony is certainly smart enough to take care of himself," Sam said. "Just wait and see, he'll turn up at our place all chipper! Maybe he's gone on a spontaneous weekend trip to visit some friends."

After a glance at his watch, he asked: "How about we visit Tina and Philip?"

"Yes, good idea!" Katja smiled briefly at her husband. She tried hard to shake off her trepidation and yet didn't succeed. She felt she had to help Tony! But how?

* * *

Tina was sitting comfortably in her garden, reading a romance novel when her friends arrived. Nellie, who was spending the weekend with her old mistress, greeted them joyfully and dashed off to look for a ball.

"What are you reading?" asked Katja, amused as her eyes fell on the book title. "A novel with hot sex scenes? You've only ever read crime novels or thrillers."

Tina blushed. "Oh nonsense! The book is rather old-fashioned and cheesy, but so beautifully romantic! Just a nice change from murder and manslaughter, because real life is cruel and brutal enough."

Sam grinned. "And where's Philip?"

"He's playing golf with some guys I don't even know yet." Her face darkened. "Lately, he spends too much time without me."

"Well, it's great if he makes new friends and you're not always hanging out together!" retorted Katja.

Tina was looking tense, and her mouth was set in a stern way. Oh dear, had the love between her and Philip already faded? Katja mused. She had been so happy for Tina when she'd fallen in love with her colleague!

"Phillip intends to go to Sydney for a whole week. He didn't even ask me if I wanted to come along," Tina said sadly. "I wonder if he wants to meet his ex-wife?"

"Aha, you're jealous!" Katja observed.

Sam watched a tiny spider on the windowsill running around a huge ant at lightning speed, trapping it in its spider web. Despite its size, the ant seemed to be losing its desperate battle. Life can be brutal indeed! Sam thought, feeling sorry for the ant.

Tina smiled crookedly. "Well, I can't take any leave at the moment anyway."

She stood up and suggested: "Let's go into the kitchen and have some coffee! Or would you rather have something cold?"

"Do you have a beer?" asked Sam.

Tina looked at him in surprise. "Already? You don't usually drink alcohol until late afternoon at the earliest!"

"I guess our dinner was too spicy last night! I'm thirsty as hell today!"

"What did you eat?"

"Sam tried out a new Indian recipe!" Katja explained with a grin.

"I'm sure Michael would have liked that!" said Tina. "By the way, we just spoke on the phone and he told me that your guest has disappeared."

Immediately Katja became serious again. "Yes, I really have a bad inkling!"

"Bullshit!" snorted Sam. "You're almost acting like a mother hen! Tony is not your kid, he's a grown man! Can't he go away for a weekend without having to tell you what he's up to right away?"

His normally warm brown eyes glared so grimly that Tina burst out laughing.

"I believe you're jealous too, Sam!"

Sam's bushy eyebrows shot up unwillingly. But then he had to laugh as well.

"You're right, Tina! I actually think it's wonderful that Katja always spoils our holiday guests! And Tony really is such a nice guy!"

Sam was looking lovingly at his wife now and she ruffled his hair for a moment.

Tina opened the fridge. "Are you guys hungry too? I still have heaps of potato salad and some meatballs left over from yesterday."

"Oh yes, gladly!" Katja replied, and Sam nodded eagerly.

Tina often wondered why her best friend could be so lean and slender despite her good appetite, while she herself gained weight far too quickly. With increasing age, it got worse. To her own horror, she had meanwhile put on a rather fat belly and 'love handles'. Now she asked herself if Philip regarded her as ugly. Did he therefore keep his distance lately? Almost angrily, she bit into her meatball.

Sam ate with gusto and said: "Some people are so lucky! A few days ago, Tony told me that Mark, his brother-in-law, had just got into financial trouble when some rich uncle of his passed away, leaving him a whole chunk of money. And so, he was able to keep his house in Sydney, buy a second property and have the brand-new house built where he's now living with his family."

"Why did he have financial problems?" Tina mumbled with her mouth full.

"According to Tony, Mark is a doctor and was quite rich until he had a huge loss on the stock market one day," Sam said, taking a sip of his beer. "Apparently, he had invested too much money in some company whose shares crashed dramatically."

"Mm, the potato salad is delicious!" praised Katja, who had never been particularly interested in the stock market.

"What kind of company was that?" Tina asked curiously. She had also invested some money in shares.

Sam shrugged his shoulders. "I've forgotten the name. It had something to do with pharmaceutical research and technology."

After a while he added:

"Tony also mentioned that Mark quit his well-paid job in Sydney after a nurse had accused him of murdering an elderly patient. Although he was completely innocent, he felt all his colleagues were constantly whispering about him. And that's why he moved to the Sunshine Coast."

Katja almost choked.

"I don't believe it!" she cried. "Why didn't you tell me, Sam? Don't you remember what Peter found out from Maureen on the train back then?"

Sam looked distressed. "Oh boy, I promised Tony I wouldn't tell anyone. After all, his brother-in-law was innocent and wanted to start a new life here!"

"Yes, but Maureen was murdered! Right here in our neighbourhood! Maybe this Mark had something to do with it! Perhaps he killed her in revenge! And now Tony is missing! He could be in danger!" exclaimed Katja excitedly.

Tina grinned. "Katja, I think you've read too many crime novels! You have a vivid imagination!"

42

Mark could hardly fathom that this darned guitar was leaning against a cupboard in his living room. He had lied to John about buying it for his daughter. No, he had in fact found it next to Maureen's dead body and spontaneously taken it. He still felt queasy when he thought of his unbelievable experience many months ago:

At the time, he had been staying at John's house in Marcoola, looking after Ernie as his friend was away on business. Although the house was quite close to the airport, it was a nice estate and far enough away from the flight path. Normally Mark felt perfectly at home there. But on that unforgettable night he'd had a bad dream and couldn't fall back asleep. He concluded that his nasty dream and restlessness were caused by a woman he had hoped never to meet again. Maureen! A few days earlier he had seen her twice, each time playing the guitar and singing, once on the beach and then in a café. That silly nurse who had brazenly accused him of killing a nice old lady in the hospital in Sydney! Moreover, she had somehow found out about his inheritance and spread another rumour, indicating that he had also bumped off his uncle!

What a mean woman! She had made his life miserable, and it was only because of her that he and his family had moved away from Sydney. Fortunately, he had quickly found a new job as a doctor in Noosa. But no sooner had he managed to banish Maureen from his memory than he had to meet her again – here on the Sunshine Coast! Was it a stupid coincidence? Or was it fate? Either way, he had stared at her with contempt and yet feeling like a fool, watching her from a distance, without daring to address her. What could he have said to her anyway?

Afterwards, in that sleepless night in Marcoola, he decided to go for a walk with the dog in a spur of the moment. Maybe that would relax him a little. The night air was pleasantly cool. The moon was shaped like a crescent, barely giving off any light. After only a few minutes, Ernie lifted his leg on a tree, and as he walked on, Mark tripped over a large object. He cursed softly and flicked on his torch – and saw a backpack, a guitar, and next to it – a dead woman!

She was lying motionless between two trees on the grass strip, dead as a door-nail!

Or could he still save her? When he quickly examined her, he realised with horror that it was Maureen! He almost threw up. His thoughts were racing and panic seized him. He was freezing and sweating at the same time, and only with difficulty did he suppress a desperate sob. Maureen, of all people! Should he call the police? Nah, no way! Everyone would think he had killed her! Ernie curiously sniffed at the backpack. The neighbourhood was quiet. What should he do? In no time at all Mark ran back to John's house, dragging the dog along, left the astonished Ernie there and got his car. He drove back, loaded the young woman, her backpack and the guitar into his car and took them to a car park in Coolum Beach.

At that hour, everything was quiet and dark there too. In the centre of town, the police might suspect someone had robbed Maureen, so he hoped. He laid her gently on the ground, feeling horrible. Only at the last moment did he remember to remove any traces that might point to him. He put on rubber gloves, which he always kept in the car for an emergency, and removed her clothes except for her knickers and her bra. Despite his earlier hatred, he was suddenly filled with pity, and he stroked her long hair tenderly as a farewell. She was still so young! Nonsensically, it seemed mean to him to leave her exposed on the floor like that. Looking around, his gaze fell on a black plastic sheet, partly hanging out of a container, so he took it and carefully spread it over her.

He was in a trance and could hardly remember the return journey afterwards. Only much later did he think of surveillance cameras, filled with horror. Had his crazy act been observed? Too late now! There was nothing he could do about it; he could only hope that he would not be arrested!

And who was responsible for Maureen's death? What had actually happened before he found her? Had someone else hated her so deeply that he had killed her? So close to John's house! Could it be dangerous to stay in this area? Mark was utterly distressed. He would have preferred to move out and escape to his own home, or somewhere else, but he had to look after John's property and Ernie.

Over the next few days, he disposed of Maureen's backpack and all her belongings apart from her cash and the guitar. He didn't have the heart to throw away such a beautiful musical instrument. He could give it to his daughter on her birthday! That date still was a long way off, so surely no one would associate a second-hand guitar with Maureen any more.

At the beginning of November, shortly before Kim's birthday, he finally collected the guitar from John, who had kept it for him for so long. However, on the way home, Mark panicked all of a sudden. No way he could give that guitar to his daughter! It had to go! He took it right away to the collection of rubbish that some neighbour in his street – quite far away from his own house – had already accumulated. It was a gloomy, rainy evening, and he didn't expect anyone to search for stuff in this lousy weather. To be on the safe side, he quickly moved some of the dumped items, namely a carpet runner, a chair and a naked mannequin, over the guitar to hide it.

What a bummer that his own children and Yolanda discovered this guitar (and also the ugly mannequin) the very next day and brought it home! He really was a complete idiot! Why hadn't he disposed of Maureen's guitar somewhere else, or taken it to a second-hand shop? And what tall tale could he tell John? He was sure the children would chat excitedly about their find the next time he'd visit, and John would be surprised!

Now, on a warm Sunday in November with cheerful weather, and a day after Kim's not-so-cheerful birthday party, Mark stared at the darned guitar in his living room, barely hearing what Debbie was saying.

"Mark!" she shouted angrily, and he winced. "What are you dreaming about? You are not listening to me!" she scolded. "I know you and Tony don't get on so well, but we have to do something! We have to go and find him!"

Mark looked at her despondently. "But where? I've already called the hospitals in our surroundings, and he is not in any of them. What else can I do?"

"I don't know! Yolanda went to his unit, but his landlords had no idea either. Where could he be?" Debbie asked in despair.

Her brother was one of the most reliable people she had ever met, and if he said he would come at a certain time, he did. And he was so fond of Kim and Daniel! At Kim's request and for Tony's sake, they had planned a small family celebration instead of a big children's birthday party, and then he didn't show up! What had happened to him? Debbie had already called his mobile phone umpteen times, but to no avail.

Mark plopped down on the sofa, feeling sick and exhausted. His stomach was aching. Despite his imposing size, he was a rather anxious, nervous man, and his arrogant demeanour was just a cover up. Although he had become a successful doctor, even chief physician, he easily felt overwhelmed and stressed. And his spontaneous reactions were often so stupid that he could hardly believe it himself! Why on earth had he secretly transported a murdered woman to another place? He was so barmy! He could end up in prison! And this time his reputation would be completely ruined! How would his family deal with that? After all, he loved them and only wanted the best for them! His life was shattered!

Suddenly he had to sob.

Debbie sat down next to him and leaned her head on his shoulder.

"Oh, Mark!" she whispered helplessly.

43

After lunch, Tina had prepared a dessert of fresh fruit and vanilla ice cream, which she and her friends were now eating on the patio. They were silent for a while, and only the fan on the ceiling above the table hummed softly. A fat fly approached curiously, briefly buzzed along and flew away. Nellie slumbered deeply and blissfully. Tina was happy about the surprise visit from Katja and Sam, feeling a sense of relief after talking things over with them. Katja was her best friend anyway, and she was very fond of Sam, too. He was a kind, patient person who often made her laugh. She also liked Philip's sense of humour and had laughed a lot with him, but in the last week her boyfriend had been very grim, reserved and quiet. Was it her own fault? she wondered.

"Do you think I'm too possessive and don't give Philip enough freedom?" Tina asked her friends. "I just don't understand why he still wants to keep his rental property, even though he moved in with me. And his rent in Marcoola is expensive as hell. But apparently he loves his own space."

"Well, everyone has his own idea of freedom and independence," Sam said thoughtfully. "But you never really struck me as a possessive person. You're very independent overall, you have a super job as a manager and you often do what you think is right without asking others first. And when you're freshly in love, it's normal to want to do as much as possible together."

"Maybe he's not in love with me anymore, because at the moment he seems to be keeping his distance. After work he usually cycles home and spends the night there, and last weekend he was seeing some other people – without wanting me to join in!"

"Oh Tina! Wait and see! Maybe Philip just needs a break, because you two really were like two inseparable lovebirds for weeks!" Katja smiled at her encouragingly.

"Perhaps it was a bit hasty that he moved in with you! After a break-up, some people don't want to get so close again straight away," Sam said. "Are he and Ronnie actually already divorced?"

"Yeah, sure! That is – hmm, well, I just assumed! Otherwise, I wouldn't have agreed to his move here. That would have seemed wrong somehow," Tina murmured meekly.

"What? You don't know if they are divorced?" Katja asked, astonished.

"Philip doesn't like to talk about his past," Tina countered snottily.

"Do they have children?" inquired Sam. "You would know, wouldn't you?"

Katja looked at her husband in surprise. Why did Sam, normally gentle and friendly, suddenly sound so cynical?

Tina cleared her throat. "They had a mentally handicapped son, but tragically he died just before his fifth birthday. It was, of course, a terribly difficult time for Philip and his wife. They loved and adored their son so much, even though he was a problem child. Or maybe they loved their little George even more because of his disability, wishing to protect him and to make his life more beautiful at all costs," Tina said with a brittle voice and tears in her eyes.

"How awful!" Katja whispered. "What did he die of?"

"He had a fatal accident while he was out for a walk with his parents. They were going to visit a relative who also lived in Sydney, fairly close to their own home. Philip was walking hand in hand with his son, a few metres behind Ronnie on the pedestrian path, when a young woman accidentally hit the boy with her e-scooter and knocked him down. George was rushed to hospital very quickly, but he died of his serious injuries shortly afterwards."

"Oh no!" Sam cried in dismay. "These barmy people whizzing around on their electric scooters at breakneck speed have no regard at all for pedestrians! Accidents like that happen too often!"

Tina nodded. "Yes, a friend of mine was almost knocked over in Brisbane once. She just managed to save herself by jumping to the side. I think they shouldn't allow these e-scooters on footpaths at all!"

"To my knowledge it is illegal in New South Wales," Katja said, frowning.

"Was the woman in Sydney punished for that incident?" asked Sam.

"She got off lightly because they considered it an accident. And she was lucky as she only got a few abrasions and a bruise. By the way, she had not been driving on the pedestrian path but on the road, where she tried to avoid a pothole and skidded. Philip, however, claimed that she had been driving much too fast. What a horrendous accident, such a catastrophe!" sighed Tina. "Philip and Ronnie could hardly comprehend that their only son was dead. Their family structure had been abruptly destroyed and nothing made sense to them anymore. Ronnie, in particular, was depressed and bitter, isolating herself more and more. Her despair and sadness turned into hatred and anger, which she also directed at her husband. In the end, Philip could stand it no longer and decided to separate from her. And then he moved here, to the Sunshine Coast, far away from Ronnie."

"How dreadful! But why didn't you tell us about it earlier?" Katja asked reproachfully.

"Well, Philip asked me not to talk to anyone about his son. He is trying to get his life back on track and the past still hurts him too much. He also avoids talking about his ex-wife and his former life in general. I only found out about this sad story one night when he was quite drunk and emotional. It suddenly just bubbled out of him. But the next morning he seemed to regret bringing it up, and he was gruff and reserved when I asked him a few more questions."

"But that's no solution either, to simply suppress your past," Sam reflected.

"Poor Philip! He must be devastated! Yet he seems so open and cheerful!" Katja wondered. "He's always very nice and friendly at work."

"And why does he want to fly to Sydney now?" asked Sam.

"He intends to visit some old friends and various relatives. When I asked for more specifics, he snapped at me, saying that I didn't know them anyway. He can be so mean!"

Now Tina had tears of anger in her eyes.

"I was so deeply in love with Philip! And most of the time he's totally loving and charming, just wonderful! But sometimes he seems like an aloof stranger to me. Was it all too good to be true? Is he a completely different guy than I imagined him to be?"

Was she always unlucky? she mused. Was it because of her looks or her behaviour that men grew tired of her? Michael had accused her of being too selfish. Or was she too bossy? She looked into the garden, without really seeing anything at all. The fat fly returned and tried to nibble at the remains in Tina's ice-cream bowl, and Sam hastily shooed it away. Nellie misunderstood his gesture and ran onto the lawn, hoping for a ball game.

"Oh, Tina!" said Katja pityingly and hugged her friend. "I hope everything will turn out well! I found Philip very likeable from the beginning, and you two seem to fit so well together!"

Sam frowned. Although he also liked Philip, he had been sad to see Tina and Michael drift apart, after being married for so many years. Nevertheless, it had been wonderful that both Tina and Michael had found new love! And so far, they had seemed so happy with their new partners! But what now? Would Tina's love affair with Philip degenerate into quarrels and dissatisfaction? Had she not found her 'dream man' after all? Sam was glad that he and Katja got along so well, rarely having any arguments.

Checking his watch, he realised that they had been at Tina's much longer than planned, and just at that moment Katja said:

"Oh dear, it's that late already? We have to go! Cheer up, Tina, don't let it get you down!"

"And remember, you are always welcome to talk to us!" Sam said as a farewell and gave Tina a peck on the cheek.

Katja hugged her friend warmly once more and then they left. It was only on the way back home that they thought of Tony again.

44

On Sunday evening I picked Nellie up from Tina's and was surprised to find my ex alone, without her boyfriend. Tina explained that Philip had been playing golf, assuming he had gone straight to his home after the game. She hadn't seen or talked to him since Friday anyway, and she had the impression that he probably wanted to keep his distance for a while. I could tell she was angry, but refused to delve into her problems with Philip. After all, I didn't want to interfere in their relationship! Besides, I was exhausted and my head was still spinning from the events on Saturday. Tina briefly told me about Katja's concern about Tony, who'd gone away without telling them.

When I woke up on Monday, Sylvie had already left for early duty. Nellie was lying contentedly in her favourite corner and I was happy to have my sweet dog with me again. Outside, the birds were singing. Why were they always awake at dawn, so early? I yawned heartily and tried in vain to remember my last dream. I often had wondrous, fantastic dreams that could easily be used as the base for a movie, a crime or adventure film or even a science fiction novel! Anyway, I kept meaning to write down all the interesting dreams, but I never did.

What did my mother dream about? Could she remember it afterwards? How did she experience her everyday life? It was such a pity that she could hardly tell me anything anymore – she who had always been so talkative! My brother was grief-stricken that he could no longer contact her by phone. He missed their chatting, their shared laughter and Mum's heartfelt sympathy and participation in the life of his family.

There are so many things in life that you only really appreciate when they are gone and you deeply miss them!

The muscle soreness in my legs (resulting from the exuberant dancing at Lisa's party) had disappeared and I did my regular home yoga practice with Nellie watching me curiously. After we had adopted her, she always snuggled up to me as soon as I laid down on the carpet, which of course was quite a hindrance to my yoga. Luckily, by now she knew that sometimes she had to give me some space. Sylvie and I once saw a film about a border collie participating in yoga, stretching in sync with his mistress' movements and the music! Very impressive! But I had never taught Nellie anything like that.

After my yoga exercises on that Monday morning, I took Nellie for our morning walk. Delicate feathery clouds decorated the bright blue sky and I was daydreaming when there was a huge bang. Instinctively (and synchronously) Nellie and I jumped to the side, then I dragged Nellie behind a tree and bent over her protectively. A stranger waved at me from his car, grinning broadly, and I realised it had just been a backfire! The next moment I heard peals of laughter and saw Mark standing at his front door. He had tousled hair, was barefoot and wore a shirt that was not buttoned properly, showing parts of his big belly.

"What's wrong with you, Michael?" he asked bemusedly. "Are you always so jumpy? Anyway, you reacted super-fast, fascinating! It was almost cinematic!"

"Well, it sounded like a gunshot!" I explained sheepishly.

Apparently, Arya's story about the shooting woman had affected me badly. Mark came closer and Nellie wagged her tail eagerly.

"Hey, aren't you feeling well? You're chalky white!" he said to me in genuine concern. His smile returned when he gave Nellie a pat.

"Oh, I'm just overtired," I replied.

"Then I am reassured! I once knew an old man who always panicked at loud noises, almost getting hysterical. He had been in the war and must have experienced terrible things! He didn't like fireworks either, because they reminded him of explosions, fires and fierce battles."

"I can imagine! I'm not usually such a scaredy-cat, but after the story about the trigger-happy woman in Marcoola ..."

"Yeah, that was incredible! Yolanda told Debbie and me about it yesterday. What a drama! So lucky that John got away with his life and Arya escaped unscathed!"

"And have you heard anything from Tony in the meantime?" I asked.

"No, unfortunately not!" he replied despondently.

"By the way, I found out last night that Ann, a neighbour of Katja and Sam, saw Tony with a suitcase on Saturday. So, I guess he's out of town?" I said, thinking back to the short conversation with Tina.

"Nah, I'm sure that was my own suitcase. I had lent it to him for his move and he was supposed to return to me."

Before I could reply, angry shouting rang out in the house and Mark quickly said: "Kim and Daniel are fighting again, I'd better go and see what's going on. Otherwise, they wake up Debbie. My poor wife had a rough night because of all her worries about Tony. Bye, see you soon!"

"Bye! Okay, we're going!" I said to Nellie, who was already getting impatient.

Almost at home again, I suddenly remembered my dream of the previous night, and I had to grin because it had been completely absurd. However, considering some of the recent incidents, it seemed to be true what my mother used to say in the past:

"Real life can be crazier than a dream!"

At breakfast, I quickly scribbled in my diary:

I wish so much that Mum mainly thinks of positive childhood events and that she doesn't suffer from horrible memories.

So many children experience war, famine, abuse, or have to endure other cruelties. How will they cope later on in life? Could it be worse for people suffering from dementia, when their memories constantly drift into the past, reliving horrible events over and over again in their minds? Can post-traumatic stress actually be exacerbated by Alzheimer's disease?

I am grateful for my mostly beautiful and carefree childhood – even if I wasn't always one hundred percent happy. (I still get goosebumps thinking of certain nasty bullies from my past!)

In general, I had so many great times, especially with my brother, with whom I could always go through thick and thin. Hopefully, I will always remember the adventures with him and our friends, the holidays with our parents, our fun cycling, swimming and playing, Dad's singing and his mischievous smile.

Lately, I've been thinking about Dad more often again. I wonder how he would have dealt with Mum's dementia. How do you cope when your wife no longer recognises you, or even rejects you? Mum is sometimes afraid of strange men, but I firmly believe that she would have been no more afraid of Dad than of me or Patrick. And I'm grateful for that too.

45

A little later that same Monday morning, Debbie got a call from the hospital. It was John asking for Mark.

"Mark is at work!" said Debbie. "Do you want me to give him a message?"

"Um, well, I've been shot, and ..."

"Yeah, we found out from Yolanda yesterday! Mark wanted to see you right away, but the doctor in charge wouldn't allow a visit. And even when he angrily explained that he was a doctor himself, she refused and said you were asleep. How are you feeling?"

"Better already! Luckily Hannah, that insane woman, only hit my arm!"

"Where did she get the rifle from?"

"From her dad! Hannah confessed to the police that she was visiting her father, who lives on a farm somewhere and was in possession of a legal firearm. She stole it from him and came to my house with full intent to murder me ... in my own bedroom, and ..." John swallowed noisily. "Yet I don't even know her!"

"Oh John, what a terrible shock!"

"For some reason Hannah assumed I'd killed her sister Maureen, and since all the police investigations so far had come to nothing, she wanted to take matters into her own hands and kill me in revenge."

"Unbelievable!" said Debbie.

"Good thing Hannah didn't learn from her dad to shoot better!" John was joking. "By the way, she and her sister allegedly saw their real father very rarely, because their mother had split up with him early in their childhood. She (the mum) supposedly couldn't stand living on a huge farm, so far away from all civilisation."

Debbie's mobile rang loudly. Was it Tony? she thought immediately. "Sorry, John, I have to take another call! I'll tell Mark you called, okay? Get well soon!"

She'd already hung up before he could say anything else. John wondered why Yolanda knew he had been shot at. Had there already been a TV report about Hannah's crime? How was Arya doing? And his Ernie? He should give Wayne precise instructions about the dog food; he had forgotten all about that yesterday. Oh yes, Ernie would also have to take his monthly worming tablet tomorrow! Excited, John called for the nurse and asked her when he could go home. He then had a long phone call with Wayne, who promptly assured him that Ernie was fine.

After Wayne had patiently listened to all kinds of explanations regarding the dog, he said: "You know what's funny? My dad took Ernie for a walk yesterday afternoon, and when they passed the property where the new neighbour lives, Ernie was acting all weird. He kept staring at the garden shed, and he was whining softly."

"What new neighbour?" asked John.

"Well, he's been living there for a while now. The guy from Sydney who works at the post office. I can't think of his name right now..."

"Philip?"

"Yeah, that's it! And on our early morning walk today, Ernie did the same thing. I had to literally drag him away from there!"

"Well, Ernie is no spring chicken and can be quite stubborn. When he gets it into his head to move into a certain direction, it's hard to change his mind." John laughed. "I must admit that too often I give in and follow my dog dutifully."

"Maybe Ernie has a particularly good nose and can smell something tasty in the shed, like fertiliser or something," Wayne said with a grin.

He had already grown very fond of the fat, friendly and trusting Ernie. And with the dog in the house, he seemed to get on much better with his father, who was usually very taciturn and grumpy. For the first time in ages, they had even heartily laughed together.

* * *

Once again, the weekend had gone by in a flash, and on Monday morning Katja was in a bad mood. On top of that, Philip didn't show up for work, so it would surely be a stressful day for her. Was he already on his way to Sydney? But neither her colleagues nor her boss had any idea where he was. Was he sick or had he just overslept? Today, of all days, it was terribly hectic at the post office, and customers were already queuing up early in the morning. Katja was annoyed by a young woman who complained loudly and vulgarly about the price of a parcel, having trouble keeping calm. Stupid cow, she thought, slapping the stamps on the small parcel.

"You stuck the stamps on all crookedly!" the woman grumbled as she paid.

"So what?" Katja replied and quickly called out: "Next, please!"

Fortunately, a petite old man was approaching her counter now whom she already knew by sight. Somehow, she found him really cute. He was always extremely polite and had a charming smile. Immediately her mood improved. She would get through the day – even without Philip.

* * *

For Tina, too, that Monday morning was rather hectic. There was so much to sort out at the hotel that she forgot her sorrows about Philip. One guest complained bitterly about a family with too noisy children who had allegedly kept him awake all night. Another guest had bitten on a dead fly in his raisin toast at breakfast and demanded (almost green in the face with disgust!) a discount for his accommodation. It wasn't until her lunch break that she discovered Katja's message on her mobile phone: "Philip didn't show up for work today. Is he ill? If so, tell him to get well soon!"

She quickly wrote back: "I don't know! I'll go and see him tonight."

What was wrong with him? Tina thought worriedly, as Leonie, an older employee of the hotel, rushed into her office. Leonie's usually smooth silver hair was dishevelled, and she shouted, "Come quickly, there's a fire!"

"What, where?"

Horrified, Tina jumped up and followed her colleague to an upper floor. Thick smoke was billowing towards them in the corridor and an alarm sounded. A woman came screaming towards them with an infant in her arms, and Tina thought frantically about what to do. She stood stock-still, and her brain felt completely empty.

"The fire brigade will be here soon!" Leonie said reassuringly to the frightened woman with the baby and led her to the nearest staircase. "Walk calmly to the exit, okay?"

"It's all right, we've already extinguished the fire!" shouted Melinda, a young, slim hotel employee with long black hair who had only been hired a week ago. She had a little girl by the hand, and behind her Tina spotted a couple with two other children. The girls looked startled; the boy somewhat guilty.

The father explained ashamedly: "It's all our fault! My children wanted to surprise me with a birthday cake and lit candles. But then my son tripped, a napkin caught fire, and suddenly a cardigan on the back of the chair was on fire too!"

"And in an instant the curtains were ablaze! It was such a shock!" the mother sobbed.

Melinda's dark eyes sparkled excitedly. "I heard a frantic scream, realized what was going on, grabbed a fire extinguisher and put out the fire!" she said. "Although that might not have been necessary, as the automatic sprinkler system switched on straight away anyway."

"Good on you, Melinda!" praised Tina. "You did a great job! Thank you so much!"

Tina was so relieved she could have danced. How wonderful that Melinda (and Leonie too) had acted so promptly and wise! Although there had been many test alarms in the hotel before, and Tina should theoretically know what to do in case of a fire, she had completely lost her head. She had been frozen on the spot! Now she managed to take control again. The family was transferred to another hotel flat, which was smaller but had a nice view, and the fire damage had to be assessed by experts. Fortunately, no one was hurt!

The guest who had been upset with the same family before, however, could not be appeased. Just when he was having a little nap after the sleepless night, he woke up from the terrifying alarm and the smell of something burning, and he moved out at once, snorting with rage.

46

Tina was glad when she finally got off work. The rush hour traffic was slow, but she was so lost in her thoughts that the drive still seemed short, and she almost missed the exit to Marcoola. She wondered how Philip would react when she showed up at his door. She had sent him a few text messages the day before and another one today without getting any replies. Would he reject her brusquely or embrace her lovingly? Oh, she wished so much to get their relationship back on track. She couldn't understand what exactly had gone wrong!

She parked her car under the mighty, picturesque Melaleuca tree in front of Philip's rental house, nodding briefly at an attractive man walking a dog across the street. The fat dog, pulling strongly on its leash and apparently eager to greet her, looked familiar, but she had never seen the man before. She strode quickly to the small brick house surrounded by palm trees and dense bushes and knocked on the door.

"Philip! It's Tina!"

No answer. Was he not at home? But his car was parked in the driveway to the garage. Her heart suddenly beat faster. Had something happened to him? Hopefully he hadn't had a stroke! After all, he wasn't the youngest anymore!

"Hello!" she called loudly, and her fear intensified.

She tried the front door, but it was locked. Something creaked as she went through the garden gate, heading to a large sky-blue painted shed that was partly screened with a tall hedge. Philip had always liked to tinker around in it. The shed's door with its pretty bull's-eye window stood ajar, moving slightly in the wind and creaking softly again.

"Philip, are you there?"

She opened the door and turned white as chalk.

"No! Philip, oh no!" she cried in horror.

Next to a wooden stool in front of the sturdy work table, her boyfriend lay on the cement floor. His face was waxy pale, and when she felt for his pulse, she recoiled from his cold skin, but then she threw herself over him, crying.

"Philip, my beloved Philip! It can't be true!" wailed Tina. Her boyfriend was dead!

"Hello?" someone called out in concern, and the next minute, the slender stranger with the fat dog was at her side.

"Oh no!" he said in shock. "I wish I had listened to Ernie!"

"What?" muttered Tina tearfully, straightening up. "Who's Ernie? Are you a friend of Philip?"

"No, I live in the neighbourhood, just a few houses down. And I'm looking after Ernie, this dog here, at the moment. Um, Ernie had been staring at the garden shed in a weird way several times before. He must have sensed something was wrong. Oh, if only I had come to help sooner, maybe I could have saved Philip!"

He too started crying, and Tina instinctively hugged him. Surprised and somewhat embarrassed, he pressed her against him and stroked her back gently. Ernie whined piteously and put a paw on Philip's arm. Tina moved away from the stranger and hastily searched for her mobile phone in her huge handbag.

"I have to call an ambulance," she said.

And then she got all dizzy and nauseous. The man caught her before she fell over and helped her sit down on the floor, leaning against the wall.

"Let me take care of that. Take a deep breath first!" he said in a soft voice. "By the way, my name is Wayne."

"I'm Tina!" she croaked.

Swiftly Wayne typed away on his own mobile phone. While talking to someone from the ambulance, he spotted a letter on the table laden with many utensils, tucked under a rusty tin box and labelled "FOR TINA". Next to it was a drinking glass and an empty tablet packet. He handed Tina the letter, which she tore open with shaky hands. She read:

My beloved Tina!

It is Saturday morning, and I have decided to say goodbye to you and explain a few things to you. Somehow, I am sure you will be the first person to find me here, and I hope you can forgive me!

I love you, Tina, and you made so happy for a while! I truly wished to get to know you much better and to grow old with you. But I did something terrible and I just can't live with it anymore. So, I'm about to take an overdose of sleeping pills.

I told you about my son who died so unexpectedly. The tragic accident has been replaying over and over in my head, and I can't stop blaming myself for not taking better care of George. And it wasn't just Ronnie's fault that we couldn't comfort each other in our despair. After the loss of our little boy, we were both so depressed, so angry and bitter, becoming more and more antagonistic. I have dark sides in me that I fear and hate!

Nevertheless, I did intend to change, to start a whole new life, and you seemed like my dream woman. Tina, you are beautiful and strong and have such a good heart! I really wanted to make you happy!

But I was not allowed to let bygones be bygones. On the very day I met you, I also saw the woman who had accidentally hit my George in Sydney. I could hardly believe it! This woman named Maureen was playing her guitar and singing nice songs in the café as if she had never killed a child! It was with the greatest difficulty that I was able to control my anger. My inner turmoil was only calmed by you and Katja, because, despite Maureen's unexpected appearance in that café, I enjoyed talking to both of you, and I was totally smitten with you! Right away I liked you so much, it was love at first sight! Perhaps my life could have changed to the better.

Unfortunately, Maureen and I crossed paths again, right here in my street. I was just getting out of the car when she trudged past me, carrying her guitar and a big backpack that seemed very heavy. Although it was already late in the evening, I recognised her in the dim light of the street lamp. Without thinking, I asked her gruffly:

'What are you doing here?'

Apparently, she had no idea who I was, but she blabbed right off the bat: 'I just introduced myself to a family, over there in the white house with the huge pool. Since they spontaneously decided to go abroad, they were looking for a house sitter at short notice. And I was keen to do it! But after we'd talked for hours, the woman suddenly said that they would rather take an older couple. I was very upset! She could have told me that on the phone, instead of making me come here. And I'd already been looking forward to the house sitting.'

Maureen looked angry, but the very next moment she giggled silly and said: 'Never mind! I already slept by the sea under the stars last night, and it was fantastic! Besides, I've got some friends on the Sunshine Coast where I can probably spend some nights. And then I will head further north.'

She leaned her guitar against a tree, took off her backpack, fiddled with the waist straps and rubbed her shoulders for a moment. Before putting it back on, she looked at me suspiciously and asked: 'Do we actually know each other?'

And all of a sudden, I was overcome with such a frenzy of anger as I had never experienced before. How could she be travelling around cheerfully, basking on the beach, playing music, laughing and having fun, gazing at the bright stars, while my little George is lying in his dark grave? Just because of her, because she had driven way too fast and recklessly on her e-scooter!

'You killed my son!' I said very quietly, and immediately she backed away fearfully. Then I grabbed her and shook her – and broke her neck! It all happened so quickly!

Oh Tina, you will now despise me deeply, and I can hardly believe myself what I did. Afterwards I just left her and ran into my house, and the whole night I lay awake, full of fear and anxiety, waiting for the police.

But strangely enough, Maureen's body was found the next morning in a car park in a different town. I have no idea how this could have happened! For a while I saw it as a good omen, hoping I could hide my cruel deed. Was fate going to give me another chance after all? Sometimes I almost believed that it had been just a nightmare.

I really tried to be a friendly, open person, wishing so hard never to do anything bad anymore. However, I hated myself, and I struggled more and more to pretend to be the nice guy. So often I just faked cheerfulness while I felt gloomy and miserable deep inside, and finally I distanced myself from you and others.

On the last weekends, contrary to what I told you, I didn't meet a soul, but retreated to my shed. I have always felt at home here. It smells so pleasantly of wood, earth and lemon myrtle leaves. Here, I find a little peace. And in the end, I will look at the majestic old eucalyptus tree, which is actually much too huge for this garden, thinking of you, my beloved Tina! I wish with all my heart that you will be happy and that you will find a new boyfriend who deserves you!

Philip

P.S. Please also tell Katja and Sam how sorry I am for everything! They are wonderful people! And my boss at the post office was very nice too. A few days ago, I wrote my last will and hid it behind some books on my bookshelf by the bed. I want you, Tina, to have most of my money. It's not much, but it's certainly more than you would have expected.

I've always been good at saving and once made a big profit on the share market. Some of the money shall be donated to an environmental organisation. Yesterday afternoon I already sent a farewell letter to Ronnie. Although we are divorced and have not parted on good terms, I also bequeath a small sum of money to her and wish her a better future. I have confessed to her too that I killed Maureen in a fit of madness.

By the way, I've only played golf once in my life and I was lousy. I never went to the golf course today. And I had no intention of flying to Sydney anytime soon. I was just looking for an excuse to withdraw from everything for a while and find a solution.

But what's the point? I had already spent far too much time thinking about my options. Should I confess everything to you and turn myself in to the police? Or should I leave you and secretly disappear to another country? No, that would be too mean! I killed a young woman and I simply can't go on living with this knowledge.

Please forgive me for having offended you and having lied to you! I love you, Tina! And thank you for the good times you gave me!

Philip

Tina's eyes were swimming in tears and she felt as if her heart would burst.

"Oh, Philip!" she stammered again and again until the ambulance arrived and one of the paramedics took care of her.

A little later, the criminal police arrived to investigate the scene.

Wayne and Ernie went home feeling terribly sad. Wayne's only consolation was that Philip had already been dead since Saturday. Even if he and his father had taken Ernie's reaction more seriously and had checked out the shed on Sunday afternoon, they would still have been too late to rescue Philip. Wayne couldn't believe that the nice and friendly looking man had snapped a young woman's neck – such a tragedy in his street! And poor Tina! How would she cope with the shock and the deep grief? Although the letter had been intended for Tina, she had given it to him and later to the police to read. He would have loved to take Tina in his arms again to comfort her.

* * *

Tina felt numb, even after the effect of the sedative had worn off. For several days she could hardly eat anything and she was unable to go to work. Her beloved Philip had killed himself! And he had broken Maureen's neck! How could he be so brutal? She didn't want to believe it! She would never have imagined such a thing! Philip had told her that he used to do various martial arts, but that had only been a hobby. He had been such a loving and sensitive man whom she had found incredibly attractive from the start. She felt sick when she remembered that he had kissed her, Tina, tenderly on the beach the very next evening after his terrible deed! How could one person have two such different sides?

Yet she could not bring herself to hate him. She felt deeply sorry for Maureen. But Philip suffered so much! First the death of his son, the marriage crisis and then his insane act! And in the end, his guilt had driven him to suicide.

"I forgive you, Philip!" she whispered.

* * *

On Tuesday I woke up from a loud ringing and sleepily reached for my phone. It was Tina! So early in the morning? Immediately I suspected bad news. It was still very dark and even Sylvie, who was on early duty this week, was still in bed. Sylvie startled, turned around and pulled the doona over her ears. Tina began to tell me a horrific story about Philip, talking in an unusually quiet, toneless voice until I hastily said, "Wait a sec, Tina, I'd better come over straight away!"

I wrote a short note for Sylvie, who was fast asleep again, quickly dressed, took Nellie along and jumped into my car. Luckily it was just a short drive. When I arrived at Tina's, she sank crying into my arms. She was completely shaken! And so was I, hardly believing that her beloved Philip had killed Maureen and himself! Such a tragedy! I didn't know how to help Tina. All I could do was listen, hug her, be there for her. It took Tina a long time to calm down a bit and my shoulder was soaking wet from her tears.

"Oh, Tina, I'm so sorry! Philip seemed to be such a cheerful, kind and warm-hearted man! What a terrible fate that he met the same woman again who'd unintentionally caused his son's death! Even though the accident back then had happened in Sydney, far away from Marcoola! Life can play some mean tricks on you!" Suddenly I thought of Bryan. "What I don't understand ... um, isn't it weird that Bryan found Maureen's body in Coolum Beach? How on earth did it get there?"

"Yes, that is a mystery! At least Bryan will be glad about the news report that reveals the real culprit, finally proving his own innocence. Surely it will be announced today that it was Philip ..." Tina sobbed. "And that's why ... that's why I wanted to tell you everything in person, before you hear about it on TV or on the radio ... ", she couldn't go on.

I stroked her back comfortingly and suggested: "I'm going to make you something to eat and a hot tea! Would you like toast or cereal?"

"Thank you, Michael! A tea would be good, but I can't eat a thing."

A few minutes later, when I brought her a cup of tea, Nellie was sitting on her lap and Tina was petting her lovingly. Off the top of my head, I said: "I'll leave Nellie with you today, okay?" Maybe Nellie could help her a little to cope with her irrepressible grief!

I kissed Tina briefly on the cheek as a goodbye. "I have to go to work! But call me anytime if you need me. Or call Katja and Sam. We are and will always be your friends, don't forget that and just don't do anything stupid!"

Tina smiled at me through new tears, squeezed my hand and whispered: "Thanks, Michael, you're really sweet!"

47

When Tony regained consciousness, he felt woozy. His head, ribs and everything else were hurting. What had happened? Only dimly did he remember his intention to go to Kim's birthday party. He had already carefully packed his present for her in Mark's suitcase and put it in the car. And then? Oh yes, gradually his memory returned:

Before going to the party, he'd planned to look at a house that was for sale. The property was actually too remote for his taste and too huge for him alone anyway, but it had something special about it. It couldn't hurt to have a look! The weather was perfect for a trip, mostly sunny but not too hot, and he felt like driving a bit through the hinterland.

Pretty soon he was out in the countryside, enjoying the scenery. After a while, he was amidst a forest, rarely seeing another car anymore. The winding asphalt road became steeper and steeper, changed into a gravel road and then descended steeply. On the way down, he stopped briefly to take a sip of water and roll down the passenger side window. His old car didn't have electric windows. Shortly afterwards, he noticed that he hadn't closed the small bottle properly as leaking water was forming a puddle on the floor. He tried to pick up the bottle but was restrained by his seat-belt. All of a sudden, a kangaroo jumped across the road. He braked too sharply, skidded, hit a tree and hurtled downhill, crashing through the forest! His car overturned and a window pane got broken. For a terrifying moment he thought he would be impaled by a large branch, and he screamed loudly in fear. Breaking branches, foliage and palm fronds performed a wild dance before his eyes, and there were crunching and cracking sounds until he felt a violent impact and then silence.

Now it all came back to him. To his amazement, however, the world was upside down! The trees seemed to be sticking up into the blue sky in the wrong place, and only slowly did he realise that his car was lying on its side. He struggled to get up and couldn't open his seat-belt. He was stuck! His right arm was injured and completely useless, and his left hand hurt like hell. What should he do? At least his car hadn't immediately exploded and burst into flames like it always seemed to happen in movies. If only he wasn't so thirsty! Where was his little bottle? It must have rolled behind the seat! But it would probably be empty by now anyway. And there was no way he could reach the large bottle in the boot of the car that he had filled with water from Sam's and Katja's rainwater tank the day before. Darn!

All around him was nothing but silence. How far away was he from the road above him? Would anyone find him here in the middle of the forest? Was he going to die? Still so young, as a prisoner in his own car? Unfortunately, he hadn't told a soul that he was going to look at the house for sale. Oh well, his family would miss him! They would surely start looking for him soon enough! At some point his kind landlords too would be guaranteed to worry about his absence. Out of the blue, he saw the pretty face of Katja's and Sam's daughter in his mind's eye. From the very beginning, he had been fascinated by the beautifully painted watercolour picture in his holiday unit. Sam was quite an artist and obviously very fond of his daughter, recently telling him with shining eyes that she'd move back to the Sunshine Coast in the near future.

With a pang of regret Tony now thought: "What a shame if I never get to meet her ..."

And again, he lost his consciousness ...

* * *

Wayne had never seen a dead person before, and the gruesome discovery of Philip's lifeless body on the floor of the garden shed had shocked him profoundly. When his mother had died, very suddenly and unexpectedly, he had just been in Norway, and he had only returned to Australia after her funeral. He had felt bad about it. On the other hand, he had seen little point in postponing his flight as he wouldn't meet his mother alive anymore anyway. But Bill, his father, had resented his decision very much, feeling abandoned by his son. Their relationship had been strained ever since.

However, in the last few days, they had spoken very openly with each other. Bill had confessed his negative emotions and sullen behaviour towards his son, and both of them had expressed their grief, anguish and disappointment. Finally, they'd started to enjoy each other's company again. And somehow Ernie, John's overweight and yet adorable dog, had contributed towards their reconnection, often making them smile or even laugh out loud. Naturally, Wayne had been absolutely shattered by Philip's suicide, and Bill had hugged him lovingly and comfortingly. It seemed aeons ago since father and son had been so close!

On Tuesday morning Wayne decided to go on a trip with his dad. Perhaps that would help to take his mind off the chilling events from the evening before. Not only the sight of the dead man, but also the image of the completely distraught Tina had affected him deeply, causing him to toss and turn restlessly during the night.

After a hearty breakfast of coffee, toast and scrambled eggs, they set off. Bill, who lived on the Gold Coast, already knew many nice places on the Sunshine Coast from previous tours into the hinterland. They both loved the outdoors and particularly the picturesque countryside near Montville and Maleny, from where they could catch magnificent views of the imposing Glasshouse Mountains. They'd used to do a lot of hiking in the past, and Bill still liked to go for little walks, although his legs were not as strong anymore. On this day, however, they just wanted to drive around a bit and explore new areas.

It was sunny and warm, and they opened all the windows to let in the fresh forest air.

"Off into the countryside!" Wayne called cheerfully, turning into a narrow road.

Ernie was sitting in the back seat sticking his nose curiously into the breeze.

"I'd never been here before, that's for sure!" said Bill gleefully as the car was moving up a very steep hill.

Wayne looked at him briefly and smiled. His father was a lean man, quite wiry and fit for his age. His thinning soft hair was snow-white, his skin wrinkled and blotchy, but his ice-blue eyes sparkled, full of zest for life. A small goatee sprouted on his chin. Wayne, who towered over his father by head length, had blond, short hair, blue-green eyes and was clean-shaven. He was extremely happy that his father was no longer as grouchy as on his former visits.

The street narrowed and reminded Bill of old times.

"Do you remember our holiday in Scotland? You were still a tiny boy back then! We were driving on a single-track road high up in the mountains, where everybody honked his horn before a tight bend. And your mum, who was always so reluctant to reverse, once had to back up almost a hundred metres or so, as she had to give way to oncoming traffic! She had a stiff neck afterwards, she claimed!" He grinned. "She was an excellent driver, but nevertheless I was sweating in fear at the time, even though it was so cold! Or was that on another holiday in Ireland? Because there were also hair-raising roads with a steep drop-off on one side! Well, it's been a long time! How old are you now? 51? Gosh, back in Scotland you were only nine, I think! How time flies!"

Just then, someone honked and a truck thundered past them by a hair's breadth.

"Phew, that was close! Thank God Ernie was sticking his head out on the other side of the car!" Wayne said. "John would rip my head off if anything happened to his beloved dog!"

"Ernie is just awesome! He's the friendliest dog I've ever met!" Bill enthused, turning around and petting him.

Wayne concentrated completely on driving for a while. The road was no longer asphalted, but partly gravelly, partly clayey, and in some places a little washed out by rainwater. Bright sunlight flooded through the trees, almost blinding him, at other times they drove through deep shadows. Wayne pushed his sunglasses onto his forehead to see better in the dark forest and turned on the radio. Shortly after, they reached the crest of the hill, and then they went down a very steep hill.

Tree ferns lined the side of the road, and lush green palms were scattered in the undergrowth of the tall trees. Wayne drove slowly and carefully to avoid falling rocks. Bill was happily humming along to a song, albeit a little off-key and hoarse, when he suddenly spotted a skid mark.

"Hey, can you pull over? Do you see that? It looks like someone's been in an accident!"

"Yeah, you're right! That one skinny tree is bent over!" replied Wayne. "I can't stop here, though. Hmm, hang on, I'll drive a bit further."

He found a spot that, although not ideal for parking, was at least relatively easy to see from both sides of the road. They quickly went back, with Ernie on a leash, and examined the location near the damaged tree. Indeed, a car must have crashed here! Apart from the bent tree, they saw broken branches and fresh marks on tree trunks. Bill looked anxiously into the abyss and Ernie sniffed the ground. And then his ears perked up. They all listened tensely.

"Did you hear something too?" Bill asked, frowning.

"It sounded like someone calling for help! But it was really faint!" said Wayne worriedly. "I'll have to climb down there."

Ernie pulled on the lead, keen to go. Bill held him tight and said: "No, you stay here with me!"

Without a second thought, Wayne began the descent. The slope was densely vegetated, but on a particularly steep section with loose scree he slipped, managing to grab hold of a puny, half-dead shrub just in time. He cursed as he scratched his hand on a sharp thorn from a climbing plant.

After a while, he shouted excitedly: "Now I can see it! There's a car lying on its side!"

"Can you reach it?" his father asked. "Just be careful!"

Wayne shouted something again, but his father couldn't hear him because another car was approaching. Bill stepped into the middle of the road, waving his arms frantically and shouting: "Stop!"

"What happened?" An old man with weather-beaten skin, a light brown shirt and a large dark blue floppy hat leaned out of the window. The clay-encrusted, rusty Ford looked like it had been through a lot, too.

"A car has crashed down the hillside and my son is on his way to help."

"Oh my god, I'm calling 000 right now!" the man said. "How many people are in that car, and are they badly hurt?"

"I don't know! But at least one must still be alive, because we heard a faint voice."

The stranger was already on the phone and Bill felt a little relieved. At least he and Wayne were not all alone in the bushland! And it was a brilliant idea to call for assistance straight away. But it would certainly be difficult to rescue an injured person. Would they have to use a helicopter? Hopefully there would be no fatalities! His poor son had already been shaken up just the day before, both by Philip's suicide and his confession to killing a woman. Bill was shuddering.

"All right, that's done! It may take a while for a rescue party to arrive, though. I'll move my car to a better spot and put up some warning signs on the road, just in case!" the man said. "See you in a bit!"

"Okay!" Bill replied, sitting down on a large tree stump. Ernie sniffed at it and abruptly lifted his leg.

"Oi, don't piss on me!" scolded Bill, pushing Ernie's rear end aside quick-wittedly.

Ernie was too baffled to continue peeing. After a while the man with the floppy hat came back, handed Bill a cup, put a small bowl on the floor and filled both with water from a thermos flask. Ernie drank greedily.

"Thank you very much!" said Bill, sipping from his cup.

"I wouldn't have thought of that at all. I've never had a dog, although I've always wanted one. By the way, I'm Bill, and this is Ernie. My son's name is Wayne."

The other man, who introduced himself as Geoff, smiled. "Ernie seems like a nice chap, but he's far too fat! Is he your son's?"

"Nah, we're just looking after him for a neighbour who's in hospital at the moment."

Concerned, Bill peered into the abyss. Had Wayne reached the car by now? What would he find? Oh, his son should have taken a first aid kit and a bottle of drinking water along!

"I go and help them," he decided, jumping up impatiently.

"Nah, you'd better not, or you'll break your bones! We old folks can't climb down there!" Geoff said, eyeing Bill bluntly.

Bill almost flew into a rage, but then he laughed good-naturedly.

„You are right. I still walk without a stick most of the time, but my legs have become a bit weak. And my hips are pretty stiff too."

Geoff found a place in the shade to sit down as well, and then they waited. Ernie was dozing off.

Wayne, meanwhile, had almost reached the wrecked golden-brown Holden. The car was stuck in thick brush, still many metres above the valley floor, with two wheels in the air. A boulder had apparently prevented it from sliding further downhill. Wayne could see the driver, slumped down motionless in his seat. Oh no, was he too late again? Would he find another dead body – or even several? His legs suddenly felt like pudding.

But then he heard a soft voice: "So thirsty!"

"Hello! Are you hurt?" asked Wayne, continuing to struggle through the terrain. Again, he pricked himself on some thorns, this time from a large Lantana bush. Finally, he reached the man, who looked quite young but terribly miserable and weary. At least he was alive!

Tony could hardly believe that someone had finally come to the rescue. He would have preferred to cheer loudly, but his throat was so parched that he could only whisper hoarsely. "The stupid seat belt got stuck!"

"We'll manage!" said Wayne reassuringly.

Fortunately, he was able to open the door without difficulty, but the car jerked unexpectedly and he cried out in shock. Could it slide down further or even tip over? He bent over Tony trying to free him. Darn, the seat-belt wouldn't move at all! If he had a sharp knife, he could cut it open, but he didn't have one.

Silly me! Wayne thought, angry with himself for not taking any tools, water containers or fire extinguishers with him! However, climbing down the steep slope had been difficult enough as it was. Tony was now muttering something about his boot, and Wayne stepped cautiously to the back. With some effort he was able to push a thick branch away from the battered car and open the boot. There he found a water bottle in an esky. He returned to the driver and assisted him to take just a few sips.

"Nice and slow, better don't drink too much at once!" said Wayne, frantically thinking of what he should do.

Wasn't it wrong to give water to an injured person? Or to move him? How could he help the poor guy? Wayne was at a loss! Even if he could undo the seat-belt, he wouldn't be able to carry the exhausted man up to the road. He cursed himself for rushing off instead of calling the police or an ambulance first. Now his mobile phone was far away, in the glove compartment of his car. Would his father be smart enough to look for it and call an ambulance?

"Dad!" he shouted loudly, but got no answer.

Unsuccessfully, he fiddled with the jammed seat-belt until his fingers hurt. Later, he examined the boot more closely, hoping to find a suitable tool that he could use to undo or loosen the seat-belt. But all he saw was a jack, a spare tyre, the little Esky and a suitcase, which he opened with a somewhat guilty conscience, feeling a bit ashamed to touch the belongings of a stranger. Inside he found only a dark green towel wrapped around an oblong object in wrapping paper. Nothing useful for his purposes! He sighed and carefully wrapped the gift back in the towel. A crow was watching him from a nearby tree and emitted a plaintive sound. The sun rose higher, but the car remained in the shade. Tony was unconscious again.

It took about half an hour for the rescue team to arrive at the place of the accident, where Bill, Geoff and Ernie were waiting, and then another hour or so before Tony could finally be loaded into an ambulance. When the sweating and hard-breathing helpers finally carried him on the stretcher past a fat dog, Tony thought he was hallucinating. Had Ernie come to his rescue? Had the friendly dog his brother-in-law so often looked after found him here?

"Dear Ernie!" he croaked gratefully.

Bill and Wayne were completely perplexed. How did the injured man know the dog?

Tony was taken to the hospital in Nambour. He was suffering from dehydration, had a broken arm, some bruises, bumps and scratches, but overall, he was in a surprisingly good condition. Wayne had cut himself on a piece of broken glass while climbing up the slope and had to be treated by a paramedic. But he was beaming with joy at the successful rescue. Effusively, he hugged his father, Ernie and the stranger with the floppy hat, one after the other.

In the evening, Bill taught his son a card game that he and Geoff had used to pass the time while waiting by the side of the road. The two old men had got on splendidly.

* * *

On the same evening, Yolanda, Debbie, Mark and their children came to visit Tony in hospital. Chatting away, they stood around Tony's bed and were overjoyed to see him again.

"We were so worried! Already on Sunday morning I couldn't stand it anymore and called the police," Debbie said. "And Mark called several hospitals, but no one knew anything about you. What a blessing that these two men discovered the accident site and found you today! In the middle of the forest!"

She and Yolanda smiled lovingly at their brother.

Tony replied: "Yes, it was! And great that the third man called in the rescue crew and that I have such a robust old Holden! Otherwise, it would have turned out worse, guaranteed. And luckily the kangaroo got away too!"

Then he addressed Kim: "I'm sorry I couldn't come to your birthday party, but we'll make up for it sometime, okay? Oh dear, my gift for you must have been broken in the accident! I had packed it extra carefully into your old suitcase, Mark, and even wrapped a towel around it!"

"What is it?" Kim asked curiously, spontaneously reaching for her uncle's hand.

"Ouch, careful!" Tony winced, pulling back his bandaged hand.

"Here!" Mark grinned broadly and handed his daughter Tony's present, which he had hidden in a large bag. "Tony, your car has already been towed to our mechanic's garage. Bob will give me an estimate for the repair tomorrow. He thinks it won't be that expensive unless you want him to fix each and every little dent on your old car. Anyway, he was surprised that it's not a total loss despite the wild slide. And even though your seat-belt was jammed, he said it surely saved your life."

Kim was carefully unwrapping her present. It was a laptop that looked brand new and unscratched.

"Thank you, Uncle Tony!" Very gently, knowing about his bruises, she hugged him.

"It didn't break at all!" marvelled Tony.

His throat was still hurting from all the screaming as he had tried to make himself heard at every sound of a car. It seemed like a miracle to him that he hadn't died all alone out there in the bushland!

48

On Tuesday morning, John was discharged from hospital. As soon as he came home, Wayne and Bill knocked on his door, with Ernie by their side. Both John and his dog were grinning broadly, so happy to be reunited and to be safely back in their own house! Ernie curled up contentedly on his bed, while Wayne and his father told John about the drama in his neighbourhood, and also about their exciting trip to the countryside.

On Thursday, there were two letters in John's mailbox. One was from Hannah. John opened it straight away, feeling curious and anxious at the same time. She had written to him in custody to apologise for her crazy attack on him. It was a thick letter, and John sat down in his living room to read all the pages that were filled with a dense, fairly neat handwriting.

Hannah admitted that she had wrongly assumed he had killed Maureen. She had loved her sister dearly and was heartbroken about her dreadful end. And why could the detectives not solve the case? Would the police never catch the murderer? For months, she had done her own research, desperate to find out who Maureen might have been seeing shortly before her death. But no one in the circle of friends she knew had a clue. It was so depressing!

Hannah was visiting her father when she found an old address book of her sister in Maureen's former room. Flipping through the pages, she spotted the name of a school friend she hadn't even thought of. She called him immediately. And he actually had some news that made her blood boil:

During one of their occasional chats over the phone, Maureen had mentioned her intention to get free accommodation as a house sitter for a fortnight. He even knew the name of the street in Marcoola where she was going to introduce herself. Furthermore, he thought that this meeting had been scheduled for the evening before she was found lifeless in the park. Hannah was appalled! She couldn't believe that this guy hadn't reported his knowledge to the police. When she snapped at him, he excused his behaviour with a bad experience. Some time ago, there had been a stabbing in front of a hotel in Mooloolaba, and the policemen had brutalised him too. They'd almost arrested him, although he had just happened to be in the area. Nah, since then he wanted nothing to do with the police!

His news made Hannah's head spinning. Should she get in contact with the criminal investigation department? But would they be interested after such a long time? Or would they just laugh at her? No, she would have to find out more by herself! With new energy, she began to browse the internet for ads of people seeking house sitters in Marcoola. She quickly detected an ad from a man called John, who was looking for an animal-loving, responsible, honest house and dog sitter.

Hannah was so excited she could hardly think straight. She absolutely had to track him down! She had no trouble finding John's address. And her anger was mounting. He was living in that same street Maureen's friend had mentioned!

She'd revealed the murderer! she thought with an explosive mixture of triumph, sadness, hatred and desire for revenge.

At the end of the long, somewhat confused letter, Hannah wrote to John:

I secretly unlocked my father's cupboard, stole his rifle and ammunition, and locked it again so that my father would not notice the theft. The next day I went to your house to confront you. It was quite easy to climb through the window into your bedroom, although I was trembling with fear and excitement. Suddenly my courage left me and I wanted to run away. After all, it would be completely wrong to take the law into my own hands! But then I heard voices. By chance, this young woman was with you at the time, and I overheard your conversation. You called her a few times by her name: 'Arya'. When I noticed that she was getting tipsier and tipsier, while your voice continued to sound normal, it only reinforced my delusion that you liked to murder women. That you'd killed my sister! And you know the rest of the story!

I am such an idiot! It didn't even occur to me that someone else in the same street might have been looking for a house-sitter back then. I was filled with such blind hatred! Besides, I imagined that I absolutely had to save Arya from you, and so I shot you.

Now I've heard about the man who killed Maureen. And that you were completely innocent! Oh, I'm so sorry, John! And although I'm sure I'll have to serve a long prison sentence for attempted murder, I'm so glad you survived! I will never pick up a rifle again!

Of course, I will pay for all the damages to your house. And I hope that you and also Arya will get over the shock well. Please forgive me! I don't like to think about my parents and my dear stepfather. They have already been through so much, and now I have caused them additional grief!

Unfortunately, I can't undo that terrible day, as much as I wish I could. With this letter I want to show you that I deeply regret my mindless act. (By the way, my defence lawyer advised me not to send you a letter, but I insisted. What have I got to lose? I am admitting my guilt anyway!)

John, I wish you a speedy recovery (for body and soul)!

Hannah

P.S. I am no better than Philip, Maureen's killer who seems to have been overcome by insane rage and vengeance just like me! And even if I had shot him and not you, I would still be ashamed. I believe that revenge can only give short-term satisfaction. In the end, it only makes the whole situation worse, increasing the intense feelings of sadness, inner emptiness, pain and futility, instead of improving anything. In any case, Philip must have been very unhappy since he committed suicide, although no one had a clue that it was him who'd killed Maureen.

My poor sister! She always wanted to help everyone, and that's why she became a nurse. She was inconsolable about the terrible accident with the e-scooter that led to the death of Philip's child. Afterwards she was in psychiatric treatment for a long time to cope with her feelings of guilt. I think her singing and playing the guitar also helped her a bit to become happier again. Oh, I miss Maureen so much!

John put Hannah's letter aside, deeply moved by this tragic story. But he wondered about the people who'd apparently discussed the advertised position of house sitting with Maureen. He guessed it was the family who had rushed to England, after a close relative had fallen ill. He only knew these neighbours from occasional chats as they lived further down the street. Why had they concealed the fact that Maureen had been in their house, so shortly before her death? Had they been afraid to get involved? Did they fear the police and rather remained silent? He should ask them one day.

The other letter was from Mark. He had written a detailed story about the nurse and her guitar, admitting that he had taken it from Maureen. He described his fear of being falsely arrested as her murderer, and how he'd moved her dead body to Coolum Beach. Mark asked him to forgive him for all his lies, and at the same time to keep quiet.

John was stunned! And yet he was glad that his friend had confided in him. In the evening, he had a long telephone conversation with Mark, promising him not to tell anyone about his deeds. Mark was his best friend after all, and it wouldn't help Maureen anymore if the whole truth came out.

Only much later did it occur to John how lucky it was that Hannah hadn't seen her sister's guitar in his house! Stored away in a cabinet, he had kept it for Mark for such a long time, unknowing about its origin, assuming it was a second-hand acquisition intended as a gift for Kim! Only recently Mark had taken it – and then he'd tried to get rid of it, as he had told him in the letter.

Suddenly John had to laugh out loud, imagining Mark's shock when his own kids found the very same guitar in the kerbside collection! It was a crazy world!

49

Sometimes I thought my life was boring. Sometimes I was sad or even desperate, sometimes angry and disappointed. And certainly, I could have done some things better. Afterwards you are often wiser! However, Lucas asked me the other day if I would like to start all over and be a child again, and to my amazement I immediately replied fervently: "No way!"

That same evening, I filled several diary pages with my spidery handwriting:

Before I forget everything, I'd better write down what's on my mind. Lately so much has happened in my own little world! Life is almost like a huge colourful jigsaw puzzle: some pieces fit together amazingly easily, others make your head spin, and some don't want to fit, no matter how hard you try.

It was a big relief when Tony reappeared who'd been missing, stuck in his car for days after an accident in the bushland. I like him and his sisters! Even Mark seems like a nice guy, and he surprisingly invited Sylvie and me to a Christmas party.

Katja and Sam were also very happy that Tony's accident turned out relatively well. Luckily it happened in the shady forest, and the car windows were open. Otherwise, he might not have survived the heat of the hot summer days. Tony will stay in their holiday unit until he has properly recovered and can go back to work. Katja will definitely mother him!

Maybe I'll let Tony do my next dental treatment.

At last, the tragic case of Maureen has been solved, although the police (as far as I know) never found out who brought the dead woman to Coolum Beach.

After Philip's death, Tina was completely distraught! She became quite thin because she could hardly eat anything for a while. I was very worried about her! She loved Philip, and she would never have expected him to be capable of manslaughter. His suicide too was such a shock to her! But I believe she is on the road to recovery.

And she has made friends with the man who happened to be with her when she found Philip in his shed. I have an inkling that Wayne could become her new 'dream man'. He seems like a great guy! He is gentle and honest, and very handsome to boot. By the way, his heroic deed was praised on TV because he had scrambled down the steep slope to Tony's crashed car. Wayne, however, was quite modest, saying that they should rather thank his father who had spotted the skid marks, and Geoff who'd had the presence of mind to call 000 straight away.

My mother's illness is progressing inexorably. For some time now, she can no longer walk at all. She is confined to a wheelchair, needing somebody to push it as she can't move it by herself. Only extremely rarely does she recognise me as her son.

I visit her as often as possible and go on short trips with her. (Patrick has bought a light, foldable wheelchair for Mum that we take for our tours in the car, but we prefer to explore nearby places on foot.) Recently, we were at a viewpoint by the sea, enjoying the fresh sea breeze, the sight of the white-crowned waves and the fluffy cumulus clouds. It was a gorgeous composition of clouds: brilliant white tufts against the blue sky and dramatic dark grey colour schemes. Mum's eyes lit up when she saw a manta ray swimming in the water below us. Later we spotted a bird of prey in the air, carrying a fish in its beak with obvious effort.

She no longer recognises Patrick and Sarah either, but she always seems delighted to see them. I am so happy and grateful that I don't have to take care of Mum alone and that I get on so well with them!

Communicating with Mum can be difficult. Repeatedly she is in her own world and we don't know what she is thinking, feeling and getting from us. Occasionally, especially on rainy days, we read to her from a book. It's nice to see her smile. We try to take pleasure in little things. Of course, it's a struggle, and we often are terribly sad. Some days Mum is so apathetic that we just can't get through to her. It's depressing when she wants to tell us something but we can't understand her.

More and more, she depends on others for her care. She's incontinent and frail, and sometimes she has trouble swallowing, making eating and drinking an onerous task. She has become very thin (even thinner than Tina).

Will there ever be a real cure for Alzheimer's disease? This terrible dementia! Patrick and I often feel despondent, and we wish we could better assist our mother. However, we do believe that she is well looked after in the 'Puzzle House', and all the staff members treat her lovingly and with respect. Sylvie and Yolanda in particular are incredibly sweet and caring.

Patrick and I hug our mother much more often and tenderly than before. We do love her, and our close bond remains, even if she no longer knows that we are her children.

Every now and then, a volunteer called Katharine (an elderly lady who is always very smartly dressed, carefully coiffed and overly made up) comes to visit Mum with a cute dog called Benny who reminds me of Bella. Mum always loves to pet Benny (and Nellie too). With dogs, communication can work well without any words!

Katharine started to learn Spanish a few months ago. She has particularly taken a resident to her heart who's originally from Spain. He moved into the retirement home after his wife had passed away. As his dementia progresses, he frequently falls back into his mother tongue. Although Katharine still has great difficulty speaking and understanding Spanish, it is marvellous to hear them both chatting away and chuckling happily together.

Maybe I should learn a foreign language as well!

Lesley has given in to Hazel's fervent pleas, putting in a good word for Ann with the nursing home's top management. Now Ann is allowed to visit her sister again (with little Bella). But she is strictly forbidden to enter other rooms. Once I met her in the corridor and she seemed subdued before she gave me a shy but genuine smile. Occasionally, I also visit Hazel. It's remarkable how well her brain still works. She likes to discuss current politics, although she talks a lot about her own life too. It's a pity that I don't know more about my family history. Now it's too late to ask my mother about her and my dad's past.

Bryan, my father's old friend, still goes swimming in the sea every day. In general, he and his wife Julie try to keep as fit as possible, and they have adopted a tiny elderly poodle named Rosie, with whom they walk a lot. Every now and then they push Mum around the park in her wheelchair, usually with Rosie comfortably on her lap. Julie has finally acquired a hearing aid. Bryan was indeed relieved about the revelation of Maureen's killer. But he is saddened by her death, as her music had evoked such fond memories in himself. And of course, he and Julie are shocked that it was Philip, Tina's lover, of all people, who killed first Maureen and later himself.

Yolanda has got a new boyfriend, namely the nice, handsome singer from Fiji, whose velvety voice already triggered many a tear of joy and emotion among the seniors in the nursing home (and apparently also enchanted Yolanda).

The kids of Debbie and Mark are taking guitar lessons, and both have been given brand new guitars. Mark gave away the guitar that they had found in the kerbside collection. I have no idea why. However, they kept that mannequin and use it as a scarecrow in their garden now, dressed in an old jumper, shorts and a frayed straw hat.

Three weeks ago, I moved in with Sylvie. I love her and can still hardly believe that I have found such a wonderful friend!

I also liked her two daughters straight away. They are lovely, natural and humorous women who quickly accepted me as their mother's partner. So, theoretically I have become a 'father' (or 'stepfather') at an advanced age after all! I don't know if Sylvie and I will ever get married, but in any case, I want to grow old with her!

We have made friends with Sylvie's new neighbours and often play Brändi Dog with them. We all love that board game! (And not just the winners are the grinners!)

Furthermore, I regularly meet up with a group of players (young and old) for pickleball, which is great fun. Overall, I seem to do more sports and interesting things, and I laugh more often than I used to! Somehow, I feel that my whole life has changed, meeting more and more warm-hearted, helpful people, and that I myself have become more attentive and open-minded.

My brother and Sarah also get on very well with Sylvie. After much deliberation, we decided not to tell Mum that Simon, her grandson, now lives in her former unit in Brisbane. But she never ever inquired about it, and we don't want to make her sad. Sometimes it's hard to know how honest we should be.

Recently Sylvie happened to meet Noelene while shopping. Noelene told her in a whisper that the nasty guy who had sexually harassed her mother in the Brisbane nursing home died of a stroke a week ago, admitting that she and her husband were really happy about it. She said she was sure several others in the home were feeling the same way as they'd all hated his guts. She would have liked to wring his neck herself! Well, a bad ending for one person can obviously mean a relief for others. At the same time, I wonder how many people could be capable of manslaughter. Can any human being turn into a brutal monster? It's easy to believe so when you watch reports on wars and crimes. However, I already feel guilty about killing a fly! And both Patrick and I were appalled when we once met a man catching and killing butterflies for his butterfly collection. As far as I can remember, my brother and I were rather peaceful even as kids, rarely getting into fights anybody. Is that because of our upbringing or are we naturally better people?

My beloved Nellie delights me every day and often makes Mum smile. And although Nellie is an old dog, she has learned some new tricks, mainly certain hand signals, very fast. Since she has become hard of hearing, she is no longer afraid of thunderstorms. But every time Sylvie sneezes loudly, she takes off in fright!

Life goes on – let's make the best of it!

Note by the author

The novel 'Bra over Jumper' is set in Australia in 2017. The protagonist Michael expresses his thoughts about the well-known doctor and psychiatrist Alzheimer and about Alzheimer's disease. Michael's perception is based on my research and understanding of this disease and treatment during that time (prior to the publishing of my German book called 'BH über dem Pulli'). I'd like to apologise for any errors in this novel, and if there is other clinical evidence regarding Alzheimer's (at present or in the future) that I am unaware of.

The following is a list of organisations in Australia (at the current date of October 2023) that may provide advice and support with regards to various issues that I have addressed in my story.

Examples of organisations in Australia

Beyond Blue
BlueCare
Dementia Australia
Lifeline
National Aged Care Advocacy Program
National Domestic Violence and Sexual Assault Helpline
Older Persons Advocacy Network (OPAN - for incidents that are related to the aged care system)
RUOK
The Elder Abuse helpline
The Salvation Army
The Seniors Legal and Support Service (SLASS)

Emergency phone line: 000
(Australian phone number for life threatening cases)

Published books by Marion Birkenbeil

Scheherazades Finger Food
ISBN-13: 9783734740367 and ISBN-13: 9783738689013
Books on Demand. Language: German

Unser Schweigen schützte die Täter
ISBN-13: 9783734761911 and ISBN-13: 9783738676204
Books on Demand. Language: German

Der Mann mit den gelben Turnschuhen
ISBN-13: 9783750413825 and ISBN-13: 9783750474970
Books on Demand. Language: German

Bake a Cake – Backe einen Kuchen
ISBN-13: 9783750440937 and ISBN-13: 9783751946940
Books on Demand. Language: bilingual, German and English

BH über dem Pulli
ISBN-13: 9783750413825 and ISBN-13: 9783750474970
Books on Demand. Language: German

Marion's website:
https://m-birkenbeil-autorin.jimdofree.com

Other English crime novels by Marion Birkenbeil

Deadly Datura

The Kuhlmanns, a German family of four, have immigrated to Australia. They are thrilled with the beautiful Sunshine Coast, the friendly and helpful people and the fascinating wildlife. So many animals are unique to Australia! A dream comes true for Anna and Sebastian when their parents adopt a dog. Taking Susi for long walks on the dog-friendly beaches, they feel as though they were living in paradise.

But then a grisly murder occurs, right in their own coastal town! The locals are shaken. Who could have killed the woman? Lizzie is upset that her children keep talking about the case, making wild accusations and playing detective.

Note: 'Deadly Datura' is a translated and edited version of the third part in Marion's first German book called 'MORD UND BRAND, FLUTEN UND SAND', published by Shaker Media in 2013. Refer to Marion's website for further information.

No Fun

The Kuhlmanns have been living in Australia for a while. Despite occasional bouts of homesickness, they adapt very well to their new lifestyle, and they get a lot of joy from their own dog Susi and various foster dogs. Unfortunately, Susi is terrified of the parachutes that keep landing on their favourite beach in Coolum Beach, a coastal town in Queensland. Sixteen-year-old Anna suffers from love-sickness, while her thirteen-year-old brother Sebastian falls in love for the first time. Both get into a real turmoil of their feelings. And then, on a bright sunny day, somebody discovers the dead body of a young man! He was a seventeen-year-old vegan who was committed to animal and environmental protection. Why was he murdered? And why was he wearing a flipper on his foot? Somehow, the Kuhlmanns get heavily involved in the mystery, meeting strange people and unusual animals ...

Note: 'No Fun' is a translated, edited and reduced version of Marion's German book called 'Der Mann mit den gelben Turnschuhen'. Marion intends to publish this book in the year 2024. Also refer to Marion's website for further information.

ABOUT THE AUTHOR

Marion Birkenbeil was born in Wuppertal, Germany in 1963. After working as a horticulturist and landscape gardener for many years, she studied landscape architecture. She immigrated to Australia in 1997. At first, she lived in Brisbane and in Ipswich, later she and her husband (and their dog) moved to the Sunshine Coast. Marion is a freelance landscape architect and became a registered member of the Australian Institute of Landscape Architects in 2007. Her crime novels reflect her love of nature and dogs.